RAINMAKER TRANSLATIONS *supports a series of books meant to encourage a lively reading experience of contemporary world literature drawn from diverse languages and cultures. Publication is assisted by grants from the Black Mountain Institute (blackmountaininstitute.org) at the University of Nevada, Las Vegas, an organization dedicated to promoting literary and cross-cultural dialogue around the world.*

Gerbrand Bakker

The Twin

Translated from the Dutch by David Colmer

archipelago books

First published in The Netherlands as *Boven is het stil* by Cossee, Amsterdam, 2006
Copyright © Gerbrand Bakker and Uitgeverij Cossee 2006
English translation copyright © David Colmer 2008
Published in the UK by Harvill Secker, London, 2008
First Archipelago Books edition, 2009

Library of Congress Cataloging-in-Publication Data
Bakker, Gerbrand, 1962-
[Boven is het stil. English]
The twin / Gerbrand Bakker ; translated from the Dutch by David Colmer. –
1st Archipelago Books ed.
p. cm.
ISBN 978-0-9800330-2-1
I. Colmer, David, 1960- II. Title.
PT5882.12.A55B6713 2006
839.31'37–dc22   2008045725
Archipelago Books
232 Third Street, #A111
Brooklyn, NY 11215
www.archipelagobooks.org

Distributed by Consortium Book Sales and Distribution
www.cbsd.com

cover photo © digital vision

The quote on page 277 is from the poem "Onder water" in Gedichten (1961)
by Guillaume van der Graft

Printed in Canada

The publishers are grateful for the support of the Black Mountain Institute,
Lannan Foundation, the Foundation for the Production and Translation of
Dutch Literature, the National Endowment for the Arts, the New York State
Council for the Arts, a state agency.

Foundation for the
Production and
Translation of
Dutch Literature

The Twin

I

1

I've put Father upstairs. I had to park him on a chair first to take the bed apart. He sat there like a calf that's just a couple of minutes old, before it's been licked clean: with a directionless, wobbly head and eyes that drift over things. I ripped off the blankets, sheets and undersheet, leaned the mattress and bed boards against the wall, and unscrewed the sides of the bed. I tried to breathe through my mouth as much as possible. I'd already cleared out the upstairs room – my room.

"What are you doing?" he asked.

"You're moving," I said.

"I want to stay here."

"No."

I let him keep the bed. One half of it has been cold for more than ten years now, but the unslept side is still crowned with a pillow. I screwed the bed back together in the upstairs room, facing the window. I put the legs up on blocks and remade it with clean sheets and two clean pillow-cases. After that I carried Father upstairs. When I picked him up off the chair he fixed his eyes on mine and kept them there until I was laying him in bed and our faces were almost touching.

"I can walk," he said, only then.

"No you can't."

Through the window he saw things he hadn't expected to see. "I'm up high," he said.

"Yes, that's so you can look out and see something other than just sky."

Despite the new room and the clean sheets and pillowcases, it smelt musty, *he* smelt musty and moldy. I opened one of the two windows and used the hook to set it ajar. Outside it was quiet. A fresh chill was in the air and there were only a few crumpled leaves left on the topmost branches of the crooked ash in the front garden. Off in the distance I saw three cyclists riding along the dyke. If I had stepped aside he would have seen the three cyclists as well. I stayed put.

"Get the doctor," Father said.

"No," I replied, turning to walk out of the room.

Just before the door closed, he shouted, "Sheep!"

In his former bedroom there was a rectangle of dust on the floor, slightly smaller than the dimensions of the bed. I cleared out the room, putting the two chairs, the bedside cabinets and Mother's dressing table in the living room. In a corner of the bedroom I wriggled two fingers in under the carpet. "Don't glue it," I heard Mother say an eternity ago as Father was about to go down on his knees with a jar of glue in his left hand

and a brush in his right, our heads already spinning from the pungent fumes. "Don't glue it, ten years from now I'll want new carpets." The underlay crumbled under my fingers. I rolled up the carpet and carried it through the milking parlor to the middle of the yard, where suddenly I didn't know what to do with it. I let it drop, just where I was standing. Startled by the surprisingly loud bang, a few jackdaws flew up out of the trees that line the yard.

The bedroom floor was covered with sheets of hardboard, rough side up. After quickly vacuuming the room, I used a broad, flat brush to paint the hardboard with gray primer, without bothering to sand it first. While doing the last section, in front of the door, I noticed the sheep.

Now I'm in the kitchen, waiting for the paint to dry. Only then will I be able to get the gloomy painting of a flock of black sheep down off the wall. He wants to look at his sheep, so I will hammer a nail into the wall on one side of the window and hang the painting for him. The kitchen door is open and the bedroom door is open too. From where I am sitting, I can look past the dressing table and the two bedside cabinets at the painting on the wall, but it is so dark and discolored that I can't make out any sheep at all, no matter how hard I try.

2

It's raining and a strong wind has blown the last leaves off the ash. November is no longer quiet with a fresh chill in the air. My parents' bedroom is my room now. I've painted the walls and ceiling white and given the hardboard sheets a second coat of primer. I've moved the chairs, Mother's dressing table and the bedside cabinets upstairs. I put one bedside cabinet next to Father's bed and stowed the rest in the spare room next to his bedroom: Henk's room.

The cows have been inside for two days now. They're restless during milking.

If the round hatch on top of the tanker had been open this morning, half the milk would have shot out like a geyser, that's how hard the tanker driver braked to avoid the rolled-up carpet that was still lying in the middle of the yard. He was swearing quietly to himself when I came into the milking parlor. There are two tanker drivers, and this was the older one, the gruff one. More or less my age, I think. A few more years' driving and he can retire.

. . .

Apart from the bed, my new bedroom is completely empty. I'm going to paint the woodwork: windows, door and skirting boards. I might do it the same color as the floor, but I'm not sure yet. I have a bluish gray in mind, the color of Lake IJssel on a summer's day with ominous storm clouds in the distance.

In what must have been late July or early August, two young lads went by in canoes. That doesn't happen often, the official canoeing routes don't pass my farm. Only ambitious canoeists get this far. It was hot and they had taken off their shirts, the muscles in their arms and shoulders gleamed in the sunlight. I was standing at the side of the house, unseen, and watched them trying to cut each other off. Their paddles slapped against the yellow water lilies. The canoe in front turned sideways and got trapped with its nose against the bank of the canal. The lad glanced up. "Look at this farm," he said to his friend, a redhead with freckles and sunburnt shoulders, "it's timeless. It's here on this road now, but it might just as well be 1967 or 1930."

The redhead subjected my farm, the trees and the field the donkeys were grazing at the time to a careful appraisal. I pricked up my ears. "Yes," he said after a long while, "those donkeys are old-fashioned, all right."

His friend backed his canoe away from the bank and turned it in the right direction. He said something in reply, something I couldn't make out because a redshank had started to kick up a fuss. A late redshank: most of them are gone by the end of July. The redhead set off after him slowly, still staring at my two donkeys. I was stuck with nowhere to go, there was nothing I could possibly be working on around that side of the house. I stood there motionless and held my breath.

He saw me. I thought he was going to say something to the other lad, his lips parted and he turned his head, but he didn't say a word. He looked and left me unseen by his friend. A little later they turned into Opperwoud Canal and the yellow water lilies drifted back together. I walked up on to the road to watch them paddle off. After a few minutes I could no longer hear their voices. I tried to see my farm through their eyes. "1967," I said quietly, shaking my head. Why that particular year? One of the boys had named the year, the other, the redhead with freckles and burnt shoulders, had seen it. It was very hot that day, mid-afternoon, almost time to bring in the cows. My legs felt unexpectedly heavy and the afternoon was empty and lifeless.

3

Dragging a grandfather clock up a staircase is a hellish job. I use rugs, pieces of foam rubber and long, smooth planks. Everything inside the case pings and rattles. The ticking of the clock drove me mad, but I didn't want to stop it every night. Halfway up I have to rest for a few minutes. It might drive him mad as well, but then of course he'll have his painted sheep to calm him down again.

"The clock?" he says, when I come into the bedroom.

"Yep, the clock." I put it right behind the door, pull up the weights and give the pendulum a nudge. Immediately, the bedroom is filled with time, slowly ticking away. When the door is shut, Father can count the hours.

After a glance at the clock face, he says, "I'm hungry."

"I get hungry too sometimes," I say. The clock ticks on calmly.

"The curtains are closed," he adds.

I walk over to the window and open the curtains. It's stopped raining and the wind has died down a little. The water in the ditch is up and flowing over the causeway. "I have to do the windmill," I say to myself and the window. Maybe I'm saying it to Father too.

"What?"

"Nothing." I set a window ajar and think of the bare spot in the living room.

In the kitchen I make a cheese sandwich and wolf it down. I can hardly wait. With the water still dripping through the coffee maker, I go into the living room. I am alone, I'll have to do it alone. I lift the sofa on to one of the rugs I used for the clock and drag it through the hall to the scullery. I carry the two armchairs out of the front door and set them at the side of the road. The rest goes in the scullery with the sofa. I have to empty the sideboard completely before I can slide it. Then, finally, I'm able to wriggle my fingers in under the carpet. This one was more expensive and doesn't crumble in my hands. As I roll it up, I consider keeping it – can't I put it to some use somewhere? Nothing springs to mind. The roll of carpet is too heavy to pick up: I haul it up the gravel path and over the bridge to the road. When I come back I notice the telephone in the hall and phone the council to tell them I've left out some bulky rubbish. The coffee is steaming on the warming plate.

On my way to the windmill I see something I've seen several times in the last few days – something disturbing. A flock of birds flying neither north nor south but all directions at once, swerving constantly. The only noise is the sound of flapping wings. The flock is made up of oyster-catchers, crows and gulls. That's what's strange: never before have I seen these three species flying together. There's something ominous about it. Or have I seen it before without it leaving me with such an uneasy feeling? After watching longer, I see that it's actually four species: between the large herring gulls there are also black-headed gulls, which are a good bit smaller. They skim past each other every which way, there are no separate units, it's as if they're confused.

The windmill is a small, iron Bosman windmill. "Bosman Piershil" is written on one side of the iron tail. "Pat. No. 40832" on the other. I used to think Pat was the name of the maker, short for Patrick, but now I know it stands for patent. If the tail is at right angles to the vanes the windmill seeks the wind automatically and keeps turning and pumping water until you fold the tail forward along the guide rail. But now I fold the tail back, using a bar attached for that purpose. It's a beautiful, slender windmill, with something American about it. That's why Henk and I used to come here so often in the summer, because it seemed foreign and because of the concrete base built in the ditch and because we loved the smell of grease. Things were different here. Every year a Bosman man would come to check the windmill and even now, years since the last Bosman man came, everything runs smoothly. I stop for a moment to watch the water bulge in the canal.

I take the long way back and count the sheep. They're still all there. Twenty-three, plus the ram. The ewes' rumps are red, I'll take the ram away soon. They walk off at first, then follow me when I get closer to the causeway. I stop at the gate. About ten yards from me they stop too, lined up on either side of the square-headed ram, staring at me. It makes me feel uncomfortable.

I see the rain-sodden carpet in the yard and decide to take that up to the road as well.

Just before milking I give the gravel in the front garden a quick rake. It's already getting dark. The two boys from next door, Teun and Ronald, are sitting under the carpet – the expensive one – which they have half unrolled and thrown over the two chairs. Not so long ago they came to the front door around seven p.m. to hold up red hollowed-out sugar beets and croak out a song. The soft light from inside the beets made their excited faces look even redder. I rewarded them with two Mars bars. Now they've got torches. "Hey, Helmer!" they shout through the hole they've cut in the carpet – with a knife? – "This is our house!"

"Great house," I shout back, leaning on my rake.

"We've even got light!"

"I noticed."

"And there's a flood too!"

"The water's already going down again," I reassure them.

"We're going to sleep here."

"I don't think so," I say.

"I think so," says Ronald, the youngest.

"No, you're not."

"We're going home soon," I hear Teun whisper to his little brother. "We haven't got anything to eat."

I look up at the window of Father's bedroom. It's dark inside.

4

"I want to celebrate Saint Nicholas," he says.

"Saint Nicholas?" There haven't been any Saint Nicholas celebrations in this house since Mother died. "What for?"

"It's nice."

"And how do you imagine it?"

"You know," he says, "the usual."

"The usual? If you want to celebrate Saint Nicholas, you have to buy presents."

"Yep."

"Yep? How are you going to buy presents?"

"You'll have to buy them."

"For myself as well?"

"Yep."

"Then I'll know what I'm getting." I don't want to have long conversations like this with him. I want to look in briefly and get away fast. The ticking of the grandfather clock fills the room. A window-shaped block of light shines on the glass of the case and reflects on the sheep painting, making it a lot less gloomy. It's a strange painting. Sometimes it looks like winter, sometimes summer or autumn.

When I'm about to close the door, he shouts, "I'm thirsty."

"I get thirsty too sometimes." I close the door firmly behind me and walk downstairs.

Only the sofa has made it back to the living room. On the bottom shelf of the built-in linen cupboard in my bedroom I found a big piece of material. Mother might have been planning to make a dress from it, although it seems a bit large for that. It's perfect for covering the sofa. The floor is primer gray. When the bedroom door is open, the color is continuous over the freshly painted sill. I've done the skirting boards, window frames and doors with primer as well. The sideboard is somewhere else, with the low bookcase on top of it. I've thrown all the flowering plants on the muck heap. That didn't leave much. When I go to buy paint, I'll have to look for venetian blinds or roller blinds as well; the heavy dark-green curtains in the bedroom and living room leave me gasping for breath, and I have a vague suspicion it's not just because of the years since they were last beaten. I took the remaining contents of the linen cupboard upstairs and brought my own clothes downstairs.

There are cats here. Shy cats that shoot off. Sometimes it's two or three, a few months later it will be nine or ten. Some are lame or missing their tails, others (most, actually) are incredibly mangy. It's impossible to keep tabs on them: it's no surprise if there're ten, but two is just as likely. Father used to solve the cat problem by shoving a litter in a gunny sack, adding a stone, and tossing the sack in the ditch. Long ago he would also stuff an old rag in the sack after first drenching it with some liquid from the poison cabinet. I don't know what it was, that liquid. Chloroform? But how did he get his hands on a bottle of chloroform? Were you able to go out and buy things like that thirty years ago? The silver-gray cabinet with the skull and crossbones on the door is in the barn and hasn't contained poison for a long time: poison is out of fashion. I keep paint in it.

Last spring I saw him shuffling around the barn with saucers of milk. I didn't say anything, but sighed deeply, so deeply he must have heard. Within a few days he had the kittens drinking from a single saucer of milk. He grabbed them and stuffed them in a bag. Not a gunny sack, we don't get them any more. It was a paper feed bag. He tied the bag on to the rear bumper of the Opel Kadett with a piece of rope about three feet long.

Seven years ago when his license needed renewing they made him do a test. There were all kinds of things wrong with him and he failed. Since then he hasn't been allowed to drive. He still climbed into the car. There was a green haze on the trees that line the yard and narcissuses flowering around the trunks. I stood in the barn doorway and watched him start the car, which immediately shot off, throwing him back against the seat, then jerking him forward so that he hit his head on the steering wheel. Then he reversed without looking over his shoulder or in the rear-view mirror. He did that for a while: driving forward, changing into reverse (the gearbox howled) and backing up, turning the steering wheel just a little. Up and down and back and forth until a cloud of exhaust fumes hung between the trees. He climbed out of the car, untied the paper bag very calmly and tried to throw it on the muck heap. He had to pick it up again no less than three times, his arms were no longer strong enough for a hearty swing. "Good riddance to bad rubbish," he said, coming into the barn. He wiped his forehead and rubbed his hands together in his one-chore-out-of-the-way gesture; it made a rasping sound.

It took me a while to get moving. Slowly I walked over to the muck heap. The bag wasn't right at the top, it had slid down a little, and not just from gravity, but partly from the movement inside. I could hear very quiet squeaking and almost inaudible scratching. Father had made a mess of things and I could fix them for him. Damned if I would. I turned and walked away from the muck heap until I had gone far enough to be well out of earshot and then stayed there until there were no more sounds and no more movement.

He wants to celebrate Saint Nicholas, because "it's nice."

5

I don't know what's going on here, but now a hooded crow is staring at me from a branch in the bare ash. It's the first time I have ever seen a hooded crow around here. It's magnificent, but it is really getting on my nerves, I can hardly get a bite down. I go and sit somewhere else, with a view out the side window. There are four chairs around the table, I can sit where I like, the other three aren't used.

I always sit where Mother used to sit, on the chair closest to the stove. Father sat opposite her, with his back to the front window. Henk sat with his back to the side window and could look through to the living room when the doors were open. I sat with my back to the kitchen door and often saw Henk as a silhouette, because of the light shining through the window behind him. It didn't matter, my spitting image was opposite me and I knew exactly what he looked like. I'm back in my old spot at the kitchen table now and I don't like it. I stand up, push my plate across the table, and walk around to sit down on Henk's chair. Now

I'm visible once more to the hooded crow, which turns its head slightly to get a better look at me. Being watched reminds me of the sheep that stood there staring at me a few days ago, all twenty-four of them. It gave me the feeling that the sheep were my equals, that they weren't just animals looking at me. I've never felt like that before, not even with my two donkeys. And now this strange hooded crow.

I slide my chair back, walk through the hall to the front door and step out onto the gravel path. "Kssshh!" The crow cocks its head and moves a leg. "Go!" I shout, and only then do I look around uncomfortably. Weird, semi-elderly farmer shouts at something invisible from his open front door.

The hooded crow stares at me condescendingly. I slam the front door. When quiet has returned to the hall, I hear Father saying something upstairs. I open the staircase door.

"What d'you say?" I yell.

"A hooded crow," he calls.

"So?" I yell.

"Why chase it away?" Whatever else, he's not deaf.

I close the staircase door and go back to the kitchen table, sitting in Father's place, with my back to the front window. I chew my sandwich stolidly while doing my best to ignore Father, who's still talking away.

In the space of ten minutes I've sat on every chair. If someone saw me, they'd think I was trying to be four people at once to avoid eating alone.

. . .

Before doing the woodwork, I painted the living room walls and ceiling white. I needed two coats to cover the pale rectangles that emerged when I took down the paintings, photos and samplers. After buying paint and a new brush from the painter's, I visited the DIY shop, where I found wooden venetian blinds that fitted the bedroom and living-room windows exactly. Apparently the dimensions they used a hundred and fifty years ago are still common today. Before putting up the blinds, I took the plants I'd left on the windowsills and threw them on the muck heap as well. Now it's empty and bluish gray in both rooms and the light enters in horizontal strips. Instead of pulling up the blinds in the morning, I just rotate the narrow slats.

I go upstairs with a box of nails, a hammer and a big, heavy potato crate.

"What are you doing?" Father asks.

I take the paintings, photos and samplers out one by one and start hanging them. "You think Saint Nicholas is nice," I say, "but we can make it nice in here too."

"What are you doing downstairs?

"All kinds of things," I say. I hang the first photos up around the painting of the sheep, but soon have to move on to the other walls. Framed photos of Mother and Henk, champion milkers with rosettes, our grandparents and me, samplers made for our birth (not one, but two) and Father and Mother's wedding. The paintings include six watercolors of mushrooms, a genuine series.

"What's the idea?"

"This way you'll have something to look at," I say.

When they're all hung, I look at the photos more closely. There is one of Mother in an armchair. She has seated herself like a real lady, hands clasped respectably in her lap and legs pressed modestly together and angled slightly – obliging her to turn her upper body a little. She's looking at the photographer in a way that doesn't suit her at all, with an expression that combines arrogance with a hint of seductiveness, an impression reinforced by her angled legs. I take the photo down from the wall and lay it in the empty potato crate, together with the nails and the hammer.

"Leave her here," Father says.

"No," I say. "I'm taking her back downstairs."

"Have we got any mandarins?"

"Would you like some mandarins?"

"Yes."

I fold out the stand on the back of the frame and put Mother on the mantelpiece. Then I get two mandarins from the scullery and take them upstairs. I put them on the bedside cabinet and walk over to the window. The hooded crow is still in the ash: from here I'm looking straight out at it.

"Does that hooded crow look at you?" I ask.

"No," says Father. "It looks down a bit more."

Suddenly I remember what I had forgotten. I go downstairs and into the kitchen. In the corner next to the bureau is Father's shotgun. I pick it up, wondering whether it's loaded. I don't check it. It feels odd to be holding it. In the old days we weren't allowed to touch it, later I didn't want to. I take the gun upstairs and lean it against the side of the grandfather clock. Father has fallen asleep. He is lying on his back, his head has drooped to one side, a thread of dribble is trailing onto the pillow.

6

Mother was an outrageously ugly woman. Someone who hadn't known her would probably consider the photo on the mantelpiece laughable: bony, pop-eyed farmer's wife with thrice-yearly hairdo does her best to assume a dignified pose. I don't laugh at the photo. She's my mother. But sometimes I have wondered why Father – who, when awake, no doubt lies there staring at the handsome figure he cut in those ancient photos – ever married her. Or rather, now that I've been looking at her photo for a while and thinking about the man upstairs, I wonder why *she* married him.

There isn't much else left on the mantelpiece, which is black marble. A bronze candlestick holding a white candle, and an old pencil box with a picture of a belted cow on it. All the other knickknacks are in a box in Henk's bedroom, along with other superfluous stuff. Henk's room has become a storeroom. His bed, which has never served as a visitor's bed, is hemmed in by all kinds of things he also saw and knew.

His bedroom has become one big gathering point for the past, and the living museum piece in the adjacent bedroom just keeps on breathing. Breathing and talking. Even now, here, I can hear him muttering. Is he talking to the hooded crow? To the photos, or the six watercolor mushrooms?

Henk and I were born in 1947; I'm a few minutes older. At first they thought we wouldn't live to see the next day (May 24th), but Mother never doubted us. "Women are made for twins," is what she supposedly said after putting us on the breast for the first time. I don't believe it: statements like that always emerge from a mass of events and comments finally to remain as sole survivor. Plenty of other things must have been said at the time and this was most likely a variation on something Father or the doctor said. Mother probably didn't say much at all.

I have a memory I can't have. I see her face from below, above a bright, soft swelling. I'm looking at her chin and, especially, at her slightly bulging eyes, which are directed not at me but at a point in the distance, nowhere in particular: the fields, maybe the dyke. It is summer and my feet feel other feet. Mother was a taciturn woman but she noticed everything. Father was the talker and he hardly noticed anything. He always just yelled his way through.

Someone taps on the window. Teun and Ronald are standing in the front garden, shouting and gesticulating. I walk to the front door.

"Helmer! The donkeys are loose!" Ronald says, in a tone that tells me he wishes the donkeys got loose every day.

"They're still in the yard," Teun says, in a tone that tells me that he too has heard what his little brother really wants.

They run ahead of me around the corner of the house. "Take it easy!" I call.

The donkeys are between the trees, about five yards in front of the partly open gate. The rope that usually keeps the gate shut is dangling from the concrete post. I realize what has happened.

"Well," I say. "You'd better get them back in the paddock."

"Who?" asks Ronald.

"Who do you think? You two."

"Why us?"

"Because."

Now that the donkeys have broken out, Teun and Ronald are scared of them. It's like faucets: when you're little they're great things until you turn one on and have no idea how to shut it off again and panic about all the water that comes gushing out.

"Because?" says Teun. "What's that mean?"

"It means," I say, "that I know that *you* opened the gate because you were too lazy to climb over it, and that Ronald followed you, and that *he* opened the gate a little bit more."

"Uh-huh," says Ronald.

Teun shoots him an angry glance.

"Go on," I say. "Push."

"Push? The gate?"

"No, push the donkeys." I stroll over to the gate, lift it and walk it around until it's wide open. The boys don't move and look at me disbelievingly and a little scared.

In the winter the donkeys often spend long periods in the donkey shed next to the chicken coop. Donkeys absolutely hate having wet feet. In the shed it's dry and there's a layer of straw on the ground. The shed is sixteen feet wide and twenty feet deep. It is open at the front, with an overhanging roof. The donkeys have a sixteen-by-fourteen stall and in the six feet that are left, at the front, there are hay bales and a bag of oats. I generally keep some sugar beets and winter carrots in a box. On a shelf I have a large knife, a currycomb, a brush, a coarse rasp, a hoof pick and a scraper. When the donkeys are inside, Teun and Ronald don't let a day go by without visiting the shed. They sit on the hay bales or on the scattered straw in the stall. They like it most when it's getting darker outside and I've turned on the light. Once I found them lying flat on their backs under the donkeys. I asked them why they were doing that. "We want to conquer our fear," said Teun, who was about six at the time. Ronald sneezed because the donkey's long winter coat was hanging in his face. Now the donkeys are out they are afraid.

"How?" Ronald asks.

"Nothing special. Just go and stand behind them and give them a push."

"No way," says Teun.

"They won't do anything," I say.

"You sure?" asks Ronald.

"I'm sure."

They both go around behind a donkey and Ronald immediately starts pushing with all his might. Teun carefully taps his donkey's backside to make sure it won't kick. I'm curious to see what happens.

Nothing happens. I walk to the barn.

"Where are you going?" asks Teun.

"I'll be right back," I say.

In the barn I scoop a few handfuls of feed into a bucket and peek around the corner at the boys to check on things before going back. Nothing has changed. When I see Teun looking around anxiously, I stroll up to them. "Not working?" I ask.

"No," Ronald says. "Stupid animals."

"What?" I ask.

"Well . . ." he says.

"They won't budge," says Teun.

I walk into the paddock and shake the bucket. Ronald falls over, that's how fast the donkey he was pushing rushes over to me. I empty the bucket and close the gate. Afterwards the three of us spend a while leaning over the gate watching the donkeys eat the feed. I'm standing on the ground, Teun's on the bottom bar and Ronald is on the second-to-bottom bar.

"You won't do it again, will you?" I say.

"No," they both say at once.

They jump down and walk into the yard. When they're almost at the causeway, Teun turns around. "Where's your father?" he shouts.

"Inside," I say.

He doesn't need to know any more. They cross the causeway and turn right.

I stay behind with the donkeys. They don't have names. When I bought them, years ago, I couldn't think of any names and after a while it was too late, they had already become "the donkeys." Father asked me if I'd gone mad. "Donkeys?" he said. "What do we want with bloody donkeys? They'll cost us a fortune." I told him they weren't our donkeys, but my donkeys. The livestock dealer was more than happy to arrange it – something different for a change. The donkeys are mixed breed, they're not French, Irish, Italian or Spanish purebreds. They are very dark gray and one has a light-gray muzzle. I click my tongue at them and whisper, "Where's your father?" They come up to me and nudge me on the head with their different colored muzzles.

The cows are restless, two of them kicked out when I went to attach the teat cups. Until recently I was sure it was because they weren't getting out any more, but now I've begun to suspect that it's me who's restless. In that regard cows can be just like dogs – dogs are supposed to be able to sense their master's state of mind as well. I don't have a dog. We've never had dogs here.

Father hasn't eaten the mandarins. I don't want to know. I carried him upstairs and now he can go and perch on the roof as far as I'm concerned, and then, from there, he can carry on to the tops of the poplars that line the yard so that he can blow away on a gust of wind, into the sky. That would be best, if he just disappeared.

"I can't get the peel off," he says.

I try not to look at the mandarins on the bedside cabinet or the crooked fingers on the blanket. It really is starting to stink in here, despite my always keeping the window ajar. If he won't disappear, I'll have to wash him. Before drawing the curtains, I cup my hands against the windowpane to block out the light from the lamp. With my face pressed against my hands I peer out at the ash in the front garden. The hooded crow has gone. Or is it so dark that it blends in with the branches and the night sky?

Then I see someone walking. There are lampposts along the road, one for each house or farm. That makes a total of seven lampposts. There has been something wrong with my lamppost for a few weeks now. It glows, but that's all; even if you stood right under it, the light wouldn't reach you. The venetian blinds in the living room are closed. It is so dark outside that I can only see that someone is walking and, now, that they have stopped in front of the farm. A dark patch, barely visible against the canal in the background. I can't even see which direction the patch is looking in.

"What is it?" asks Father.

"Someone on the road," I whisper.

"Who?"

"I can't see properly." Then the patch moves and suddenly acquires a bicycle's red back light. I follow the back light until it disappears past the window frame. I jerk the curtains shut. My heart is beating in my throat. "All right then," I say, picking the mandarins up from the bed-side cabinet. I peel them both, remove the bitter white threads and hand them to Father in segments. Soon the juice is running down his chin.

"Delicious," he says.

7

I've been scared all my life. Scared of silence and darkness. I've also had trouble falling asleep all my life. I only need to hear one sound I can't place and I'm wide awake. Still, I've never really stopped to think about what happens outside at night. Of course, in the old days I used to see all kinds of things pass the window, even though I knew that the window was high above the gravel path. I saw shoulders: the tense, hunched shoulders of someone climbing up the front of the house. Like a panther, sometimes with one arm hooked over the window ledge. Then I'd listen to Henk breathing next to me, or later imagine him asleep in the bedroom next to mine, and the shoulders or whatever else I thought I had seen would disappear. In the back of my mind I knew that I saw things that couldn't possibly be there.

Now, after what I saw on the road and after feeding Father, I lie in my bed with my eyes squeezed shut. Sleep, I think, sleep. But I see sheep lying in the field, groaning and chewing the cud, gray smudges in a greenish-black expanse, and crows in the poplars with their feathers fluffed up around their heads, and the donkeys facing each other, close to the gate, necks bent as if they were sleeping on their feet with their heads touching, and the Bosman windmill, which I have stopped again, standing by itself in the far corner, gleaming pale gray when there are breaks in the clouds, and someone by the windmill, looking up at the tail and reading "No. 40832." When I see that before me, I open my eyes. Is that a common occurrence, someone standing motionless in front of the farm on autumn nights? And would I have ever known if I hadn't happened to look out of the window?

Later I think of the lads in canoes. The first, the one who said it is time-less here, is vague and soon gone. The other one, the redhead with sunburnt shoulders, sticks in my mind. He said something, but what he said doesn't matter. He saw it, and he saw me. A fairly old farmer in faded blue overalls with the top buttons undone because it was a hot day. Standing next to a farmhouse, in the shade, with no reason to be there except to look on motionlessly, holding his breath. Who has grown older every day since 1967 without anything else changing. No, one thing has changed, the donkeys, and it was the donkeys, of all things, that he commented on. He called them old-fashioned. So it does matter what he said. They paddle out onto Opperwoud Canal, laugh-ing, young, self-obsessed and quick to forget. At the end of the canal the sun is setting. That's impossible because the canal runs eastwards, from here the sun never sets in Lake IJssel, but it can now, and the boys turn into silhouettes with voices that grow weaker and weaker. Then they're gone. Now, I think, now I'll fall asleep. If you think it, you can forget it. The imaginary sun reminds me of the sea, twenty miles to the west as the crow flies. Long ago we went there, twice in one summer. On both days it grew cloudy during the afternoon. Mother wanted to see the sun sink into the water and convinced Father to let the farmhand do the milking by himself. I have never seen the sun go down in the sea, although I could, hardly any distance away.

I hear something. I think it's beneath my window and the hair on the back of my neck prickles. I think of Father, upstairs. He's no use to anyone any more, but I need him now, after all, to conquer my fear.

Maybe the red-headed boy thinks of me sometimes: that old farmer who just stood there, on that beautiful summer's day.

8

"Old? Helmer, you're nowhere near old." Ada, Teun and Ronald's mother, is sitting opposite me at the kitchen table. "Your father, okay, he's old."

Ada has heard things from her sons. Things about donkeys and "wooden strips" in front of windows. She is curious. "You know who else is old? Klaas van Baalen, who lives just outside Broek. He's your age and lives in complete squalor. He can't look after himself. Just the other day they took away his sheep, completely neglected, balls of wool and rattling bones."

I had forgotten that Ada drinks her coffee black these days, and put it down to getting old.

Ada thought it was "fantastic," all the things I'd done in the bedroom and the living room. The blue of the floors and the woodwork was "just gorgeous" and she was especially impressed by the spaciousness. I *did* need to buy a duvet, in her opinion. Blankets, *no*, that really wasn't on any more, that was "very, very old-fashioned" and sleeping under a duvet was "much comfortabler." ("Is that actually a word?" she wondered afterwards.) She wanted to know how much I had paid for the venetian blinds and considered getting rid of her own curtains at home ("those dust traps"). Had I just thrown away the chairs? No, wait, actually she already knew that, she suddenly remembered one of Teun and Ronald's stories, something about a "carpet house." She'd "simply adore" it, just throwing things out, making space, instead of always hanging on to everything. She walked into the bedroom one more time. Why did I still sleep in a single bed? In a double I'd have "room to stretch." She gave me a mischievous look when she said that. And that duvet, "you really should, you know," because then I could buy some nice blue duvet covers and that would make it even "fresher" and more beautiful.

On her way to the kitchen she spread her arms to indicate the bare walls of the living room. Art. Why didn't I buy "some art"?

Ada is still young, about thirty-five. Her husband is at least ten years older, maybe fifteen. She's bursting with energy. If she had her way, she'd come to my house to clean once a week instead of once a year, in April, as she does now. She's treasurer of the local Women's Institute, makes quilts, is a member of a reading group, supports her local community and is busy planting "the most beautiful garden in all of Waterland." She reminds me of Mother because she is almost as ugly, but in Ada's case the cause is a harelip that wasn't corrected all that neatly. Her boys are beautiful, with blond hair, long lashes and perfect mouths. She's not from round here, and maybe that's why she knows everything about everyone for miles around.

I pour us a second cup of coffee and suppress a yawn. I like Ada, but her enthusiasm and open-hearted chatter still overwhelm me, especially when I've just done the milking and fed the yearlings.

"So you've swapped bedrooms with your father. How is he? Can I pop up to see him?"

"Fine," I say, then lie to her. "No, he's asleep, don't disturb him."

Ada drinks her coffee and eyes me over the rim of her mug. "Old..." she says. "What gave you that idea? You've got a handsome face, a nice full head of hair and not an ounce of fat on you."

I turn red, I feel it and can't do a thing about it. Not just because Ada says I have a handsome face, but most of all because I've lied and my lie could be exposed at any moment by Father. He's not asleep.

"And you're blushing like a schoolboy!"

Ada is sitting in my old spot. That's where she always sits when she's here, so she can see her husband's farm through the side window and feel like she's keeping an eye on things, even though the farm is more than five hundred yards away. I'm sitting in Mother's place. The hooded crow has been perching on the same branch in the ash for more than a week now. Saint Nicholas came – but not to our house – and went. It's a Saturday, the sun is shining and there's no wind. A clear December morning with everything very bare and sharp. A day to feel homesick. Not for home, because that's where I am, but for days that were just like this, only long ago. Homesick isn't the right word, perhaps I should say wistful. Ada wouldn't understand. Not coming from here, she doesn't remember days long ago that were just like this, here.

"Have you ever seen a hooded crow around here?" I ask.

"What's a hooded crow look like?"

"There's one in the ash."

She gets up and looks out of the front window. "It's enormous," she says.

"It's been sitting there watching my every move for days now."

"Nice," says Ada. She couldn't care less. She turns and sits down again. When she talks it's as if she's got a ball of cotton wool in her mouth. That must be something to do with having had a cleft palate. "What was that about the donkeys?"

"They left the gate open."

"I'll tell them not to do it again."

"I already have."

"Has the doctor been back?"

"Yep."

"What did he say?"

"Old. He's just old. Old and forgetful. He's been saying funny things lately as well."

"Like what?"

"Ah, just things. About the old days. Sometimes I have no idea what he's on about." I make a vague gesture at my forehead.

"And now?"

"And now what?" I put my coffee down and try to rub the warmth out of my forehead with my left hand. Left – to get my hand between Ada and me.

"Should I drop in now and then? I'd be happy to help look after him a little."

"No, I can manage. It's almost winter, I've only got the milking to do."

"All right." She's finished her coffee and slumps a little on her chair. She stares out of the side window. "No, Klaas van Baalen, he's old. You can look after yourself just fine." She keeps staring, she's thinking. Maybe she's wondering why Father is in bed upstairs and why I have painted the floors bluish gray. "He never even talks to anyone," she adds, "he's shy and lonely, and now that they've taken his sheep away he doesn't have anything any more." She shivers. "Terrible."

"Yes," I say. That is terrible.

"Why didn't you ever get married, Helmer?"

"Huh?"

"Married?"

"You need a woman for that," I say.

"Yes, but why haven't you got one?"

"Ah . . ."

"That brother of yours, he had a girlfriend, didn't he? Weren't they going to get married?" If Ada really is thirty-five, she was born the year Henk died. 1967.

"Yes," I say. "Riet."

"Henk and Riet," says Ada. "That has a nice ring to it."

"Yes," I say.

"So he had a girlfriend and you didn't?"

"No."

"Strange."

"Ah, things are like that sometimes." I hear the scullery door open.

Before anyone appears at the kitchen door, we both know who is coming in.

"Don't yell like that," Ada calls out.

Teun and Ronald come into the kitchen together and take up positions on either side of their mother, their shoulders drooping. "Hi, Helmer," says Teun. Ronald doesn't say anything, he just stares at the packet of cake on the table.

"What are you two here for?" asks Ada.

"Dad wants you to come home," says Teun.

"Why?"

Teun thinks for a moment. "I don't know."

"Do you not know or have you forgotten?"

"Forgotten," says Ronald.

"We'd better go then," says Ada. She stands up. "Have you seen Helmer's new room yet?"

"No," says Teun.

"Go and have a look." She follows the boys into the living room.

Teun and Ronald try to outdo each other shouting "Oh" and "Ah" because they think I'll like it. They're right. I also like sitting here in the kitchen while people are walking around and talking in the living room.

They go out through the front door. Halfway up the gravel path, Ada turns around. "I completely forgot to tell you that the Koper boy, you know, from Buitenweeren Road . . ."

"Shoot, Jarno, shoot!" shouts Ronald. A football hero. He himself plays in the E or F team.

"That's right, Jarno, he's going to Denmark to farm. Or did you already know that?"

"No," I say, "I hadn't heard that."

"Jutland, I think. There's room to breathe up there. Will you say hello to your father?"

"I will," I say, closing the front door.

I stand in the doorway of my bedroom and look at the woollen blankets on my single bed. The top blanket has frayed edges. I turn around and look at the bare walls in the living room. Some art.

"Helmer!" the old man upstairs bellows.

I lie down on the fabric-covered sofa and close my eyes. Denmark.

9

Denmark. Jutland, Zealand, Funen, Bornholm, the Great Belt, the Little Belt, Odense. Ada has got me thinking. Rolling hills, lots of room, heathland. Jarno Koper is a farm boy who has had enough here. Dark-haired, he must be about twenty-five. When I speak to him – which is hardly ever – he always says things like "slush and muck here." He's leaving, he's brave enough to go to Denmark. An old country: if I'm not mistaken the *mark* in the name is something Germanic, I'll check in the dictionary. I get up off the sofa and look behind me. The low bookcase with the rural novels Mother used to read is no longer there. I'll have to go upstairs.

"Helmer!"

"Yeah, yeah," I mumble, pulling the dictionary out from between the rural novels. I sit on Henk's bed with my knees touching the bookcase. I'll have to rearrange things in here, there's almost no space to move and the dressing table is pushed up against the door of the built-in wardrobe. The stuff in the wardrobe is mine. The kind of things you want to keep or can't bring yourself to get rid of, but never actually need. There's *mark*. From German *Mark* and Goth *marka*, borderland. The dirty Germans – that bit of land on the edge of *our* empire, *that* bit of land where the Danes live. It also means a landmark, a boundary or a tract of land held in common by German peasants. Is that how Marken came to be called Marken?

"Helmer!"

I clap the dictionary shut, slide it back between the rural novels and walk to the door. Mother could read for hours in the evenings. "Romantic soul," Father would sometimes mutter when heading off to the bedroom hours before her. It always sounded nasty.

I shit twice a day. First, just after milking, the second time after coffee. On very rare occasions I get an urge to go again later in the day, usually in the evening, but I always ignore it.

If I think of it, I carry Father downstairs to put him on the toilet. I shut the door and wait in front of it like a faithful dog – dogs are supposed to be faithful but I wouldn't know, we've never had dogs here – until he shouts "ready." He has to go when I put him on the toilet. That can be once every two days; sometimes four days go by. He hardly pisses either, now and then I find a splash of urine in the bedpan. I empty it and rinse it out with boiling water. I don't know how and when that thing came into the house, but it is handy.

. . .

"What is it?" I ask as I go into Father's bedroom.

"Nothing," he says.

"What are you calling me for then?" I walk over to a straight-backed chair with armrests next to the window, under the sheep painting, and turn it around. I try to avoid breathing through my nose.

"Get the doctor."

"No."

"I want to get out of bed."

It's not something I would normally let myself be drawn into, but right now his wish suits me fine. I fold back the blankets and the sheet. The fumes that rise from the warm bed leave me gasping. I slide my arms under his body, pick him up and carry him over to the chair. His bony hands grab hold of the armrests. I pull the covers off the bed and take the sheets downstairs. I stuff them into the washing machine with a load of whites and set the temperature to ninety degrees. Then I take a bucket from the cupboard under the sink and fill it with lukewarm water. I fetch a towel and flannel from the linen cupboard and go back upstairs. Father is drooped forward in the chair. Apparently unable to support his own weight with his arms, he must have slid forward slowly and saved himself from falling by grabbing the chair legs. I put the bucket down and push him upright. First I take off his pajama top, that's not too difficult. The gray hairs on his sunken chest are lying flat on his skin. I go around behind him and lift him with one arm under his arm and around his chest. I use my free hand to slide the pajama bottoms off his bum. The trousers are stained. Then he's sitting naked on the chair. His penis is clamped between his legs. Compared to his body and the skin on his arms and legs, it is remarkably large and smooth.

"Was Ada here?" he asks, finding it hard to keep his head up.

"Yes."

"Why didn't she come upstairs?"

"She didn't feel like it."

"Did she say that?"

"Yes, she said that." I look from Father to the bucket and from the bucket to the floor, which is covered with dark-blue carpet, and from the floor to the flannel lying on the stripped bed. I'm not getting anywhere like this. I go back downstairs and move a plastic stool from the kitchen to the bathroom.

"Cold," he says.

I hold one hand under the spout and turn the hot water on a little more. I haven't planned things properly: I'm still fully dressed and now it's too late; if I let go, he'll fall. We don't want that, a falling father, here on the tiled floor. The stool is up against the wall, in a corner, so I can keep him upright with one arm. He raises an arm to protect his head from the jet of water, just as I'm turning off the taps.

"I'm going to wash you," I say.

He says nothing.

I lay the flannel on his knee and squirt a good squeeze of bath gel on it. It's called Badedas and smells of menthol. It's not easy, with one hand. I start to wash him. Again he reminds me of a newborn calf, smooth and slippery, jerky. I want to run the flannel over his bum and to do that I have to lift him with one arm the way I did to take off his pajama bottoms, except that now I'm standing in front of him instead of behind him. I'm glad I didn't plan it properly and that I still have my clothes on, otherwise my naked torso would be pressed against his gaunt, naked chest. After running the flannel over his bum a couple of times, I feel his balls against my fingertips through the wet material. I lower him back onto the stool. God almighty, his penis is getting hard. I should really rinse out the flannel, but I use one foot to push his legs apart and quickly wipe his groin, making his penis get even harder. I throw away the flannel and turn on the taps.

"Cold," he complains again.

"It's your own fault," I say.

Slowly his penis sinks back down between his legs. After rinsing him off, I wonder whether I need to wash his hair – "still a fine head of hair" Ada would say. No, enough's enough. I dry him off. He manages to stand on his own two feet for a moment.

Poised in the doorway of his bedroom like an old-fashioned bride-groom, I realize I've done things the wrong way round. I still have to make the bed. I put Father, with the wet towel wrapped around his waist, in the chair by the window. His dirty pajamas are in a pile next to one of the chair legs. I make the bed with clean sheets from the cup-board. Then I lay him on the bed and dress him in clean pajamas. My wet clothes make it awkward and it's cold in the bedroom. I put the two pillows against the headboard and pull the blankets up over him.

"I wish I was dead," he says softly.

"Now you're nice and clean?" I ask.

"It's that crow," he says, pointing with a trembling finger.

"What about it?"

"It's waiting for me."

"No, it's not."

"Yes, it is."

"Whatever," I say.

Father wouldn't hear a word about central heating. Mother disagreed, but her vote didn't count. There are two oil heaters: one in the kitchen and one in the living room. Now he can feel the consequences, upstairs. In the old days, when there was a frost outside, he'd leave the heater on low at night with their bedroom door ajar. When Henk and I woke up we couldn't see outside, so exuberantly had the ice flowers blossomed on the window.

Our hot water comes from a boiler. I haven't wasted all that much on Father, so there's nothing stopping me. I can't remember the last time I showered in the middle of the day. Now I smell like menthol myself. I feel young and strong, but when I take hold of my penis, I feel strangely useless and empty. I can't help comparing it to Father's. Mine is larger and that conclusion alone is enough to make it grow. Just when I'm wondering what that signifies, the doorbell rings. I feel my balls shrink in my hand. Almost no one rings the bell here, at first I don't even realize what it is. I turn off the taps and await developments. I can feel an artery throbbing in my throat, the water dripping on the tiled floor sounds like thunder. All quiet. I dry myself slowly and pull on a pair of underpants. My clothes are in the bedroom. I open the bathroom door and don't see anyone standing in front of the rectangular frosted pane in the front door. Before going into the living room, I peer around the doorpost to see whether there is anyone at the window. No one. I walk to the bedroom where the blinds are closed. Pulling on dry clothes, I again notice the frayed edges of the blankets. Once I'm dressed, I walk to the hall and open the front door. The road is empty. The hooded crow stares at me.

According to the handbook it makes a loud "krraa, krraa," but I haven't heard it do that once.

All afternoon I hear the sound of the bell, echoing through the empty hall. I go to count the sheep and, although there are only twenty-three of them, I have to start again three times. A few days ago I separated the ram from the ewes and returned it to the farmer who lends me one every year. I've hung up the ram harness in the barn. It's only in the afternoon, when it's already dark and I've started milking the cows, that I think of the motionless figure I recently saw in front of the farm.

10

The other tanker driver, the young smiling one, is in the milking parlor.

"Ah, Helmer," he says when I come in. I generally stay away from the milking parlor when the old, gruff one is there. He's leaning with one hand on the edge of the storage tank and keeps looking from the inside of the tank to the hose at his feet. I'd like to greet him by name but whenever I see him I forget what he's called, and end up nodding hello.

"Arie's dead," he says. Even news like this doesn't dim his smile.

"Dead? How?"

"Heart attack."

"When?"

"Day before yesterday. At home."

"Just the other day it occurred to me that he'd be retiring in a few years."

"Yeah, he wanted to stop at sixty."

"How old was he?"

"Fifty-eight."

"Fifty-eight."

"Way too young." The tank is empty. He unscrews the hose and the last bit of milk runs down the drain. Then he winds the hose around the reel on the back of the tanker. "Way too young," he repeats. He comes back to stand in front of me with his legs apart and his hands on his hips. Always that smile, a crooked smile that shows his teeth. "You'll have to make do with me for the time being," he says.

"God help me," I say.

Now the smile changes into a laugh, showing even more teeth. He doesn't say goodbye as he walks to the cab. We've laughed off the news of the death and that's not the kind of thing you follow with small talk. He opens the door and jumps up smoothly. His blue trousers tighten around his take-off leg, a leg that could belong to a skater. I walk out of the yard, following the tanker as it drives away. If he looked in his rear-view mirror he'd see me standing there, like the red-headed boy last summer. It's raining, the donkeys are at the gate with their heads bowed. If it doesn't stop I'll put them in the shed. I look out over my wet farmyard.

Old, gruff and dead, I think.

Until his death we were Henk and Helmer, even though I was the oldest. Until recently I took regular afternoon naps on his bed. I've stopped doing that because of all the junk in his bedroom and because of Father's proximity. I would lie on my side with my legs pulled up, like in the old days when we shared a bed. Now I use the sofa in the afternoons. Since Ada's comments about my bed, I no longer feel comfortable in it, especially not in the daytime. A few days ago I went to Monnickendam to buy a new bed. I settled on the kind that's really only two mattresses, with very short legs under the bottom one. They're going to deliver it soon – they said they'd call me. "Definitely before Christmas," according to the jovial bed salesman. From another shop I bought a duvet and two duvet covers, one light blue and one dark blue, I trust Ada's judgment. The duvet is still wrapped in plastic in a corner of my bedroom. I haven't unpacked the two pillows either. I asked for one pillow, but the female shop assistant (a young thing with black braids) said "One?" so emphatically that I had no choice but to say, "No, two, of course." I won't unpack it until the bed has been delivered and for now I carry on sleeping under the frayed blankets and the single sheet.

Henk and Helmer, not Helmer and Henk. I'm the kind of person who doesn't have any memories at all of the first four or five years of their life. And if I do have memories, I suspect them of being contaminated, suggested by things other people have told me. My memory only starts in the fifties. I don't know how often Father beat us before then.

He found the two of us together infuriating, he always had to deal with two boys forming a united front. He thought we were conspiring against him, that that was our goal in life, and that we met his eye to provoke him. I got the most blows because I was the oldest, so I "must have cooked it all up." He'd pound away at us with his bare hands, and if he had time, he'd pull off a clog to hit us on the bum and sometimes on the back. It was partly to do with my name, I thought. Helmer is a name from my mother's side. Henk was named after *his* father.

Before doing the milking, I bring in the donkeys. There's not much to it. I just open the gate and walk to the donkey shed. Before I get there, they're standing waiting for me. I let them in, cut up a sugar beet and throw the pieces into the feeding trough. Then I stuff a few handfuls of hay into the rack. I've taught Teun and Ronald to always ask whether they're allowed to feed the donkeys. If I gave them free rein the donkeys would be fat in no time, or ill. The rain taps on the corrugated roof. When I scratch their ears, they ignore it, they're too busy eating. Before leaving the shed, I turn on the light. They don't watch me walking away.

11

In Monnickendam I take the N247 and follow it to Edam, where I drive through the village to the dyke, because if I don't get off here I'll be stuck on the main road to Oosthuizen. Near Warder I stop the car for a moment to have a better look at a flock of birds: oystercatchers, crows, herring gulls and black-headed gulls. The horn of a car that wants to pass on the narrow dyke makes me jump.

"Why did you stop on the dyke anyway?" asks Ada, who can't tell a great tit from a blue tit. She's wearing a black mid-length coat and looks a little pale.

In Hoorn I have to leave the dyke for a while. The weather is still and misty, in the distance the water of Lake IJssel merges imperceptibly with the sky. Something is rattling under the bonnet of the Opel Kadett, I'll have to take the car to the garage again. At Oosterleek I turn left and ten minutes later I park the car in front of the Venhuizen funeral parlor, which is next to an old people's home.

"How could they come up with something like that?" asks Ada. "How can they be so cruel?"

There are a lot of farmers, you recognize them right away from their clothes, they're almost all wearing "a good sweater" over a clean shirt. From the funeral parlor we follow the hearse on foot to the Roman Catholic church, where Arie's wife addresses the coffin, or rather, tries to address the coffin, because once she's said, "Arie is dead," she can't go on. Two young women – her daughters, presumably – get up and lead her back to her pew. The priest takes care of the funeral service and a local choir sings a sad song. After a brief silence, six pallbearers in dark-gray top hats come in, lift the coffin onto their shoulders and carry it out. Ada walks beside me, as my wife. She has taken me by the arm and is crying. Wim, her husband, didn't want to come. According to Ada he's scared of death and always keeps a safe distance. What's more, he had better things to do. The cemetery isn't directly behind the church, we have to walk a fair distance. On the way we pass a De Boer's super-market. It's a good funeral: the pallbearers lower the coffin and Arie's wife and daughters throw earth into the grave. When we're walking back to the church the young tanker driver comes up behind us. "I'm glad you could make it, Helmer," he says. "And you too, Ada. Solidarity is a beautiful thing."

"Ah, Galtjo," says Ada, her voice sounding more like cotton wool than ever, "it's the least you can do."

I don't say anything, I'm touched by the young tanker driver's reaction. *Galtjo*, no wonder I keep forgetting his name. Even here, at the cemetery, he's smiling. He can't help it. We've fallen a little behind.

When I turn around, I see that two men have started to fill the grave, not carefully one handful after the other but with enormous shovel loads.

Then everyone returns to the funeral parlor to offer their condolences to the wife and daughters and the rest of Arie's family. We drink coffee and Ada eats a slice of cake. I eat two.

Ada wants to take a different route back. We drive through Hem and Blokdijk to Hoorn.

"Let's go through the Beemster," she says. "The Beemster is lovely."

I cut through Berkhout to Avenhoorn and Schemerhoorn. I follow the signs for North Beemster. "The villages?" I ask.

"The villages," says Ada.

I turn right and take the road through North and Middle Beemster. "Imagine living here," Ada says. "Just look how much space there is. And the land is so nice and high, ours is always wet. Cramped and wet."

"Has Jarno Koper gone to Denmark yet?" I ask.

"No, he leaves in January." She looks around longingly. "Wim would love to have something bigger. Not a lot bigger, just a bit. Ten or so cows, a few hectares."

"You should go to Denmark too then."

"God, no. Can you see Wim ever leaving?"

"No," I say. "I can't see that happening." Wim's lived next door all his life, but I hardly know him.

Just before we turn off to Southeast Beemster, Ada asks me to slow down so she can have a good look at The Unicorn. "Yes," she says, peering at the renovated farmhouse, "we drive off home, but they're left behind, without a husband and without a father."

I stop the car just before the junction and get out. The bare branches of the windbreak bordering the field opposite The Unicorn are damp. I can't see the end of the row of trees, the trunks blur in the thin mist. A car races past. Then it's quiet again. On the other side of the junction, standing next to a less beautiful farmhouse, are three horses.

Ada is right, the Beemster is lovely, even in late autumn, but I'm thinking of Denmark. I have the idea that it's often misty in Denmark.

Ada opens the car door and gets out of the car. "What are you doing?" she asks.

"Nothing special, just standing here," I say.

She looks at me. "Are you okay?"

"Sure," I say.

"Funerals are weird."

"Yeah."

"Especially when it's someone you didn't know very well."

"Uh-huh."

"It makes you feel more alive afterwards than you did before."

"Where does this Galtjo guy live?"

"No idea. I didn't know that Arie came from as far away as Venhuizen either. What do we know about these people?"

"Not much," I say.

"Shall we go home?"

"Let's do that." I take the middle road to the North Holland Canal, which I follow past Purmerend, Ilpendam and Watergang, until Het Schouw. Then through Broek and home.

· · ·

Walking into the milking parlor, I hear the phone ringing. I hurry through the scullery to the hall to answer it. Nothing. "Hello?" I say. It stays quiet on the other end of the line, the kind of silence in which you hear someone holding their breath. "Who's there?" No one responds and I hang up. The newspaper is lying unread on the kitchen table. I can't sit down. I have to do something. It's afterwards now: I'm more alive than I was before.

I have a beautiful, small handsaw that is exceptionally well suited to pollarding willows. It's stayed very sharp for a very long time and must have been expensive. There are willows on the south side and at the back of the farm, and I pollard them every two or three years. I haven't got round to it yet this year and today is a perfect day for pollarding. Hopefully tomorrow will be too, because I can't get it all done in just one day. Halfway through the first willow I'm warmed up and when I start on the second I'm already sweating. I don't need a ladder, a potato crate is high enough. When it's almost time to start milking, I've done the six willows at the side of the farm and have no idea what I've been thinking about the whole time. I throw a few shoots in the donkeys' trough and phone Ada. She has started work on a wooded bank in what is intended to become Waterland's most beautiful garden. I tell her that she can have my willow shoots if she comes and gets them herself.

12

Father is standing at the window. That's not right. He is leaning on the narrow windowsill and his forehead is pressed against the glass. There is a washed-out light in the bedroom, the weather is like yesterday's: misty with the sun trying vainly to break through.

"How'd you get there?" I ask.

He says something but I can't understand him.

"What?"

He pushes himself up a little with his arms, straightening his back and pulling his head back from the glass. "The hooded crow's gone," he says.

"What?"

"The hooded crow, it flew away."

Looking past Father through the bedroom window, I now see what I didn't see through the front kitchen window: the branch of the crooked ash is empty.

"It wasn't waiting for me."

"No, of course not, what kind of rubbish is that?"

"That's what I thought." His arms start trembling and his head shakes.

"But it would have been wonderful," I say under my breath.

"What?"

"Walk back to bed," I say.

"I can't."

"Why not? You got to the window, didn't you?"

Slowly he turns around, keeping his right hand on the windowsill. He looks at his bed like a hesitant long-jumper eyeing the take-off board. Inch by inch he shuffles away from the window. "I'm not going to make it," he says, halfway.

"Yes, you will," I say, "don't give up."

He doesn't make it. I'm there to help him. I lift him up and walk around the bed. When I'm about to lay him down, the phone rings. Let it ring. If I answer it, I'll probably just hear that pent-up silence again. It rings seven times. I lay Father down on his bed.

"I can walk," he says, still panting.

"You know who died?" I ask.

"No."

"Arie."

"Arie who?"

"The tanker driver."

"No!"

"Yes."

. . .

There is no key in his bedroom door. There isn't one on the outside of the door to Henk's bedroom either. I walk in and sit down on his bed. The key is in the keyhole on the inside of the door. I lie down. The curtains are drawn, it's dark in the room. Staring up at the ceiling I realize that everything would be very different if I had someone, if I was married with children. When you have a family, you can get rid of your father without feeling guilty.

I stand up and pull the key from the keyhole. I go out onto the landing and stick the key into the lock of Father's door. It fits, but it's only when I turn it that I feel that it really fits. No remarks from inside the bedroom. I take the key out of the lock and stand there for a moment with it in my hand, then I put it back in the keyhole.

The two bedrooms are on the right side of the landing. Opposite the staircase is a skylight that doesn't let in much light: upstairs it's always evening. At the end of the landing on the left, next to the skylight, is a third room, smaller than the two bedrooms. This room covers maybe a third of the milking parlor beneath it. "The new room," Mother called it to the day she died. I can't remember what the room was supposed to be for, but ever since it was built along with the milking parlor, some time in the sixties, it has remained unused. I never go in there. The door is always shut. The floor is covered with the same dark-blue carpet as the two bedrooms. It is a very strange room, I feel that when now, for once, I go into it. Although it's musty, there is also a lingering smell of newness about it, of its being newly built. There is a fairly large Velux window in the sloping wall, making the room a good deal brighter than the landing. But it's empty, there is no reason to go inside.

Through the window I see the donkeys in the far corner of the donkey paddock. I put them out again early this morning. They're always together, it's only when walking or trotting around that they occasionally separate and then they're so shocked they can't wait to get back together again. Before going downstairs I open the window a little.

It was the bed shop. Later in the day the jovial bed salesman calls a second time and says that he tried earlier. The bed is coming tomorrow. I want to know what time. He can't say exactly, "some time in the morning." Before hanging up, he advises me to buy an answering machine, so it's more convenient when people want to leave a message.

Behind the chicken coop, the donkey shed and the muck heap, there are eight willows in a row along the ditch. Seven stand up straight, one overhangs the ditch. For years now I have tackled that tree the same way: I lay the two sections of a ladder next to each other over the ditch and attach a short beam at right angles across the ladders, hammering in a few long nails to keep it in place (the sides of the ditch are at different heights). Then I lay a wooden pallet on the ladders, resting one side on the beam so it's as good as horizontal. By resting the wooden crate on the pallet, I can then reach the branches of the willow. I always start with the crooked willow, once that's done the rest are easy. The razor-sharp steel of the handsaw cuts smoothly through the young, tender wood. After the six trees yesterday, my arms and shoulders aren't moving quite as smoothly. I do a couple of willows, then rest, watching the sheep in the field near the Bosman windmill.

Twenty-three, that's an odd number actually, twenty would be more beautiful.

13

It took them a while, the men who came to deliver the bed. This one doesn't come apart. The front door was easy enough, the turn from the hall into the living room harder. I'd removed my old bed straight after milking. I put the mattress on its side in Henk's bedroom and threw the pieces of the wooden frame on the woodpile next to the muck heap. It's getting pretty big, I might have to have a bonfire on New Year's Eve, if the wind's right and it's not raining. The deliverymen left muddy tracks in the bedroom and the living room, and didn't want coffee because they had more beds to deliver. It was cold in the house for a long time afterwards because no one, me included, thought of shutting the front door during all that messing around in the hall. A cold easterly wind is angling in on the front windows. There'll be a sharp frost tonight.

The bed has a Swedish or Danish name I've forgotten, something with dots on an A. It is blue-and-white check and extremely wide; no matter which way I lie, my feet don't stick out over the edge. While I'm making the bed, Father keeps shouting. He's desperately curious. I get a fright for a moment because I think I've forgotten where I put the key, but then I remember leaving it in the keyhole. After slipping a pillowcase onto one of the pillows and laying it in place, I go and sit in the kitchen. If I sit on Mother's chair and lean across the table, I can see into the bedroom through the open doors. Two pillows. What do *I* want with two pillows? But one pillow looks funny, somehow it makes the big bed look unbalanced. And they weren't cheap. After reading the front page of the paper and drinking a cup of coffee, I walk to the bedroom to put the pillowcase on the second pillow.

In the afternoon the livestock dealer's truck drives into the yard. The livestock dealer is a strange fellow who hardly ever says anything. He wears a tidy dustcoat and a cap, which he takes off when he comes into the house. If he finds me outside or in the shed, he raises his cap. He always makes some kind of remark about the weather and then clams up. It's up to me to say whether I have anything for him. If I don't have anything for him, he leaves again immediately, without another word. He has never – and he's been visiting the house for more than thirty years – sat down at the kitchen table. He leaves his clogs next to the hall door and, when standing on the linoleum in the kitchen, puts one foot on top of the other and wriggles his toes in his knitted woolen socks. Today we are standing in the middle of the yard and I've got something for him. A few sheep.

"They been tupped?" he asks.

"Yes. I took the ram away at the end of November."

"Three?"

"Three. What's a sheep bring these days?"

"Hundred and twenty if you're lucky. More likely a hundred."

"That's not much."

"No, it's not much. Have you got them at the house?"

"No, they're in the back field."

He's happy to lend a hand, although he could have come back tomorrow. Together we walk into the field and drive the sheep to the causeway gate. He grabs one, I grab two. The other twenty rush off. After opening the gate and releasing his sheep into the next field, he takes one from me. We herd the sheep to the causeway gate close to the yard. I climb over it, fetch two sections of fencing out of the barn and set them up on either side of the lowered tailgate. There's fifteen feet at most between the barriers and the causeway gate. I open it and one of the sheep walks straight up into the back of the truck. The other two follow. The livestock dealer raises and bolts the tailgate.

"That went smoothly," he says.

"For once," I agree.

The livestock dealer raises a finger in farewell and gets into his truck. He drives slowly over to the causeway, then turns onto the road even more slowly.

I shut the gate. The remaining twenty sheep are huddled together near the windmill, in the very far corner of the farm.

That night, just before going to bed, I cut my fingernails and toenails and have a long shower. I leave the gas fire on low and my bedroom door open. In the big mirror above the mantelpiece, I look at myself naked, head to toe. Suddenly I feel like skating. I miss the heavy feeling you get in your backside and the muscles of your legs from long-distance skating. The fire's warmth glows on my penis. Then I crawl in under the duvet for the first time. The glow in my crotch fades fast; the duvet is scratchy new and I hardly sleep a wink all night.

14

Teun and Ronald are bundling up the willow shoots. They lay a length of baler twine on the ground, each throw an armful of willow shoots on it and tie it tight. They carry the bundles through the front garden to the yard. Every time they pass a window, they wave. In front of me on the kitchen table are a telephone bill and a hand-addressed letter Ada has brought in. The postman drove off just before she turned into the yard with a trailer hitched to the back of her car. It's Saturday.

I'd like to open the letter, but Ada is still standing on the threshold of my bedroom. She just felt the duvet cover. "You have to wash these covers first!" she calls to me. "They're always so stiff!" I nod at Ronald, who is waving as he walks past the front window. I follow him in my thoughts and he appears in the side window just when I expect him to. He waves again. He is wearing a woolly hat and snot is trailing from his purple nose. He's happy, he's always happy, even when his fingers are cold and he's trampling kale in my vegetable garden.

"It's lovely."

She makes me jump.

Ada is standing in the doorway with her head a little to one side, as if listening for something. "I miss something," she says. "In the living room."

"Chairs?"

"No." She thinks for a moment. "A sound."

"The clock?"

"Yes, the clock. Where's that got to? You didn't throw it on the wood-pile, did you?"

"No. It's upstairs with Father."

"Oh," says Ada. She looks at my hands. "Who's the letter from?"

"I don't know, I haven't opened it yet."

"How is your father?"

"The same."

"Does he ever come downstairs?"

"Sometimes. He sleeps a lot."

"I see." She looks at me with her head to one side, but this time not as if she's listening for something. "I'll go and load up the trailer." She turns and walks into the hall. I wait for the sound of the door opening into the scullery, but instead her head reappears around the corner of the kitchen door. "Two pillows, Helmer," she says. "Two pillows." Ada looks funny when she gives you a meaningful look, with that harelip. Then she really does disappear. I turn the letter over and over in my hand. There is no name on the back.

· · ·

Dear Helmer

Don't be shocked, I know you looked at the sender first, I always do that when I get letters too, but there's no reason for you to be shocked by my name. Maybe you don't even know who I am any more! We haven't seen or spoken to each other for more than thirty years and that makes writing this letter difficult.

I'll start by honestly saying straight out that I am finally writing to you because I think that your father has probably passed away by now. Am I right? Your father has always been the obstacle that has stopped me from getting in touch with you. I'm not trying to be nasty about this, and maybe you find it hurtful, if you are sad about your father's death (if he has died).

And do I really need to write down all the things that have happened to me? Okay, in a nutshell then. I went to stay with relatives in Brabant, where I soon married a pig farmer. We had two daughters and, much later, a son. My daughters left home long ago. My husband (he was called Wien, I know, it's a bit of a strange name) died last year. My son still lives at home, he just turned eighteen.

I may as well be honest and tell you that I already tried to get in touch with you before writing this letter. Once I cycled out to the farm in the middle of the night and stood there looking at it for a while. I saw you at the bedroom window upstairs (no sign of your father). I was staying at my aunt's in Monnickendam. (Yes, she's still alive, she's eighty-three. Do you know her? She doesn't know you.) I hadn't seen her for fifteen years and she couldn't understand what she owed the honor to. The next day I rang the bell, but suddenly panicked and left in a hurry. I also phoned you and then I heard your voice and hung up like a real coward. But I'm sure you'll understand that it's not easy for me to see or hear you. When I heard your voice, I pictured Henk standing there in your hall.

A letter seemed like the simplest solution, but now I'm writing it I find it difficult. Would you mind if I wrote you another letter later? Or shall we talk on the phone? I'll put my telephone number at the bottom of the letter.

That's all for now,

Best wishes,

Riet

P.S. There's something I'd like to ask you.

Like the envelope, the letter is handwritten. No address, just a telephone number. I don't open the bill.

In the afternoon – on a Saturday of all days – a council cherry picker arrives. One man operates the contraption from the ground while the other unscrews the lamppost cover. I stand behind the blinds in the living room to watch them, I don't think they can see me. It's only when they're finished that I leave my spot at the window. I lie down on the new bed. I'm restless, I have the same feeling in my body as the day I saw that flock of different birds and my sheep stared at me like the members of a firing squad. Sleep is out of the question, all kinds of things keep running through my head, nothing stays put. Painting the living room and the bedroom, pollarding the willows, Jarno Koper in Denmark, the old tanker driver's funeral, the hooded crow in the ash. Buying the new bed, which I am now lying on, and that should be enough to send me to sleep, but I'm too restless.

A letter from Riet.

15

On April 19th, 1967 I was halfway through the third term of the first year of my Dutch language and literature degree. I think I was the hardest working student in my year, not because of any ambition or drive of my own, but to show Father. *I* wasn't eligible for a grant because *he* had too many assets. That was what it said in the rejection letter from the Ministry of Education and Science, Board of Study Grants, and he and I both knew what those assets were: land, buildings, cows and machines. "Am I supposed to sell cows to send *you* to university?" said Father, when I showed him the letter. He didn't wait for an answer but crumpled the letter up without another word and, since there were no bins to hand, threw it in the kitchen sink. If he'd had a lighter or matches on him, he would have set fire to it. Henk was standing in the kitchen too and didn't know how to look at me from under his dark eyebrows. Mother retrieved the letter from the sink and tried to smooth it out, then put it in the bin after all.

So I stayed at home, rode my bike to Amsterdam, attended lectures and did all kinds of jobs to pay the tuition fees. When I sat at the kitchen table in the morning bleary-eyed because I had come home late the previous evening after unloading a delivery truck at a large department store, Mother would sometimes ask me what I got up to in Amsterdam – Amsterdam, the city you were better off avoiding. She didn't actually have a clue what to ask me, but at least she tried. Until that 19th of April, Father might have asked me three times how many big words I'd learned now, without waiting for an answer before resuming his conversation with Henk. Conversations about cows that had gone dry, yearlings that needed moving or other farmers in the neighborhood. Things that really meant something. To him and to Henk.

Henk was the farmer. Henk was Father's son. What he was supposed to make of me or what I was supposed to make of myself were questions he could ignore.

And Henk had Riet. Until December 1965, when he met her in a pub in Monnickendam, Henk belonged to me and I belonged to Henk. I was in the same pub and that was a source of some confusion for Riet. It was Christmas Eve, *the* night out for people who didn't attend Midnight Mass. Henk got talking to her and, as the evening progressed, they slid further away from the group that had started the evening together, the group of farm boys I was left with. Henk was facing away from me. I could tell from the back of his head that he was talking nineteen to the dozen, while now and then over his shoulder Riet glanced at me with a bewildered look in her eyes. She was the most beautiful girl I had ever seen. He talked, I was silent, it was a typical Henk and Helmer evening, and not the other way round. We were eighteen and still looked as alike as two lambs, but then from different ewes, and after that Christmas Eve I was left behind, alone.

Riet got her driver's license at the start of April. On April 19th she wanted to show Henk that, despite what he thought, despite what so many men thought, she hadn't passed the test because of her smile. I'd had a philology lecture that afternoon and rode my bike home. It was blowing from the south-west, a tailwind, my coat wasn't zipped up.

Mother was sitting in the kitchen, alone. "Henk's dead," she said.

At Murderer's Breach, between Edam and Warder, Riet went off the road because a car coming from the other direction didn't pull over. The car slid down the dyke, rolled and landed neatly, the right way up, in Lake IJssel. Henk was knocked out, the passenger door was twisted and the roof on his side was dented. Just there, the water was deeper than most places, perhaps because of the flood that once washed away this section of dyke, creating the lake called Murderer's Breach on the inland side. Even with the help of the driver who hadn't given way, Riet was unable to get him out of the car. The car, which wasn't winched out of Lake IJssel until the next day, was Father's dark-blue Simca.

As long as Henk was laid out in the living room, Riet spent every day at our house. She arrived early in the morning and went home late at night. We couldn't leave the coffin open for long because Henk had drowned. The temperature had plummeted during the night of the nineteenth and we kept the two sash windows ajar. Mother and Riet sat in the kitchen doing nothing all day. Now and then someone would visit, grandparents mostly, three of whom were still alive in 1967. Father and I avoided each other and did our best to stay outside as much as possible. Being inside the house was unbearable. The two women sat silently in the kitchen, Henk was laid out in the cold living room, and at night I couldn't sleep because I was afraid I would start to smell him. Two days after the accident I cycled to Amsterdam to attend a couple of lectures. On the way there I stood for a long time at the top of Schellingwoude Bridge, staring at the Orange Locks. I know with absolute certainty that I had a philology lecture on the nineteenth because when I came home Mother said that Henk was dead. The lectures I had before or after that date have completely faded from my memory. On the way back I stopped again for a long time at the top of Schellingwoude Bridge, now staring out over the Outer IJ, postponing the moment I would start pedaling again. That year the bridge was celebrating its tenth anniversary. I felt that I would be forgotten: Father and Mother were the parents, Riet was the almost-wife, I was just the brother.

Since that day almost every journey I make is north, I no longer go south of the village.

After the funeral Riet was still shivering, chilled to the bone by guilt and the icy water of Lake IJssel. Everyone else had left, the four of us were sitting in the kitchen: Riet in Henk's place, with the light from the side window behind her. Father raised his empty coffee cup and jiggled the spoon back and forth, staring down at the tabletop. Mother got up and silently poured another cup. Henk could do that too, make his spoon jump in his cup, but he smiled at me while he was doing it and he thanked Mother after she'd filled his cup. I saw Riet looking at Father. He stirred the milk skin into his coffee. Then she looked at me. In her eyes I saw again the bewilderment with which she had looked at me the night she met Henk. I don't remember talking to her. She did her talking with Mother. It was a week of silence.

She must have had a job, I don't remember. Three days later she was still at our house, as if she didn't know what to do next. She infected Mother with her mood. They'd walk around together, often to the Bosman windmill, as if they knew it was a place that meant a lot to Henk. She ate with us, and that was completely natural. At least for Mother and me. Not for Father. That evening, if I'm counting properly it must have been the 26th of April, he worked his way through his meal in silence. Just after shoving a forkful of potato into his mouth he spoke to Riet, it was virtually the only thing he said to her in that whole week of silence, "I want you to go away and never come back."

She put down her knife and fork – she was the only one who ate with knife and fork – neatly alongside her half-empty plate, slid her chair back and stood up. "Fine," she said calmly, as if she'd expected it, as if she'd been waiting for it. She walked to the hall, put on her coat and left through the front door. Mother started to cry. I got up and walked over to the front window. I saw her turning onto the road, on her bike. That's how I remember Riet: her back bent (she had a headwind), her blonde hair fluttering, riding her bike down a narrow, empty road that got emptier and emptier towards the dyke. She disappeared, just like the red light had in November, behind the window frame.

Father had more to say, "And you're done there in Amsterdam."

I became Father's boy. Mother didn't stop crying.

16

I'm skating. After four nights of frost Big Lake has frozen over except for an oval-shaped hole in the middle. If I keep an eye on the ducks, coots and moorhens, I'm safe enough. The Amsterdammers haven't shown up yet, they don't know it's already skateable. During the last real freeze, years ago, I bought a pair of racing skates because I wanted to skate corners. You can't skate corners on Frisian skates. Now I'm skating corners, faster and faster, wider and wider. I go down a little lower on my stiff knees. The faster I go, the less cracks appear in the ice, which is black in places. Skating before Christmas – it's been a long time. About a dozen Shetland ponies watch me stupidly, they don't see ice, they see smooth water. When my knees and lower back can take no more, I finally have to brake to stop myself from flying into the bone-dry undergrowth along the east side of the lake. If it stays this cold, I'll be able to skate to Monnickendam in a few days and maybe do a circuit around Watergang or Ilpendam.

I learned to skate without Henk and without Father. Father is scared of frozen water, although he'd never admit it. We did everything together, Henk and I, except skating. The farmhand taught me how to skate, Mother encouraged me. She skated on figure skates, turning elegant pirouettes, doing figure of eights and regularly shouting, "That's right!" The farmhand didn't pull me along, which I think is the usual way of teaching someone how to skate; he pushed me. His big hands enclosed my bottom like the seat of a chair, he bent his knees so much he was almost squatting. When I shouted stop, he braked and held me back by wrapping his hands around my hips. As I remember it, he skated around with me like that for hours. Long after Mother had finished her figure of eights. But it can't have been like that. Father must have strode out into the field to remind him sharply that he had more important things to do than entertain himself on the ice. He would have glared at me – a six- or seven-year-old kid – because Henk was doing the yearlings. Or collecting eggs, perhaps tail docking. Mother would have been downcast in the kitchen, back at work, because even she would have had an earful. Skating with the farmhand, what *was* she thinking?

That might have been the day that Father – simply because I was having fun doing something else – decided for himself that Henk would be the farmer, even though I was the oldest, if just by a couple of minutes. Henk helped Father, I went skating and treated the farmhand as an equal. Maybe it was just one incident in a series of events that made Father conclude I wasn't suited to succeed him. After Henk died Father had to make do with me, but in his eyes I always remained second choice.

· · ·

A few long strokes carry me to the place in the reeds where I have left my clogs. I take my skates off and look out at the water birds. Father calls coots *and* moorhens "water hens" because he always gets them mixed up. Later today I'll go and see how the frost flowers on his windows are doing.

Frost flowers remind me of Henk and his warm bed.

Even before I reach the road I see the livestock dealer's truck turning into the yard. I don't hurry. He'll go looking for me but, before he's been everywhere, I'll be home. My thoughts catch on the word "everywhere," and immediately I see the livestock dealer standing on the blue carpet next to Father's bed, cap in hand, silent, wriggling his toes and looking serious. Father isn't silent, he jabbers and gabbles and keeps talking until I come into the room. I hurry, the frost-covered grass crunching under my clogs. I swing my legs over the last gate and run into the yard.

The livestock dealer emerges from the barn. When he sees me he makes to raise his cap but changes his mind. "You've got a few good calves in there," he says.

"Yes," I say, still panting.

"Cold," he adds.

"Yes."

"Been skating?"

"Yeah. Big Lake's already frozen."

"I sold your sheep."

"That's fast."

"Ah, one of those hobby farmers. A hundred and twenty-five a head."

"Not bad."

He pulls out his wallet, an enormous thing that's chained to his belt. He licks his thumb and index finger, pulls out five fifties and digs a handful of change out of his pocket. He takes thirty per cent, whatever the price.

"Thanks," I say. "You going to declare it?"

"No."

"Good."

He walks over to his truck, parked in the middle of the yard. Before climbing into the cab, he says, "Have a good Christmas." He's talkative today.

I vaguely remember an art shop at the start of the Prooyen and park the car. It's called Simmie's. I notice that I'm feeling nervous and open the door without looking through the windows. A large woman in loose-fitting clothes approaches, the artist herself from the look of her. Was there something I wanted to ask? "No, I'm just looking." It doesn't take me long; if these colorful splotches are art, I'm a gentleman farmer from Groningen. Back on the street, I smell the wood fire from the smokehouse. I buy a pound of eel, which the fishmonger rolls up in old newspaper and puts in a plastic bag. Then I carry on along the water-front. There's a gallery near the English Corner. The soapstone statues on the shelves along the wall are beautiful, especially to touch, but I am still thinking of a painting. I head back to the middle of town. Banners announcing "FIREWORKS" have been hung everywhere. A crib with life-size cows and donkeys has been set up in the roofed outdoor section of The Weighhouse. A child touches the nose of a donkey and almost tumbles off the raised floor with surprise when its head rocks back and forth. In the old harbor there is an enormous Christmas tree on a barge, all lit up. The barge is stuck in the ice.

Walking back to the car, I pass an antiques shop. I go in, even though the last thing I'm looking for is more old junk; I've just tossed a load of that on the woodpile or stowed it away in Henk's room. An elderly man looks up from a dark corner, but doesn't say a word. I put the plastic bag with the eel down on a chair near the door and look around. There is a pile of old maps on an oak table. No idea what I would want with an old map, but I still leaf through the pile: North Holland, land reclamation, something I don't immediately recognize, Marken, the Beemster. I drop the maps one after the other until I'm back at the one I didn't recognize. It's Denmark, an old Denmark and mostly in green, with three insets: Iceland, Bornholm and the Faroe Islands. Iceland and the Faroes are in shades of brown. The map is in good condition, just slightly yellowed along the edge. I buy it and even get change from the fifty I give the old man. Then I cross the road to the picture framer's. I find a wide frame in the right size that has been painted with clear varnish. There is no one else in the shop; the frame-maker has time to cut a piece of non-reflective glass for me. He packs the frame and the glass separately. I don't get any change from the four fifties I give him. Before returning to the car, I pop back into the antique shop. In all the excitement I forgot my smoked eel.

Driving home I think of Jarno Koper. In Jutland.

. . .

I quickly eat a few slices of bread and cross the fields to Big Lake for the second time today. The light is different from this morning and a flock of geese have settled near the open spot in the ice. I pull on my skates. By my second lap around the lake, I'm going so fast that I don't need to skate any straight sections at all. I skate one big loop, a corner that never ends. I keep going until I'm exhausted.

After milking, I eat half of the pound of eel on bread. I drink a glass of milk with it. When I've finished I go upstairs with an apple. I turn on the light in his room. He is lying on his back with his eyes wide open, the blanket pulled up to his nose. He gives off almost no warmth, the bottom of the window is covered with frost flowers. Maybe he'll freeze to death in the coming night.

"I've got an apple for you," I say.

"Cold," he says.

"Yes, it's freezing." I lay the apple on the bedside cabinet and leave the room. It's only on the stairs that I think of a knife. I'm not going back up again, not to take him a knife and not to turn off the light either.

The framer has stuck a paper bag with little nails in it to the glass. Now everything is spread out on the kitchen table I notice that something is missing. A back. I measure up the frame and go out to the barn with a pencil and tape measure. I find a piece of thinnish plywood among some old timber and cut it to size on the workbench under the silver-gray death's-head cabinet. The activity keeps me warm. I hammer two small nails into the plywood and attach a thin wire to hang it up with.

I lay the frame face down on the kitchen table, then slot in the piece of glass, followed by the map (which fits perfectly, so that most of the yellowed edge disappears behind the frame), finally laying the piece of plywood on top. I haven't left much leeway and four small nails are enough to anchor it tightly in the frame. Then I carry the framed map into the living room and hold it up against the wall here and there. It's lost between the windows and it can't go to the left or right of the mantelpiece without making the other side look empty. It will have to be the bedroom. I bang a large nail into the wall next to the door and hang the map where I can see it from my bed.

The donkeys are waiting for me, even though I don't go out to them every evening. I've left the light on and it casts a broad track into the yard. My very own crib. They snort when I enter the shed. I give them a couple of winter carrots and a scoop of oats. Their breath billows up out of the trough as a cold cloud. I sit on a bale of hay and wait for them to finish feeding. Quiet cackling noises come from the chicken coop next to the donkey shed. Strange.

I've got cold from sitting still. When I take off my clothes in the scullery, I do it slowly, to get even colder. I shiver in the bathroom until the water has warmed up. I wash my hair and clasp my hands together behind my neck to make a bowl that I empty again and again, splashing hot water over my shoulders and down my back. I dry myself off and walk to the living room, where I turn off the lights and turn up the fire. I stand up straight and study myself in the mirror in the light coming from the bedroom. This is my house now. I can stand naked in front of the mirror whenever I like. The warmth from the fire glows on my penis, the muscles in my bum and legs feel heavy and strong. It's as if I can feel the farmhand's hands on my bum again. The sensation is so real that I can't help putting my own hands there to make the imagined hands disappear. Riet's letter is on the mantelpiece. I take it to the bedroom and read it yet again in bed (under the second duvet cover, which I have washed in the meantime). Before turning off the light I look up at the map of Denmark. That's three sheep hanging there, I think, rolling onto my left side and pulling my knees up in the dark.

17

A second letter has arrived:

Dear Helmer,
Brabant is horrible. I don't know if you've ever been here, but take it from me:
it's terrible. Nothing but pigs and sociable people, but their kind of sociable is
nothing like what we used to have at home in North Holland. Carnival, for
instance, can you imagine? Can you see me dressed up in funny clothes, a clown
suit with a mask on? And everyone keeps on smiling the whole time, as if they've
got anything to smile about.

Our two daughters are Brabant born and bred, but because they're our
daughters, and I get on with them really well, it doesn't matter so much. They're
both very warm and they both have nice husbands and young children (yes, I'm
a grandmother!). They live a stone's throw away so I can drop by whenever I
feel like it.

Our son (I've only just noticed that I've written "our," although Wien has been
dead now for almost a year) doesn't fit in quite so well in Brabant. I don't know

why, maybe it's because he takes after me more than Wien. After Wien's death I sold up and now I live in the village, together with my son. That's strange: husband dies, you move, and then all you've got is time on your hands.

I'm writing this letter because you haven't written back or called. I'm curious about how life has treated you. I don't even know if you're married, but I suspect not, because just before my mother died, she told me you weren't. Yes, you can see that I tried to keep up with you as best I could. And there's something I'd like to ask you, but I'd rather not do that in a letter. Won't you write or call?

I'll just say it straight out: I would like very much to drop by. To see you, but also to see the farm I visited so often (and where I, if things had gone differently, would now live). But then the problem with your father (which I wrote about in my last letter) needs to be resolved.

Hoping to hear from you,

Love,

Riet

This time there is an address on the back of the envelope. The name of the village doesn't ring any bells. I don't understand what she wants from me. Like the previous letter, this one is muddled. The first time it was "best wishes, Riet," now it's "love." It's as if she's trying to arouse my curiosity. Is the thing she wants to ask me about, which she also mentioned in her first letter, simply whether she's allowed to drop by? Or is it something else. The sentence "and where I, if things had gone differently, would now live" (in brackets, of all things, as a passing comment) annoys me. I interpret the end of her letter as meaning that I have to inform her that Father is dead, otherwise she won't come.

·　·　·

A fitful thaw has begun. Now and then the temperature creeps above freezing. It's misty with occasional rain, but most of the day it stays below zero. There's a layer of water on the ice, but at the same time the yellowish-white frozen edges in the ditches keep widening. The mist is strange; with mist you expect warm air. I can forget about my Monnickendam–Watergang circuit, I've already put away my skates. The donkeys stay indoors. The chickens are hardly laying. The frost flowers in Father's bedroom have slid off the window, there's a pool of water on the windowsill. He ate the apple. I don't know how he managed it. He must have been very hungry.

Twenty cows. A pre-war tie stall barn. A few calves and a handful of yearlings. Twenty-three sheep. No, twenty. I'm not even a smallholder. But the paintwork is in good condition and the tiles on the roof are straight.

In the afternoon the young tanker driver arrives. I don't go into the milking parlor. I watch him through the round window, which was moved from the outside wall to the wall between the milking parlor and the scullery when the milking parlor was built. With the doors to the shed, hall and milking parlor shut, it's dark in the scullery, the only light comes in through that same round window. Mist seems to be streaming along the sides of the enormous tanker and into the building. The driver keeps smiling, despite the pitiful amount of milk flowing into his tanker through the hose from my tank. I've forgotten his name again and the harder I try to dredge it up, the further it sinks. There's an O in it, I know that much. He sticks a little finger in his nose; I actually feel like turning away. He doesn't look like he's waiting for me, he doesn't seem to care whether I come to make small talk or not.

Is it enough to have the paintwork in good condition and the roof tiles straight? The willows neatly pollarded and the donkeys warm and well fed in their shed?

Of course I am curious about Riet. Of course I want something to happen. I want to know what has become of the beautiful girl with long blonde hair – the young woman who was going to marry my brother. I want to hear what she has to say, I want to see the look in her eyes. I wait until the young driver has leapt up to his cab, as lithe as ever, before going into the parlor to spray the storage tank clean. The hot water drives the cold mist back outside.

After milking I go into the vegetable garden to pick some kale. It's had more than enough frost. I straighten up and look through the kitchen window into my own house. The lights are on in the kitchen and the living room. In the distance – I can see it because all the doors are open – the new bed is like a throne in a palace. It's Christmas Eve and in seven days the new year will start.

II

18

"There's no such thing as a pig farmer."

"What do you mean?"

"Pig keepers, maybe, but you can't call them farmers."

"Why not?"

"Did that husband of yours have land?"

"Yes."

"How many acres?"

"A bit between the sheds and another bit around the side."

"That's what I mean. A farmer has land and he does something with that land. Pig keepers keep pigs in sheds for slaughter. That's got nothing to do with farming . . ."

"The clothesline was on one bit of land and the silage clamp was on the other."

". . . it's all about money." I'm standing in the hall and looking out of the kitchen window. It's raining. The fitful thaw has finally set in and any ditches with ice left in them are now steaming. Funnily enough it was sunny all day yesterday and the temperature dropped below zero again last night. I have no idea what Riet is looking out at. The telephone conversation isn't going well. Riet (who answered using the name of her deceased husband) mentioned pig farmers and I couldn't help myself. I feel like hanging up.

"Come on, Helmer, let's change the subject."

"Yes," I say.

"Would it be all right if I dropped by?"

"That's what I'm calling about."

"How . . . is your father . . ."

"Dead." I'll sort that one out later.

"Oh," says Riet, as if she's suddenly intensely sorry.

"It's no big deal."

It's quiet for a moment, somewhere in Brabant. "Did you have a good Christmas?"

"Yep."

"And last night?"

"I lit a New Year's bonfire."

"Just like the old days!"

"That's right. The two boys from next door came to watch. And help, of course."

"That must have been fun."

"It was. Except the youngest, Ronald, burned his hand."

"Oh . . ."

"Not badly. He even managed to laugh about it, he thought it was cool. Fortunately his mother was there too."

"When shall I come? I can any time."

I can any time. Half my life I haven't thought about a thing. I've milked the cows, day after day. In a way I curse them, the cows, but they're also warm and serene when you lean your forehead on their flanks to attach the teat cups. There is nothing as calming, as protected, as a shed full of sedately breathing cows on a winter's evening. Day in, day out, summer, autumn, winter, spring.

Riet says "I can any time" and those four words send everything toppling. I see her emptiness, and her emptiness shows me mine.

Of course it's Father I'm cursing, it's not the cows' fault, especially not the cows we have now.

"Helmer?"

"Yes," I say. "I'm here"

"When shall I come?"

"Whenever you like."

For a long time that afternoon I sit with the donkeys, feeding them pieces of mangold. Although it's stopped raining, it's still gray. The light is on in the donkey shed. I recognized her voice.

Yesterday evening, before I poured diesel over the woodpile, Ada, Teun, Ronald and I stood by the donkeys for a while. Cold stars were shining over the shed. Ada's husband wasn't there, he wanted to keep his eye on a cow that was about to calve. Plus – according to Ada – he doesn't like "the festive season," I had made doughnuts, a task I have taken upon myself every New Year since Mother's death. Father was sitting very briefly at his old place at the kitchen table. He worked hard to keep himself upright on his elbows and ate two doughnuts. I sat in Mother's old spot and stared at him while he and Ada talked. Teun and Ronald shared the other kitchen chair. Ronald kept his eye on Father and seemed a bit scared, he had trouble swallowing. Father told Ada no less than three times that he wanted to see a doctor. When she shot me a questioning glance after the third time, I raised my eyebrows significantly.

"I hope you get better soon, Mr. van Wonderen," she said as I carried him out of the kitchen.

"Do you have heating upstairs?" she asked in a concerned voice when I came back down.

"No," I said. "But he's a tough old codger. A shame he's not altogether with it any more. He's going downhill fast."

"Is he dying?" asked Ronald, eating a doughnut at top speed now there was nothing to hold him back.

"Ronald!" Ada said.

"When are we going to light the fire?" asked Teun.

And then the donkeys, and then the New Year's bonfire, and then a smoldering board (from my old bed) falling on Ronald's hand. He'd got a little too keen while poking the fire with a thick branch.

"Finished!" Father calls. The flush gurgles dully, as if the lid is closed.

I've been standing for a good while in the hall, in front of the toilet door. The doughnuts have got his bowels working. I contract my nostrils, open the door and lift him up. He pulls up his own pajama bottoms. "Wash your hands," I say.

He picks up the piece of soap on the sink and I turn on the tap.

Carrying him upstairs, I ask, "Do you actually know what day it is today?"

"Christmas?" he says.

"New Year's Day. You're not right in the head any more."

"No?"

"No."

"You're the one who's not right in the head. I'm not mad."

"Have it your own way," I say, laying him on the bed.

"Ada was here last night," he says.

"Yes, she was." I sit down on the chair in front of the window. Maybe I should buy an electric heater after all, it's damp in here. Before you know it he'll have all kinds of terrible fungal infections. I rest my elbows on the armrests and rub my hands together. The wall with photos, samplers and paintings is a big rectangle with little rectangles and squares on it, I can't see any detail. I stand up and turn on the light. With my hands behind my back, like someone visiting a gallery, I walk along the wall extremely slowly before sitting down again. "Why did your mother embroider two samplers instead of just one?"

"You'd have to ask her," Father says reluctantly.

"I can't."

"No, you can't," he says with a sigh.

"Did she think one of us wouldn't make it?"

"I don't know."

"Was it so you could throw one of them out?"

"Shouldn't you be milking?"

"Soon. The cows aren't going anywhere."

"Hmmm..."

"It was economical of her," I say. "No, not economical, practical."

"Yes, practical," says Father.

"But still, when someone dies at nineteen, you don't take their sampler off the wall."

"No."

I talk, but hardly hear what I'm saying. The telephone conversation with Riet is on my mind. That's what I want to talk about, I wanted to taunt him with it and instead I'm taunting him with our samplers. Until five minutes ago I'd never stopped to think why grandmother Van Wonderen embroidered two separate samplers. One sampler must have been a big enough job as it was. Did Mother actually know she was going to have twins? I sigh and open my eyes. I am really not in the mood for tormenting Father. It's New Year's Day.

"What's the matter?" asks Father.

I open my eyes. "Nothing." I get up and walk to the door. I pull up the weights of the grandfather clock. "Kale tonight?"

"Delicious," says Father. He looks happy. It's unbearable.

"Light on?"

"Yes."

"Curtains closed?"

"Yes."

I walk back to the window and draw the curtains. The lamppost in front of the farm is already on. Now it's been fixed, no one can stare in unseen.

The bulb in the scullery casts a dim glow up the staircase and onto the landing. The door of the new room is open. As an invitation: come and fill me. I look at the key in the lock of the bedroom door. I look but don't turn it. I hurry downstairs.

I ring Ada to ask about Ronald's hand.

"It's fine," she says, "it's not that bad at all."

I'm glad to hear it. It was my fire.

19

Mother was not just outrageously ugly. She was outrageously kind-hearted too. Her eyes were always a little watery, a bit moist, perhaps because of the slight bulge. There was something wrong with her thyroid, and those moist eyes softened her view of the world. Father beat and scolded, Mother only had to look at Henk and me to make things better again. She looked at us a lot.

Henk was Father's boy; I was not Mother's boy. She didn't differentiate, although I did notice that, during the period when Riet joined us at the table, she looked at me more often than she looked at Henk. It wasn't a look of consolation, it was a look of encouragement, like a hand on my back to push me forward. Mother got along perfectly well with Riet, but her presence also placed Mother in a dilemma: through no fault of her own, her boys were no longer equal. Father had no such scruples, he had taken sides long before.

When she died (not from an overactive thyroid, but from a heart attack), Father could no longer make his spoon jump in his coffee cup the way Henk had as well. After all, there was no one there to answer the call. I was there, of course, but he wasn't reckless enough to provoke me like that. We just stopped drinking coffee, or we drank coffee separately. Ada hadn't moved in next door yet, she never knew Mother.

She had the heart attack in the shower. That means it was a Saturday. I wasn't at home and it wouldn't have occurred to Father to go and check, despite her staying in the bathroom much longer than usual. Some people have a heart attack and just keep on going, some people collapse and never get up again. Mother never got up again.

I never blamed her for not speaking up the day Father sent Riet away and told me I was done "there in Amsterdam." What if, instead of crying, she had said something to protect me from spending my life milking cows? Would I have seized the opportunity? I don't think so. I was nineteen, I was already a man. I could have stuck up for myself. I didn't, I stayed as silent as Mother. Long after Riet had disappeared behind the window frame (by then she was sure to be up on the dyke and I'd had plenty of time to commit to memory a place where I might find a nest of peewit's eggs), I turned around. To the left of Father's back I saw her half-emptied plate, the cutlery placed neatly on either side. To the right of Father's back sat Mother, looking at me even more moistly than usual. At that moment an alliance was sealed. I couldn't say exactly what that alliance involved, but it definitely included some we'll-get-through-this-together. I sat back down at the table and we finished the meal in silence. The next morning Father and I milked the cows together. After the milking I put my textbooks in a cardboard box and put the box in Henk's built-in wardrobe. Weeks later a letter from my tutor arrived, asking where I was and whether I was planning on coming back. I put the unanswered letter in with the books. I've ignored the cardboard box ever since.

The alliance held until her death. It was an alliance of glances, not words. Mother and I looked at each other when he disappeared into the bedroom after calling her a romantic soul; when he growled while cutting the gristle off a piece of braised steak; when he raged across the fields while moving the yearlings or sheep from one field to another; when he went to bed at ten o'clock on New Year's Eve; when he barked the day's jobs at me (as if I was a fifteen-year-old kid and not a forty-year-old man); when he said "I wouldn't touch it with a barge pole" in discussions about anything at all, before going to sit in his chair in the living room like a lump of rock.

On very rare occasions she avoided looking at me, and that was almost always after Father had asked if it wasn't time for me to start looking for a wife. I took that to mean that for once she agreed with him.

After her death I didn't have anyone left to look at, to look *with* – that was the worst of it. The alliance had been unilaterally dissolved. I found it – and find it – very difficult to look Father straight in the eye. In Mother's eyes I always saw Henk's shadow and I assumed that she saw the same in mine. (Of course, she also saw Henk in my body as a whole, in my eyes she saw him double.) Father's eyes never gave away anything – after Mother's death even her shadow was absent.

20

For Riet I make an exception: I drive south. South-west, to be precise. To the ferry in North Amsterdam. We have agreed on a time and long before that time I am already parked in front of a chip stand on the IJ. Futuristic ferries cross back and forth, streamlined butter dishes in blue and white, nothing like the pale-green boats they had in 1967. Back then they still took cars, the ferries were sailing motorways. I see "Municipal Ferry No. 15" before me, and the narrow, roofed sections for bikes and motorbikes. They were only pale green inside the deck, the outside was a filthy white. I'd forgotten that.

I try to think my way further into the city. Faces and names of fellow students don't come back and I can't even picture the building I had lectures in. It's all gone, there across the water.

I described the Opel Kadett to her, but, faced with the stream of pedestrians and cyclists, I start to worry. Who will discover who? Should I stay in the car or get out and stand next to it?

Earlier this morning, when I was in the middle of the yard with Father in my arms and he asked me through chattering teeth and trembling lips where I was taking him, I decided to carry him back to his bedroom. I was going to put him in the loft of the yearling shed. His question and the inquisitive looks from the donkeys (one of the two started to bray loudly, waking the chickens from their morning snooze) were enough to make me abandon the plan. How was I going to get him up the ladder anyway? The return journey went smoothly, all the doors were wide open. I put him back in bed (still warm) and was going to leave the room without a word. At the door I changed my mind.

"I'm going to pick up Riet," I said.

He looked at me with a blank expression.

"At the ferry in Amsterdam. She's coming to visit."

"Riet?" The name croaked out and he went a bit pale.

"Yes, Riet. And you're dead."

"Dead?"

"I told her you're dead."

"Why?"

Now I tried to look at *him* blankly. "Do you need to ask?"

He thought about it.

"If I were you, I'd keep quiet," I said ominously. "Otherwise there's a chance she'll come upstairs."

"What for?"

"Payback."

"Oh . . ."

"And you're not all there, remember?"

"Oh..."

"I'm going now."

Que será, será, as Doris Day would say, I thought on the stairs. Whatever will be, will be.

I'm old, I thought in the scullery.

A ferry arrives every six minutes: five since I've been parked here. A lot of women in their fifties have got off them, fortunately I can exclude the ones with bikes. They're all wearing thick coats and scarves. It's been a long time since I've seen a winter like this: the temperature has fallen below zero again and there is even snow on the ground. The sixth ferry approaches the quayside. I check my watch; this will be the ferry that brings her to me. Where are all these people going on an ordinary weekday? Riet is one of the last to get off the ferry. I feel a little dizzy, I was expecting someone who looks like Ada (why that should be, I don't know), but it is Riet just as she rode away thirty years ago. Without the long blonde hair, a little plumper, and with a different way of walking. I sit rigid behind the steering wheel, which I have involuntarily grabbed with both hands. She walks straight up to the car. I feel like falling to one side, crawling under the dashboard, putting the car in reverse and disappearing backwards into the IJ, straight through the chip stand if necessary. Maybe she'll try to save me.

She stops in front of the car and looks in through the windscreen. I wait for a moment, then open the door. She approaches with outstretched arms.

"Hello, Helmer," she says.

"Hello, Riet," I say.

Very old fury, a fury I can't remember having, whose existence I didn't even suspect, rises up inside me. Riet isn't troubled by fury, I can see that. She is moved and confused, that's what's troubling her. The longer Henk is dead, the more I look like him, simply because there is no longer any comparing.

No, fury is too big a word, outrage is closer.

What is it like to have a relationship with a twin? I wouldn't know – apart from some childish carry-on at primary school – I have never been involved in anything like it. That Christmas Eve was followed by a Christmas Henk filled with absent-minded humming, not even stopping during meals. Over the roast beef and cauliflower cheese, he answered all of our grandparents' questions in such detail that Father looked up with surprise and Mother looked at me with an expression which would only become normal later, during our alliance. He was home on New Year's Eve, but two minutes into the New Year he disappeared without telling me where he was going. Late at night, when I was crossing the bridge near The Weighhouse with the group of farm boys we had both been a part of until the week before, I saw them. They were sitting holding hands on a bench in the drizzle. I tried to hide behind the brawniest farm boy and spotted something further along – a snot-colored Volkswagen Beetle two or three steps away – that I might be able to reach without being seen. As the brawniest farm boy was also the one who had drunk the most, he pushed his way through the others to talk to Henk, leaving me exposed. I can still picture the snot-colored Beetle perfectly, I have no idea what was said. There are two other things I haven't forgotten. One: Henk saw me there – at the back of the group, while he was talking to the drunk youth and keeping Riet's hand firmly clasped in his – and wasn't able to look me in the eye. That had never happened before. Two: a little later Riet noticed me as well and I realized that I was the last person she wanted to see, she wanted to forget that there was someone else walking around who looked just like Henk. I broke away from the group and turned down a lane behind the Beetle, fortunately Monnickendam is full of lanes. About a hundred yards later, I put a hand on a damp wall, bent forwards and spewed up all the beer and doughnuts. Then I went off in search of my bike, finally finding it where we had started our pub crawl. Someone had set off fireworks between the spokes of the back wheel. I hoisted the bike up onto one shoulder and walked home, swapping the bike back and forth between my right and left shoulders on the way. I licked drops of water off the bell to get the dirty taste out of my mouth. Late at night had changed to early in the morning. Drizzle isn't much more than mist with delusions of grandeur, but I was still saturated by the time I got home.

It was months before Henk finally brought Riet home with him. Our farm was at its best for her first visit. It was the time of year when eager lambs dive at the ewes in the field next to the farmhouse, peewits and godwits call their own names while defending their nests, the willows have already sprouted and the crooked ash in the front garden is about to come into leaf. A light-green spring in which even a muck heap can look fresh. Father kept his distance; Mother welcomed Riet with moist eyes and open arms.

I had seen her a few times since New Year and been clumsy and insecure in her company. She was awkward and quiet in mine. Now that she was going to be in our house I had even less idea of how to act. Henk took her to the Bosman windmill, our windmill, that very first time. They came back with a peewit's egg, and after that things were never really right between Riet and me.

Worse still, things between Henk and me were never right again either.

Later Riet spent her first night at our house, it must have been some time in August.

"Colts and fillies separate," Mother announced one night at the kitchen table. The night before Riet was expected.

"What?" said Henk.

"Colts and fillies separate."

Henk had to think it over for a moment. "But you're a colt and a filly too?" he said with all the innocence he could muster, gesturing at Father.

Father snarled.

Riet slept in Henk's room, Henk slept in mine. On a mattress on the floor. I couldn't think of anything to say, I had trouble breathing, something I put down to the oppressive heat. The window was wide open, the curtains weren't drawn, a full moon was shining straight into the room.

Henk was lying half under a sheet, his upper body bared and bluish. He was beautiful, so beautiful. After a long silence, almost as oppressive as the temperature, he whispered something I didn't understand.

"What?" I said.

"Shhh!"

"What did you say?" I whispered.

"I'm going next door."

"To Riet?" I said numbly.

"Where else?" He sat up straight and pushed away the sheet. He pulled up his knees and stood up. He was wearing big white underpants. He walked to the door as if treading on eggshells and pulled it open inch by inch. It took a very long time before his body had left my bedroom and the door was shut again.

I've hated moonlit nights ever since. The bluish light that comes into bedrooms through curtains or venetian blinds and can't be kept out is cold, even in summer.

No, give me coots, there's something I like to hear at night. Their yapping drives away emptiness and next year they'll yap again, even if they're not the same ones, and ten years from now they'll be yapping still. You can depend on coots.

21

Riet is sitting at the kitchen table, in Henk's old spot. I can't tell from her face whether she has sat there deliberately. She is staring at a photo on the front page of the newspaper of a group of Koniks standing on a strip of land surrounded by the waters of the Waal. Here it's freezing, across the borders it's raining, and washlands and banks everywhere are under water.

"Polish horses," she says to the newspaper.

"Coffee?" I ask.

Only now does she look up. "Yes, please."

The sun is shining: low and cold, but a warm yellow. I have never been to Austria or Switzerland, but this is how I imagine the sun on ski slopes. The coffee machine is in full sunlight and I see that it needs a wipe with a damp cloth. I take my time, with my back to Riet I don't have to worry about the expression on my face. From the corner of my eye I see something pass the front window.

"A hooded crow!" exclaims Riet.

I turn around. It's back in the ash, perched on its old branch and rearranging its feathers. I see the knuckles of my hand, wrapped around the handle of the coffee pot, turn white. This is *the* moment for noise from upstairs. It stays quiet.

"Have you seen hooded crows before?" I ask, making more noise than necessary as I slide the coffee pot in under the filter.

"Sure, often enough. In Denmark. They're almost all hooded crows up there."

"Have you been to Denmark?"

"A few times. On holiday." She thinks for a moment. "Four times."

"What's it like?"

"I don't know what it *is* like, only what it *was* like. It must be eight years since we last went. The girls weren't with us, they'd been going on holidays alone for years. It was just the three of us."

I sit down, cross my arms and let her take her time.

Riet looks out. "Do you remember the wooden electricity poles you used to have here?"

"Yes, of course." Irritation itches in my forearms.

"They still have them there, but concrete. They're a bit behind." She keeps on staring out, without seeing anything. The water sputters in the coffee machine. "We were there in August, in the car. The farmers had set fire to piles of straw and there were swallows on the electricity wires."

"Swallows."

"Yes. Wien didn't get it at all. 'Who on earth burns straw!' he said and, 'What a waste!'"

"He's got a point."

"I don't know about any of that. I thought those swallows were so beautiful. The electricity cables hung really low." She starts crying quietly.

"What is it?"

"Ah, I'm chattering away and I actually feel very peculiar here." She hides her face in her hands.

"Relax. First some coffee." I stand up and get the best cups from the kitchen cupboard. Not the mugs, the best cups, that's what Mother would have done. Earlier this morning I put the matching milk jug and sugar pot on the table. I pour coffee into the cups and lay a silver spoon on each saucer. I arrange some biscuits on a plate. I put the coffee and the biscuits on the table. If it wasn't freezing outside, I would slide the window open. Specks of dust float through the kitchen.

"I feel strange too," I say, sitting back down.

Riet smiles. "We both feel strange."

I feel light-headed. Unreal. Take Father, for instance: he's always been just like he is now. I've seen him every day my whole life long. Every day he has grown older, but because we have grown old together, it has all been gradual. When I see a photo of my father as a young man – like the photo on the wall of the bedroom upstairs – I know it's him, but it's distinct from the father I have now. I didn't really know him when he was young, because I was much younger at the time. We've both grown old without my noticing. I haven't seen Riet for more than thirty years. It's shocking, as if I'm in bed having a bad dream.

This is what I am thinking, what is she thinking? I feel like copying her and hiding my face in my hands. "Who do you see when you look at me?" I ask.

"Henk," she says.

"I'm Helmer."

"I know. I still see Henk."

Before we got to the kitchen, I showed her the new living room. She didn't like it. "It's so bare in here," she said. "What happened to all the photos?" The door to the bedroom was shut and I had no plans to open it for her. "And the curtains and the sideboard and the bookcase with your mother's books?" She looked at herself in the large mirror above the mantelpiece and used both hands to plump up her hair a little.

"Ah, the cows," she says, as we walk through the shed. She's wearing jeans. Her hair is still blonde and even in the sunlight in the kitchen I couldn't tell whether she bleaches it. It's not permed like most women's in their mid-fifties. She walks a little stiffly. It is totally impossible for me to see her as the mistress of this house: making meatballs, running after sheep or heifers, cuddling up to Henk in bed at night, having her kids visit on Saturday mornings, a grandchild climbing the ash in the front garden.

"I broke a leg a long time ago," she says when she notices me looking at the way she walks. "It stiffens up in cold weather."

Skiing? A bike accident? A wet floor in the pig shed?

"I was cleaning the kitchen ceiling and the stepladder slipped."

Sunlight comes in through the square windows, a cow groans and a mangy cat shoots off. It's a cat I can't remember having seen before. Is it one that escaped last spring's motorized cull?

"What kind of animals are they, pigs?" I ask.

"They're not cows, that's for sure." She rests her hand on the bundled lengths of baler twine hung up on an enormous nail. "Piglets are cute, but the older they get, the nastier."

"And then they're ready for slaughter."

"Yes, then they're ready for slaughter."

"And your husband?"

"What do you mean?"

"What kind of fellow was he?"

She thinks for a moment. "He was respectable. He was a respectable man."

"Respectable?"

"Yes."

We walk into the yard. Riet pulls the collar of her coat tight. "My daughters are respectable women. Maybe Brabant brings that out in people, respectability."

"And your son?"

"What have you got there!" blurts Riet as she catches sight of the donkey shed. She walks up to it. "This never used to be here. Did it?"

"No," I say. "The donkeys are new."

"Donkeys!"

They've heard us and are standing inquisitively at the railing with their heads up. When they see us, one starts to swing her head. The light has been on all night.

"Would you like to feed them?" I ask.

"Yes, please."

I take a few large winter carrots out of the box on the bale of hay and give them to Riet. She sticks two carrots through the bars at once. They disappear in the donkeys' mouths with a snap. I scratch the donkeys' ears. For a moment everyone is happy. There's something comforting about her having established that we both feel strange.

Riet walks from the donkey shed to the chicken coop. She waves a hand at the willows, a little impatiently, maybe to let me know that she can see they've been pollarded recently. And that Henk would have pollarded them if things had turned out differently. "You used to have brown chickens here," she says, peering in through the wire.

"That's right, Barnevelders."

"And these?"

"These are Lakenvelders."

"They're beautiful. Are they good layers?"

"They're okay, not as good as the Barnevelders."

The chicken coop leads inevitably to the causeway gate. She leans her forearms on it and stares out over the fields. It's incredibly light because of a thin layer of snow on the grass. The ditches are steaming. "The windmill," she whispers.

I'm not in the mood for that at all. I turn and start walking towards the milking parlor. A little later she follows, I hear her irregular footfall on the frost-hardened yard. Now, with my left arm, I gesture at the donkey paddock. "In good weather they're out there," I say. We walk through the milking parlor to the scullery. I cut straight through to the hall door, Riet stops in front of the door to the staircase.

"You coming?" I say.

She doesn't answer.

"I thought," I try, "if we eat an early lunch, we can go for a walk to the cemetery afterwards."

She doesn't answer.

I keep at it. "Then I can take you back to the ferry on time, before milking."

She doesn't answer.

"What is it?" I ask.

"I want to go upstairs."

"To Henk's room?"

"Yes."

I pull the door open and lead the way upstairs. I open the door to Henk's room. Riet walks in expectantly. I stay in the doorway – it's so full inside there's only room for one of us. She looks around and sits down on the bed for a while.

Then I can't see her any more, she has disappeared completely under Henk and the January sunlight has made way for August moonlight. Henk's white underpants have got stuck at his knees and his body is going up and down, a movement that doesn't seem right for someone his age. I can almost smell him. He is holding his breath, the dimple above the crack of his bum is damp, he presses her deeper and deeper into the old mattress, his Achilles tendons are part of the up-and-down, as if the movement is a wave that starts in his toes.

". . . his bed?"

"What?"

"Is this the bed Henk slept in?"

I blink a few times, it takes a while for the warm August night to turn back into a January morning. "Yes."

"I don't recognize it. There's so much junk in here." She lays her hands beside her on the blanket – as if she has no plans ever to stand up again – and looks out of the window. "That hooded crow is still there," she says.

"Come on," I say.

She stands up and leaves the bedroom.

"My old bedroom," I say casually and fairly loudly as we walk past the second door. I notice the key and try to remember whether I locked the door. "Full of junk as well." I hurry on through to the new room, whose door is wide open. Riet follows.

She leans against one of the walls, knees bent slightly and her jumper bunched up around her shoulders. "His face," she says. "His face in that cold water. His hair floated back and forth like seaweed."

22

"Nothing's changed here at all," she says.

"They're not allowed to build."

"Why not?"

"Heritage area."

We're walking through the village to the cemetery. Ten minutes ago Ada just happened to be watering the plants on her kitchen windowsill. The sun has only just passed its highest point but our shadows still stretch out in front of us. "You should come back in late summer," I say. "For years now there's been a kind of competition going on here."

"What do you mean?"

"Who has the most hydrangeas in their front garden. Preferably in as many colors as possible. It's everywhere, a hedge of hydrangeas half a mile long. If you haven't got hydrangeas, you don't belong."

"I don't like hydrangeas."

In the distance is the white church, on the western edge of the village.

I feel like I've said enough and we carry on in silence. When we arrive, Riet ignores the church and walks between the poplars to the bank of the Aa.

"We went skating here in the winter of 1966," she says.

"1967," I say. "January 1967."

"Either way, that winter. Winter always goes from one year to the next."

She's right about that. Winter is a season that doesn't limit itself to the calendar year, a season that straddles years. Now, apart from a thin film between the reeds, there's no ice at all. A pair of ducks – drakes – race towards us. They jump up onto the bank like penguins. Riet watches the ducks coolly and turns away. She crosses the street and tugs at the cemetery gate. She keeps on tugging until I'm next to her, slide open the bolt on the back of the gate and, bending forward, swing it open for her. Without a word she walks into the cemetery.

When we're at the grave, I say, "You're grateful to Father now, I guess."

"Why, for God's sake?"

"He's the one who renews the rights to the grave every ten years."

"Hmm," she says.

To me Riet seems like the kind of person to run her fingers over the letters. She doesn't. Instead she sits down on a green bench on the shell path next to the church. I take a few steps backwards and stand with my back against the cold wall. I stick my hands in my pockets.

"I wasn't angry at your father," she says. "I felt humiliated. Later, sure. Later I got angry and I stayed angry."

We're in the shadow cast by the church. Only now do I feel that the sun gave warmth.

"He was so sweet, Helmer," she says.

"I know that," I say.

"And beautiful. He was a handsome young man."

It would be immodest of me to agree to that.

Riet looks at me, she sees Henk. "You're a handsome man," she says.

"Ah."

"It's true. You can take it from me."

"If you say so," I say.

Mother was buried with Henk. I was very curious what I would see. I didn't see anything. Just a white sheet, hardboard by the look of it, at the bottom of a grave that went deeper. It poured with rain during the funeral, a summer cloudburst, the water splashed up high off the coffin, the flowers drooped.

They bury people three deep in this cemetery, so there's room for one more. I wonder who Riet finds handsome, me or the young man she sees in me. I also wonder whether she's noticed anything strange about the headstone.

"What were you talking about in the car?"

"Henk said, 'Slow down,' when he saw a car coming from the other direction. I did, but only slightly. My driving instructor was a real macho and he'd told me that you had to force the other traffic to make room. 'You have to impose your will,' he said, 'through the way you act and the look in your eye.'" She slides back and forth on the wooden bench. "But she was more imposing."

"What was the last thing he said?"

"'Dear oh dear.'"

"'Dear oh dear'?"

"Yes. As if to say, silly goose, you can tell you just got your license."

I can hear him saying it, it fitted the Henk-and-Helmer pattern perfectly.

"That driving instructor tried to impose his will on me too by the way he looked at me. He wore a toupee. Of course I never took him up on it."

"Of course not," I say.

"Are you making fun of me?"

"No."

"Your father's insurance did pay for the Simca, didn't it?"

"Yes."

"Good."

I'm leaning against a cold church wall, but I see myself standing on Schellingwoude Bridge. That's because I feel forgotten. I felt forgotten then too. Riet was the almost-wife, I was just the brother. Now she's the one who is remembering things and telling her story. No one's asked me a thing.

The ducks that jumped out of the water are quacking away on the other side of the church, maybe in front of the closed gate. So many people sit on the grass under the poplars in summer – cyclists from Amsterdam, canoeists, children from the sailing school in Broek – that they are completely fearless. They'll do anything for a piece of bread. Now and then a car drives past. It sounds as if one brakes, then pulls away again.

"Do you come here often?" asks Riet.

"Birthdays and the anniversaries of their deaths. Four times a year."

"I could have come as well, of course. At first I didn't because I'd been sent away and I thought to myself: you needn't think you'll ever see me again. Childish. Later I didn't come because I had Wien, and my children, and I didn't want to be reminded of those days. I wanted to become a new person."

"You can never become a new person."

"Of course you can."

Now the irritation is itching in my shoulders and I almost rub myself against the church wall like an old, moth-eaten sheep in the summertime.

Does she want something? What does she want? Does she want me to kiss her? Am I supposed to act as if I'm Henk? Does she want me to tell her she's still a beautiful woman? Am I supposed to ask her to marry me? Does she want me to forgive her?

She's still beautiful. She's not one of the hundreds of thousands of ageing women who walk around in the same blouse and knee-length trousers, with chemically tamed hair, a premature stoop and sagging eyes. In summer they cycle past the farm with their husbands, always wobbling a little on their solid, reliable-yet-inexpensive bicycles. No matter how different their blouses and jackets, they're always the same blouses and jackets.

Riet is almost as tall as I am and her face is a less firm, slightly sagging version of the face she had as a girl. In it I can very clearly see the Riet who was long ago half hidden by Henk's head in the pub in Monnickendam. Who, even then, I saw thinking, God, he's got a twin brother, there's someone just like him, how am I supposed to deal with that? In the eighteen months before Henk died, she didn't deal with it. In her awkwardness she kept a quiet distance, avoided looking at me and made sure the two of us were almost never alone together.

On December 5th, 1966 her Saint Nicholas gift for me was accompanied by the traditional poem, but she had written something so trite and impersonal that I found it hard to keep back the tears of self-pity that welled up. Like an upset child, I read it out loud for the others with the parcel on my lap. Father noticed and – since he finds Saint Nicholas such a nice occasion – he rubbed it in a little by winking at Riet and telling her that I was used to grander things and was learning how to write poems full of long, difficult words "down there in Amsterdam." He's never had a clue. Riet looked at her feet.

"I'm starting to get cold," she says.

"Let's go home then."

She looks at the headstone once more. In her face I see the question I had expected to hear much sooner. "Where's your father buried?"

"He was cremated." The freezing air cools my hot face. "And scattered."

There is only one duck standing by the gate. The other one has been run over, steam rising from its warm body. That's how it goes, one minute you're alive and kicking and longing for a piece of bread, the next you're stone dead. Riet shudders as she steps over the dead duck. I nudge it to the side of the road with my foot. The remaining duck waddles to the water quacking loudly. When we pass the school on the way back, one of the classes is singing: fifteen or so children's faces turned to look up at their teacher in total concentration. I don't know the song they are singing and stop for a moment to listen. Riet walks on without a glance. I almost have to run to catch up with her before the bend in the road.

When Riet stayed for dinner we had to get a chair out of Father and Mother's bedroom. We put it next to Mother's chair, on the long side of the kitchen table. Consciously or unconsciously Riet has now moved her chair a little to one side before sitting down, almost to the corner of the table. The kitchen clock buzzes. "It's so quiet here," she says.

We're drinking tea. It's almost time to take her back. Is she imagining lively scenes? Children or grandchildren? Highchairs, different wallpaper, a modern kitchen?

"You were the oldest, weren't you?" she asks.

"Yes."

"It was only later, when he was dead and I'd gone away, that I wondered why . . ."

"Yes?"

"Why I chose Henk. I mean, why do things happen the way they do?"

"Henk chose you." She's annoying me again. Surely now, forty years later, she's not going to pretend she had it all under control?

She looks at me and picks up her teacup. A respectable, porcelain teacup. "And later still, I thought, why was Henk the farmer? If you were the oldest?"

"I went skating with Mother and the hand while Henk did the yearlings."

"Huh?"

"Somehow Henk always took the lead. He was quicker than I was and I have an idea he was better with the animals, even though we always did the work together. Father saw that and Henk was his boy, almost from the beginning."

"But didn't you want to be a farmer?"

"I don't know. I always just let things happen." Now that she's finally asked me something, I notice how reluctant I am to answer. I force myself to go on. "At any rate I never said anything. I never complained."

"And when he died you had no choice."

"No, I had no choice."

"The hand was gone by then?"

"Yes. Six months before."

"And?"

"What?"

"How did you like it?"

God almighty. It's as if she's asked me how my life has been. Calling me to account for the life she should have led with Henk. Next she'll ask to see the books. None of it's any of her business, especially not the way I feel about things. Why is she here? What does she hope to find? "Fine," I snap.

She sets her teacup down carefully on the saucer. "That's good," she says. Slowly her eyes fill up again and she turns her head away. For a long time she looks out of the side window at Ada and Wim's farm. Then she sighs deeply and stands up. Apparently she's finished here.

. . .

We're about to get into the Opel Kadett when Ronald comes running into the yard. "Wait!" he shouts.

We wait.

"I've come to show you my hand," he says, without looking at Riet.

"Show me then," I say.

"Can't you see it?"

"Up close."

Ronald almost shoves his hand in my face. The skin on the side, under his little finger, is pink, pale and tight.

"Does it still hurt?"

"Nah," he shrugs. "We took the bandage off 'cause the cold's good for it."

"Did your mother say that?"

"Yes." For a moment he looks past me at the other side of the car, where Riet is standing waiting. "Who's that?" he asks.

"That's Riet."

"Where's she from?"

"Brabant."

"Brabbend?"

"Brabant. A long way from here."

"What's she here for?"

"Ask her, she won't bite."

He looks at me with doggy eyes.

"I used to come here very often," says Riet. "And now I've come to have a look around."

"Oh," says Ronald, staring at my stomach.

"I was going to marry Mr. van Wonderen's brother."

"Huh?"

"That's me," I say.

"Do you have a brother?" he asks in astonishment.

"No, not any more."

"Oh."

"But now I'm going home. On the train."

"Are you taking her?"

"Yes," I say. "To the ferry in Amsterdam."

"Is she going to come back another time?"

"I don't know. Are you going to come back another time?"

"Maybe," says Riet. She gets into the car and closes the door.

"We're going," I tell Ronald.

"Okay," he says. He turns around and walks off. When he's almost at the causeway, he turns around. He's going to copy Teun, I can see it coming. "Where's your father?" he screams.

"Upstairs," I say, pointing at the sky with one finger.

23

"Upstairs," Riet says when we're parked in front of the chip stand.

"Yeah," I say.

"What a joy to be a child."

"Yeah."

"He must have died fairly recently?"

"Yes, not so long ago."

We've been parked in front of the chip stand for a good while now. The sun hasn't gone down yet, but it must be getting close. I can't see it, the train station is in the way. It's much busier than it was this morning. People are going home in both directions. If the ferries weren't operating and the Rhine barges and tour boats weren't sailing, the water of the IJ would be perfectly smooth. In the distance I see tall buildings in a place I remember as empty. It frightens me, the other side. This side frightens me less, because I know exactly which roads to take to get away as quickly as possible. Riet shows no signs of wanting to get out.

Even the bag on her lap isn't standard for women of her age. Although the double-fisted way she's holding it is.

"Henk is a bit of a problem," says Riet.

Is?

"He doesn't do anything. He's been hanging round the house for six months now. He hasn't even got any friends."

Doesn't? Hasn't?

"Sometimes he just lies in bed and then suddenly he's gone. I have no idea what he gets up to."

"Riet, what are you talking about?"

"Henk."

"Which Henk?"

"My son."

"Is your son called Henk?"

"Yes. Didn't you know that?"

"How would I?"

"Lying in bed like that, that's what gets to me the most."

"Henk? You called your son Henk?"

"Why not?"

"What did your husband think of that?"

"Nothing. Wien thought it was a good name. There was a Henk in his family too. Short and snappy, that's what he said."

A passing cyclist bumps the wing mirror. He half turns to raise a hand in apology.

"I was thinking, couldn't he come and stay with you for a while? Working, I mean."

Is this what she wanted to ask me? "With me?"

"Yes. You've got animals. Cows, sheep, chickens. I think animals would be good for him. And you're alone, maybe you could make use of someone. As a farmhand."

As a farmhand. She forgot to mention the donkeys.

"It will do him good. Working. Getting up early, going to bed early, regularity. Fresh air, although he gets enough of that at home, of course."

"Really?" I say, "With all those pigs?"

"That's true," Riet says. "It smells better here."

"What's he think about it himself?"

"He doesn't know about it."

"When did you come up with this?"

"Oh, about a month ago."

There's no reflected sunlight visible anywhere any more, not on the water, not in the windows of the tall buildings. It's getting dark quickly and the sky over the train station is turning orange. Riet lets go of her bag to open the passenger door.

"Will you think about it?" she asks.

"Of course," I say.

Glancing over her shoulder to check for pedestrians, she opens the door. She hesitates. "I've lost him," she says. "When he looks at me, it's as if he's looking at a stranger." She leans to the right, ready to get out of the car. Cold air streams in. Then she leans back to the left and kisses me on the cheek. "Thank you," she says.

. . .

I watch her go. During the interrogation Ronald subjected her to through me, I felt like I would be seeing her more often. Now I think I will never see her again. Dragging her leg slightly and not looking back, she disappears among the pedestrians and cyclists. She is crossing the harbor, soon she'll be on the other side, walking among hundreds of people who will all be traveling in different directions. Thousands of people taking different trains that will carry them all over the country. There won't be anything to see outside, it's dark. What will she do? Read? Sit there quietly and think? Talk to the people opposite her? I don't know. Before starting the car, I rub my hand over my cheek and look at my fingers.

While milking I rest my head on the cows' warm flanks more often than usual, even when the teat cups are attached and the milk is being sucked into the tubes in a soothing rhythm. I will never stand in a white-tiled milking pit wearing a plastic apron while ten or twelve cows are milked simultaneously; there will never be a big free stall barn here where you spread sawdust instead of straw; here the gutter cleaner will always shuttle back and forth slowly and the muck heap will always grow a little every day until I spread the manure with my ramshackle muck-spreader; a woman will never work in the kitchen here every day, or hang out the washing two or three times a week on the clothesline on the strip of grass next to the vegetable garden. Here, my head moves in time to the breathing of the cows, it is safe and secure. But also empty.

I think of electricity cables hanging low with the weight of hundreds of swallows. I think of Denmark, but for the first time without Jarno Koper. I think of a farmhand who saw the swallows in Denmark.

· · ·

"Old junk!" Father says indignantly when I take him something to eat after milking.

"You disputing it?" I ask, pointing at the grandfather clock, the photos on the wall and him.

"That crow's back in the ash."

"I saw it."

"How was it?"

"I don't know yet."

"You don't know yet?"

"No."

"What were you two doing in the new room?"

"Talking."

"About what?"

"Couldn't you hear us?"

"No."

It's been a long time since he's asked so many questions. Riet is on his mind, he might have spent the whole day thinking about the old days. I picture him lying here quiet as a mouse, breathing out when there's talking on the other side of his door, and straining his ears when things get said further away. Is he lonely? I shake my head, I don't want to think about things like that. All the same, the day suddenly feels like a competition with one player in concealment: Riet versus the Van Wonderens.

I draw the curtains. "Oh, one thing," I say as casually as I can, "you were cremated. And scattered."

He has to laugh. "You went to the cemetery."

"Yes. And your name was missing." Have I ever joked like this with him before? I stare at the pattern on the curtains, unable to remember any occasions.

He suddenly gets serious. "I'm dirty."

"Maybe you are."

"Where was I scattered?"

"I don't know. In the fields, behind the chicken coop, under the ash."

I let go of the folds of the curtain and turn around. His eyes are still wet from laughter. I think. He badly needs a shave. The white pillow-case is grayish.

"What did she come for?"

"Because." I walk to the door. When I turn off the light, a better answer occurs to me. "No," I say, "not because. She came for a job interview."

Smiling, I go downstairs.

24

I am the last Van Wonderen. There are many others, of course, but not in our branch of the family. I used to see the name Kees van Wonderen in the sports pages: a footballer. Feyenoord, I think. Once there was a photo of him as well. I thought I looked like him, although he could have been a good thirty years younger than me. Grandfather Van Wonderen had four sisters. They all married and they all had children. Father had, or has, quite a few aunts. I have, or had, just as many great aunts and even more second cousins. None of them was called Van Wonderen. I don't know them. Father was an only child. Henk – named after my Van Wonderen grandfather – is dead. I'm not married. After me, we'll die out.

It's raining. The second freeze was short-lived and I read in the newspaper that at least three skaters drowned. I walked to Big Lake with my skates in my hand and discovered that it was only half frozen. I didn't try the ice – I don't want us to die out just yet. Two days ago the young tanker driver had a big round bandage over his left eye. He was doing some painting at home and got a splinter in his eye while sanding a window frame. The smile on his face was still there, if a little crooked. I left the milking parlor sooner than I'd intended; seeing him like that brought a lump to my throat and I was afraid he'd hear it if I stayed talking. Yesterday the livestock dealer drove into the yard. He stood in the kitchen rubbing one foot over the other for a while, then left without doing any business. The vet came to look at a sick heifer. He emptied two enormous hypodermics into her rump and said she'd get better. I separated her from the rest.

For a few days now I've been looking round the kitchen and wondering whether I shouldn't also paint in here. Every time my survey ends at the hooded crow in the ash and my thoughts turn to the farmhand. I've started to think of him as "Little Henk." Riet phoned to ask if I'd thought about it. "Yes," I answered, "but not enough." I've never had a farmhand. I was one myself, Father's. Every now and then the crow goes off somewhere, always swooping down a little first (as if to test its wings), before starting to fly.

It's only today that Ada has reappeared in my kitchen, five days after Riet's visit. Saturday. Teun and Ronald are at football, the winter break for the junior teams is already over.

"Helmer! How lovely! What was it like?"

"Strange," I say.

"What kind of answer's that? Your sister-in-law!"

"No. My sister-in-law-to-be."

"Still." Ada acts as if Ronald hasn't told her a thing about Riet. "I saw you out walking and I said to myself, What a good-looking woman."

"Yes, she's still good looking."

"Was your father excited about it as well?"

"Very excited."

"What did he think about it?"

"Not much."

"Ah, don't be so offhand. I can tell from your face you enjoyed it!"

"It brought a smile to his face," I say. I look Ada in the eye and after a few seconds she turns away. She is more wound up than usual, flustered.

"What kind of things did you talk about?"

"Nothing special, the old days, her husband who died last year, her daughters, what a sweetheart Henk was, the donkeys and the chickens."

"Is she going to come again sometime?" Her voice is different too, pinched. I can almost see the exclamation marks.

"Maybe. That's what she told Ronald before she got into the car."

Ada blushes. These aren't red cheeks from busyness and spring-cleaning. "Great," she says.

Between the side window and the kitchen cupboards is an old electric clock. The face is brown, the case is orange, the hands are white. The clock buzzes quietly, almost inaudibly. The other day, when Riet was here, I heard it buzzing. I can't remember ever having heard it before. Now it's buzzing louder than ever. Maybe it's on its last legs.

"She didn't come here on her own account," I say.

"What?"

"When we got to the ferry, instead of getting out of the car, she started talking about her son."

"Her son?"

"Her son, Henk. Whether he could come and work for me."

"Why?" Her face has regained its normal color. She brightens up.

"He doesn't do anything at home. He hasn't got a job, he spends a lot of time in bed and sometimes he disappears."

"Why?"

"I don't know. Riet asked me whether I could use him as a farm-hand."

"Fantastic!" exclaims Ada.

"Fantastic?"

"Yes! You've had to do it all yourself since your father fell ill."

"I can do it easily, there's no work for him here."

"It would be more fun together, surely? Of course there's work for him. Take the yearling barn, it's high time that was creosoted again. Two people to do the milking, in a few months you'll be busy with the sheep–"

"I have twenty sheep."

"Still. If you're helping the kid out at the same time. And Riet?"

She says the name as if she's known her for years.

"Hmmm," I say.

"You going to do it?"

"I have to give it some more thought."

"Does she want to come and live here too?" She does her best to sound casual.

"Surely not?" I say.

"I'm asking *you*."

"No, I don't think so, she didn't say anything about that."

Ada turns to check the clock. She stands up. "I have to pick the boys up from football."

"Have they lost their hero yet?"

She gives me a baffled look.

"Jarno Koper? Is he gone yet?"

"Oh, Jarno Koper. Yes, he left."

I walk her through the scullery.

"She must have loved your brother very deeply," Ada says as she opens the door to the milking parlor.

"To call her son Henk?"

"Yes."

"It's a common enough name."

"Bye, Helmer. Say hello to your father for me, will you?"

"I will."

I watch her walk past the storage tank and out of the milking parlor. There's something elderly about the way she holds her back, something I've never noticed before.

The first thing I do when I go into Father's bedroom is say hello from Ada. Then I give him the works. I sit him down on the toilet and ask whether he wants to shave before or after his shower. Before, he says, and he wants to do it himself. I take the small mirror off the wall in the hall and put it on the sink so that he can see himself while sitting on the plastic stool. It takes forever: his hands tremble and he finds it difficult to pull the folds in his neck smooth and use the razor at the same time. Besides washing his body, I also squirt a big dollop of shampoo into his hair. Once he's clean, I ask him whether he can stay sitting on the stool. He can, as long as he clamps his hands on his knees and leans back against the tiled wall. I go upstairs, strip the bed and remake it with clean sheets and pillowcases. I catch myself whistling while I'm at it. Before going downstairs again, I walk to the window and look at the hooded crow. "Yes, have a good look," I say, when I see its eye on me. A little later Father is back in bed with fresh-smelling, combed hair.

"I want some French toast," he says.

"Do you turn over in bed sometimes?"

"Turn over? Why should I?"

"If you always lie on your back like that, you'll get bedsores and then you'll have to go to hospital, and, once you're there, that'll be it, there'll be no coming back."

"Yeah?"

"Yes."

"In Purmerend?"

"What in Purmerend?"

"The hospital."

"If you like."

"Nonsense," he says, closing his eyes.

But just before I shut the door I hear the fresh sheets rustling.

25

Strange, my making such a fuss about being the last Van Wonderen. Without a wife, without kids and with a decrepit father who's never wasted a word on family in my presence, I never expected myself to get sentimental about my own flesh and blood. Is it the farm? Our farm? A collection of buildings, animals and land I didn't want anything to do with, an entity that was forced on me, but gradually became part of me?

Next to the donkey paddock there used to be a cottage that was going to be Henk and Riet's home after their wedding. First the farmhand had to go, then later Henk and Riet would have children, starting a family that would outgrow the cottage and end up moving into the farmhouse. Everything had been planned in advance: in her mind Mother had already furnished the cottage. After the farmhand left they rented it out to Amsterdammers, who only came for holidays and weekends. When

I turned thirty, Father decided to sell it. Mother disagreed. "You never know," she said, with a sidelong glance in my direction. On a Sunday night in the autumn of 1987 after the Amsterdammers had been there for the weekend it burned down, about eight months before Mother died. It's still strange to see the gnarled magnolia flower every spring in the totally overgrown garden. One of the side walls is still half standing, but that won't last long either.

The Forestry Commission wants to buy the land.

I regret throwing my bed on the New Year's bonfire. "Another bed?" the jovial shop assistant asked yesterday when I went in for a cheap pine bed. "Yes," I said, "another bed." Did I want a mattress to go with it? No, I didn't need a mattress. In the other shop I wasn't served by the young girl with the black braids, but by an older, weary looking woman. I bought a single duvet, two duvet covers and two white fitted sheets, all in a sale. I paid no attention to the colors or patterns. Satisfied with my purchases, I bought a pound of eel at the smokehouse. I poked the long sides of the bed out of the front passenger and rear left windows and tried to get home at an even speed, without accelerating or braking hard.

Before setting to work, I open the window and spread newspapers over the blue carpet. I have brought the transistor radio upstairs from the kitchen. It's nice to paint with the radio on. When I'm painting outside in the summer, I always have Radio Tour de France on. I don't care who wins or loses, it's the commentary that matters. I start with the ceiling. It was already white so one coat is enough. The wallpaper on the walls is patterned, a sixties pattern. A tanker has turned over near Reeu-wijk, four men in yellow suits are cleaning up the slaked lime. People liv-ing in the immediate vicinity are advised to keep all windows and doors shut. The paint dries quickly and as it dries the pattern grows fainter and fainter. I was only planning on doing the walls and ceiling but, now I've started, the varnished wooden frame of the window annoys me. Thom de Graaf of Democrats '66 explains the benefits of direct prime-ministerial elections. "Will they give us a prime minister with a cute bum?" the reporter asks. The question doesn't faze De Graaf. "The only people who ever talk about cute bums are journalists," he says. I look at the radio, unable to believe I'm hearing what I'm hearing. The door is white gloss. When I've finished the first coat, I walk to the barn to get the bluish-gray primer from the poison cabinet. Lifting the tin, I can tell that there is enough left to paint the door and window. I take the primer, a sheet of sandpaper and a brush back upstairs and sand the woodwork very carefully. The paint is still wet. Indonesians may not have a word for ice-skating, but at a shopping mall in Jakarta people are skating on an ice rink. There are no signs of an economic crisis in Indonesia, but the population has still had enough of President Megawati. When I've finished the primer, I do another coat of white on the walls. The pattern re-emerges under the roller. I'll have to check tonight to make sure the second layer has really covered it. At the moment there are scattered showers across the country. Later, rain will move in from the west. Tomorrow will be overcast, clearing slightly in the course of the day.

I turn the light on in Henk's bedroom and shift some old junk out of the way to get at the bedside cabinet. I pick it up and carry it through to the new room, where I give it a lick of primer as well. Then I look in on Father.

He sniffs. "You painting?"

"Yep."

"What this time?"

"The new room."

"Why?"

"For the farmhand."

"The farmhand?"

"Yep. Didn't I tell you?"

"I just lie here, no one tells me anything."

"I did tell you, you've forgotten."

"I never forget anything."

"Have it your own way. I bought some eel, would you like a bit later?"

"Delicious," he says, grinning. It's still unbearable, but not as bad as usual.

In the evening I spend a long time in the shower. I want to be wet: warm and wet. I don't even want to think about drying myself off. The walls of the new room are finished, the sixties pattern has disappeared completely. Tomorrow morning: the Velux window, the door and the bedside cabinet. Tomorrow evening I'll assemble the bed, chuck my old mattress on top and put the bedside cabinet next to it. When I see that my fingertips have started shriveling, I turn off the taps. I dry myself quickly and hurry through the scullery. I comb my hair in front of the big mirror above the mantelpiece. The warmth from the fire glows on my legs and lower belly. I turn the knob down from 4 to 1 and walk over to my bedroom door.

"Krraa," I hear from outside. And then four more times. I leave the bedroom door open and notice while climbing into bed that the leg I'm still standing on is trembling slightly. I lie back to listen, but find myself straining to hear only silence. Calling five times was enough for the hooded crow.

26

It's ten thirty in the morning. Raining from low clouds. As usual, the weathermen had it wrong. The kitchen light is on. The crooked ash gleams. The hooded crow is hunched over on its branch. Now and then it ruffles its feathers without spreading its wings, which makes it look like a sparrow bathing in a puddle in the yard. A giant sparrow. I wait. The newspaper is lying on the table in front of me, but I can't read. I sit and stare out of the window. The clock buzzes; it's quiet upstairs, there are a few mouthfuls of cold coffee left in my mug. It's not only quiet upstairs, it's quiet everywhere, the rain taps softly on the window ledge, the road is wet and empty. I am alone, with no one to cuddle up to.

In February 1963 Father drove circles on the Gouw Sea with Henk and me sitting on the back seat. "This is once in a lifetime," he chuckled. Henk and I were sitting far away from each other, glued to our own windows. Mother had stayed behind in Monnickendam; she was too scared. When we got back to the harbor she was standing waiting for us in exactly the same spot, little icicles on her eyelashes. During the third or fourth lap Father steered right instead of left at the end of the embankment. After about fifty yards he braked. The embankment is like a dyke from Marken to Volendam that the builders forgot to complete, leaving the island and the town separate forever. Father leaned over the steering wheel and stared at the end of the embankment, the gate to Lake IJssel. He sighed. The sun was shining, it was as if the sun had shone all through that long winter. Snow drifted over the ice like sand on a wet beach. Without looking at each other, Henk and I realized what Father wanted to do. We broke free from our windows and slid towards each other on the back seat. We were fifteen years old. We saw another car driving past in the rear-view mirror, we didn't hear it. Father sighed again. The engine had stalled, it was quiet. "The ice is a good two and a half feet thick," someone at the harbor had told Father. That was unimaginably thick. Father measured it roughly for himself with his hands and mustered the courage. Two and a half feet of ice, that would hold a truck. It was more than quiet, the silence was terrifying. Father didn't know how thick the ice was past the embankment. While he sat there sighing, we crept even closer together on the back seat until we were like Siamese twins joined from the sides of our feet to our shoulders. If Father was brave enough for the big adventure, we would face it as one man, without fear, silently. Father started the car, it didn't turn over until the fourth or fifth attempt. I no longer had any sense of my own skin, my own muscles, my own bones. He could have put the car into first. But he reversed, very slowly, as if taking the time to change his mind. Henk and I saw the four mounds of snow that had blown up against the tires grow slowly smaller. Then Father did a fourth or fifth lap at top speed, with the car slipping now and then and, for a moment, a very brief moment, disrupting our Siamese unity. It was only when we saw that Mother could see us, just before Father drove the car up the boat ramp in the harbor, that we let go of each other and became Henk and Helmer again. Mother couldn't get a word out, her chin refused to lower, her lips were two strips of frozen flesh.

Before heading off, I do things I could just as well do later. I move the sick heifer, which is no longer sick, back with the other yearlings. I lift up the lid of the feed bin in the chicken coop and tip in a bag of feed. The donkeys get a few handfuls of hay, even though I already gave them a chopped-up mangold this morning. It's still cloudy, but it's stopped raining. Past Zunderdorp, the city lies before me like a plain of gray blocks.

27

In front of the chip stand. A place both Riet and I know. But driving up, I see that the chip stand has vanished and the spot in front of the vanished chip stand is already taken. I park the Opel Kadett behind the other car, a shiny, expensive model with two men in the front.

Riet sounded very businesslike during the telephone conversation, as if my yes hadn't surprised her at all. Henk already knew about it and he had said yes, too. No, she wasn't coming with him. "He wouldn't appreciate that, his mother dropping him off at a sleepover." In answer to my question as to how I would recognize him, she told me to look out for his ears and said she would describe *me* to *him*. Just before hanging up, she was more specific about that "yes" of his: his exact words were "what difference does it make?"

I get out of the car. A little further along the walk-on ferry arrives and, with the boat, the name of the service looms up from the late sixties: the Eagle Ferry. The men in the expensive car are both smoking. They're wearing suits. The kind of car and the kind of men you only see in the city. It starts raining again and I wonder what kind of behavior goes with "what difference does it make."

"My mother said you'd be wearing this sweater."

The teenager with short hair and big ears is shaking my hand. He found me, I was watching the young lad who walked off the ferry behind him and off to one side. I'm wearing my good sweater. The blue one with black stripes that I also wore during Riet's visit, on New Year's Eve, and to the old tanker driver's funeral. The lad who came off the ferry behind him looked like Riet. He had the same color hair and was looking around shyly. I was so sure he was Henk that I stepped aside to look past the person standing in my way.

"Mr. van Wonderen?" the person asked.

"Yes?" I said without looking at him.

"I'm here." He held out his hand and I accepted it. "My mother said you'd be wearing this sweater."

"Get in," I say.

"What shall I . . ."

"Just put it on the back seat."

While he takes off his backpack, I watch the boy who looks so much like Riet. He has jumped onto the pannier rack of a bike and wrapped his arms tightly around the waist of the girl who is pedaling. He even rests his head on her back.

"Get in," I say again.

We open the doors at the same time, but before he has settled down properly I've already started the car. A little later I overtake the girl on the bike. The boy is talking to her back and looks at me for a second. He looks at me the way people look at each other in passing: briefly, indifferently, their minds on something else. And still I'm thinking, Henk, why didn't you get into the car with me?

Instead of turning right at Zunderdorp, I drive straight on. In Volgermeer Polder heavy machines are tearing up knotty little trees. They've finally started cleaning up the contaminated ground. On the dead-straight road through the Belmermeer, the youth next to me says something.

"This weather stinks."

I glance at him, the road is narrow and a car is coming from the opposite direction. He must look like Wien, I think, while pulling over. His listless voice doesn't really go with his short, ginger hair. Maybe Riet sent him to the barber yesterday and when he saw the barber picking up scissors and comb, he said, "No, just use the clippers," hoping to give her a good fright when he got back home. I still have the strange feeling something has gone wrong somewhere.

Coming home doesn't really help. Coming home after you've been somewhere very different is always strange. Is that because everything at home is just the way you left it? Whereas you yourself have experienced things, no matter how insignificant, and grown older, even if just by a couple of hours? I see the farm through his eyes: a wet building in wet surroundings, with bare, dripping trees, frost-burnt grass, meager stalks of kale, empty fields and a light in an upstairs room. Did I turn on the light or did Father manage it by himself?

"This is it," I say.

"Uh-huh," says Henk.

I put the car in the barn out of the rain. Without looking around, he lifts his pack off the back seat.

"Clothes?" I ask.

"Yep," says Henk.

"I've got boots and overalls for you."

He stays there next to the car, backpack over one shoulder.

Myself aside, I've never put anyone to work. Father put *me* to work. How do you do something like that? First, lead the way. If I start walking, he'll be sure to follow. Like the outside, I now see the inside of the barn through his eyes. Sacks of concentrate feed, hay and straw in the shadowy heights, the harrow, implements on hooks, shovels, pitchforks, hoes, the diesel tank on its stand, the messy workbench (screwdrivers, chisels and hammers scattered on the work surface and the wooden board with nails and penciled outlines, empty), the silver-gray poison cabinet. Next to the workbench Father's bike is hanging on the wall. The tires are flat, the rear mudguard loose, the chain rusty. The spiders' webs are old and gray. Rainwater is trickling in through the window frame over the bike.

"You got a driver's license?" I ask.

"No," Henk answers.

The bike. That will be the first job.

. . .

The bulb in the overhead light must be at least seventy-five watts. Henk's backpack is lying on the dark-blue carpet under the window. Rain rattles on the glass. Henk is sitting on the bed. If there was anything to look at, he would probably be looking around. Only now do I notice how childish the duvet cover is, decorated with animals. African animals: lions, rhinos, giraffes and something else I don't recognize. The walls around us are dazzling white, the marble top of the petroleum-blue bedside cabinet is empty. I want to say something but I don't know what. Maybe Henk wants to say something too. It's cold in the new room. Why does it have to be such lousy weather, today of all days? He has a scar over his left ear, a hairless inch-long gash.

"Do you read?" I ask. "Would you like a reading lamp on the bedside cabinet?"

"I've got a book with me," he says.

"I'll see if I can find a reading lamp."

"That'd be good," says Henk.

"But first we'll have something to eat."

I go out onto the landing. He follows, shutting the door of his room firmly behind him. From Father's bedroom comes the sluggish ticking of the grandfather clock.

28

I scoop milk out of the storage tank with a measuring cup; Henk wants a glass of milk with his sandwich. Myself, I almost never drink milk – it's my livelihood but about the only thing I ever use it for is making porridge. The door to the milking parlor is open, outside it smells of spring. The idea of the trees turning green again and daffodils flowering around their trunks suddenly makes my stomach churn. The image of lambs under pale spring sun drains the strength from my arms, for a moment I have difficulty holding up the lid of the storage tank. Yet another spring like all the previous springs. I don't think it, I feel it. Before walking back to the kitchen, I stop to look out through the open door at the trees that line the yard. They are bare and wet. The rain keeps falling. It's late January and in February you can still get severe frosts.

When I come back into the kitchen Henk is sitting there exactly as he was a while ago, in my old spot, with his back to the door. There is a slice of bread on his plate, unbuttered, with nothing on it. I take a mug from the kitchen cupboard, fill it with milk and put it down next to his plate.

"Thank you," says Henk.

"You're welcome," I say.

I sit down. I realize there is no wardrobe in his room. Where's he supposed to put his clothes when he takes them out of the backpack? "Aren't you hungry?" I ask.

"A bit." He sticks his knife in the butter and spreads a thin layer on his bread. Then he puts it down to look at what else there is: cheese, peanut butter, jam, salami and ham. He settles for jam.

"My next-door neighbor made that," I say.

"Oh."

"It's blackberry."

Before he starts eating, he takes a mouthful of milk.

"And?"

"What?"

"How's it taste? Fresh cow's milk?"

He takes another mouthful. "Metallic," he says.

On second thought, his ears aren't so very big. They just stick out a little. That makes them look big. When he chews they move up and down.

"I milk twenty cows. That's hardly any."

"It smells good here," says Henk.

"You think?"

"Yes."

"Not like pigs?"

He doesn't answer. He looks at me and that's enough. The shed door is open. I let him go first. He's not much taller than me, but he's a good deal bigger. Brawnier. I'll stand on the trailer and stack the bales of hay, he can throw them up. Teun and Ronald will roll them to the trailer. Thinking about early summer doesn't bother me: no churning in my stomach, no weak legs.

"The yearlings are in here."

They sniff and raise their heads as we enter.

"All they do is eat, sleep and shit," I say.

"Don't you have a gutter cleaner in here?"

He's asked a question, that's a development. "No," I say.

"How do you do it then?"

"Nothing special. A shovel and a wheelbarrow."

"Oh."

I walk out and turn the corner. Before opening the side door, I point out the muck heap. "See that plank, you run the wheelbarrow up there."

"Bit narrow," says Henk.

We go into the sheep shed. The bricks and woodwork are saturated with the dry smell of sheep and manure. Even if I left the door and all the windows open for months, you would still smell it. For most of the year it's empty in here. Sheep can take anything: drought, rain, snow – although they do tend to go lame during extremely wet autumns and winters.

"In a month or two we'll bring the sheep in." *We*, I say. The tour of the farm – with Henk in the cowshed, the yearling shed and the sheep shed – has evidently turned us into farmer and farmhand.

"Why?" he asks.

"Because they'll start yeaning."

"What?"

"Yeaning. Lambing."

"Oh, lambing."

"What do you call it when pigs have piglets?"

He looks at me as if I'm not quite right.

"Farrowing."

The donkeys leave him cold. Out of politeness he asks what they're called. I tell him that they don't have names. They have stuck their heads over the rail enthusiastically, but Henk ignores them, staring intently at the shelf with the farrier's tools on it. When I say that I hope it turns dry so they can go outside again, he leaves the donkey shed. Of all the people who have ever been here on the farm, he is the first who hasn't touched the donkeys. Even the taciturn livestock dealer strolls over to their paddock occasionally to scratch them on the head, even when I don't have anything for him.

"And?" I ask.

"What do you mean?"

"What do you think of it?"

He looks around with a rather gloomy expression. "It's all a bit bare."

.   .   .

"Do you want to get started?" I ask in the barn.

"Sure," he says.

I point at the bike. "That's my father's, but it's been ages since he could ride a bike. If you can fix it, it's yours."

Henk walks over to the bike and wipes the cobwebs off the frame. "How old is this thing?"

"Oh, about twenty years old."

"Christ," he says.

He looks around. "Bike pump?"

I get the pump, which is probably pushing twenty as well, out from under the workbench and plug in the strip lights. "Come on," I say. "I'll give you some overalls."

"What do I do?" whispers Father.

"Nothing special," I say.

"Yeah, but . . ."

"What?"

"I'm dead, aren't I?"

"No, not any more."

"That boy's mother . . ." He can't bring himself to say her name.

"Yeah?"

"She thinks I'm dead."

"There were reasons for that." I feel sorry for him. I don't want to – when I'm in his bedroom I don't want anything – but I still feel it.

"Where is he?"

"He's in the barn fixing your bike."

Father is eating a cheese sandwich off a plate he tries to hold under his chin with one trembling hand. I've turned on the light. It's just past three, but the clouds refuse to break. What was I thinking when I moved him upstairs? That it would be the first step to "upstairs" as Riet understood it when I told Ronald where Father was? That here, surrounded by photos, samplers, mushrooms and the ticking of the clock, he would lie back calmly and wait? I walk over to the grandfather clock, open the door and pull up the weights.

I imagine Riet cooking in the kitchen; she's already turned on the light. Everywhere something is happening: Father is lying here; for the moment I'm not sure where I am; Henk is in the barn, in the light as well, at work; the cows are standing calm and serene in the cowshed; in the donkey shed the donkeys are eating winter carrots out of Teun and Ronald's hands; the twenty sheep are lying down near the Bosman windmill; Ada drops by, drinks a coffee with Riet and asks her whether she'd like to come over tomorrow to see her newly completed willow-shoot bank; the buzzing of the electric clock in the kitchen is less and less penetrating; the winter is far from over. And, of course, I know where I am too: I'm fixing the bike together with Henk, and Riet is more mother than wife.

"That old rattletrap," says Father.

"Yes, but it's not worn out yet."

"What's he like?"

"I don't know yet."

"That's what you said last time."

"Whatever," I say. I take the plate out of his hand and walk to the door. "Light on?"

"Light on," says Father.

"I'll send him in to you for a moment this evening."

"I don't know..."

"We can hardly act like you don't exist?"

"No."

The bike is upside-down in front of the workbench. Henk is squatting before it. He's wearing a pair of Father's old overalls, faded green with big patches on the knees, the collar turned up. He's got the chain soaking in a container next to the bike, in diesel by the looks of it. The tires are pumped up. He looks up at me as I approach. There is a black smudge on his jaw. Now he's down low, I see that he has his mother's mouth.

"It needs a new back mudguard," he says.

"I can buy one," I say.

"And the tires are almost perished."

"If they've really had it, I can buy new tires too."

"The chain's soaking in diesel."

"Did you siphon it out of the tank?"

"Yep."

Not once has he come to me with a question. What does that say about him? I don't know.

29

We eat kale with smoked sausage and mash. Once I've started on the kale, I eat it at least twice a week. The supply in the vegetable garden lasts until deep into the winter. Mother always put a beef stock cube in with the potatoes, I use vegetable. I buy the smoked sausage from the butcher. I have a lot of stuff in the deep freeze, but no pork.

"Mr. van Wonderen?"

"Yes?"

"Do you have any wine to go with this?"

"Wine?"

"Red wine. It's good with kale."

"No, I don't have any wine. Only spirits."

He spoons a large portion of mustard out of the jar. After loading his fork with mash and kale, he smears a dab of mustard over it with his knife. He spears the sausage without mustard.

"Listen, Henk..." Before I go on, I take a mouthful. Saying his name was an obstacle.

"Yes?"

"Can you stop calling me Mr. van Wonderen?"

"Okay."

"It's Helmer."

"Helmer," he says. He takes a mouthful of water, then says, "Difficult."

"What's difficult about it?"

"It's an unusual name. It sounds young."

"Henk's a difficult name for me."

"Why?"

"My brother was called Henk."

"Oh, yeah."

"You're named after him."

"No I'm not."

"No?"

"I'm named after one of my father's uncles, but a generation back."

"A great-uncle."

"Is that a great-uncle?"

"Yes. Who told you that?"

"My father."

"Did you know that my brother was called Henk?"

"Yeah, my mother told me a bit about him. But not when I was little, much later." He thinks for a moment. "I think it was only last year."

"More sausage?"

"Yes, please."

I cut off a piece of sausage and lay it on his plate. A car drives by.

"Why aren't the curtains closed?"

"Who's going to look in here?"

Henk looks straight ahead, at the side window. I see him gazing at his reflection.

"With a telescope I could look right into that house over there."

"The neighbor who made the jam lives there."

"Has she got a telescope?"

"Probably."

We eat in silence for a while.

"In Russia they eat donkeys," he says.

"What?"

"Donkeys. In Russia they eat them."

"How do you know?"

"I dunno, I read it somewhere."

"Russians are barbarians."

"Hmm." He lays his cutlery on his plate and pushes it away. He crosses his arms and looks at himself in the window. I pick up the plates and put them on the draining board. I get the washing-up basin out of the cupboard under the sink and fill it with hot water.

"There's food left over," says Henk.

"That's for my father." I'm standing with my back to him. He doesn't say anything. I slip the plates and cutlery into the washing-up basin. It's still quiet behind me. I turn around. His arms aren't crossed any more and he's sitting straighter on the chair. He's staring at me. If he hadn't been here, I wouldn't have filled the washing-up basin with hot water yet.

"My father," I say again.

"Is there someone else in the house?"

"Yes."

"Your father. I thought . . ."

"What?"

"When you said, "He can't ride a bike any more" . . ."

"Yes?"

"And that bike's so old. I thought . . ."

"What did you think?"

"I thought he died ages ago."

"No."

"Christ. Where is he then?"

"Upstairs."

"Where the light was on when we drove up?"

"Yep."

"Is there something wrong with him?"

"He's old. His legs are clapped out."

"How old?"

"In his eighties. He's starting to go downhill mentally as well."

"Christ."

I picture Riet and Henk at home in the village in Brabant. They live there together, but I find it impossible to imagine them in one room. When one walks in somewhere, the other walks out, doors opening and shutting simultaneously. They hardly exchange a word. That's good for me, I have less to explain than I expected.

"Let's take his dinner up to him now," I say, "before it gets cold."

"What, me too?"

"You too."

He looks at me as if I've asked him to lay out a dead body.

"Show me your hands."

Now Henk has to go closer to the bed. From the moment he entered the room, he kept his eyes on the things on the walls and finally he noticed the gun leaning against the side of the clock. He's been staring at it for a while now. He holds out his arms with the backs of his hands up, as if about to dive.

"No, the palms."

Henk turns his hands over.

"Hmm," says Father.

"Your bike's fixed," I say.

"Yes, my bike. Be careful with it," he says to Henk.

"Yes, Mr. van Wonderen," says Henk.

Father has put the plate with the kale, mash and sausage on the bedside cabinet. "Do you have any experience with cows?"

"No," says Henk.

"His father had pigs," I say.

"Pigs!"

"Yes," says Henk. Almost imperceptibly he shuffles away from the bed again.

"There's no comparison!" Father says. He shakes his head. "Pigs," he says quietly.

"Henk comes from Brabant," I say.

"I suppose that why he's got a Brabant accent."

I have to admit to being impressed. Rather than lying back like an old, decrepit man, Father is playing the part of a large landowner laid up with a dose of flu. In the spring of 1966 he fired the farmhand. Henk and I were eighteen and Riet was looking like a permanent fixture. He gave the hand six months to find somewhere else to live. That was very obliging of Father, considering the way he treated him otherwise.

"I'm the bloody boss here! You follow my instructions."

Father and the farmhand were standing in the cowshed, opposite each other. I was behind Father and to one side, squirming, and when I dared to glance up quickly at the hand I saw that, like me, he was keeping his head bowed. I remember being surprised by the phrase "follow my instructions." Father didn't usually talk like that. I had no idea what the hand had done wrong.

"Who's the boss here?"

"You are," said the hand, not looking up but seething inside. "You're the boss."

I was young, young enough to get tears in my eyes. I couldn't stand my father, I wanted to stick up for the man who had taught me how to skate. But I was young and had no idea what the disagreement was about. Not too young though to notice the trembling muscles in the farmhand's neck. It was a recalcitrant trembling, somehow provocative. After his subjugation he straightened up, but he didn't look at Father. He looked at me. His eyes were still smoldering.

Now Father is trying to resume his old role. Maybe he's not even trying, maybe the master-servant relationship comes naturally. To him.

"Get out of here," he says. "Then I can eat in peace."

Henk reaches the door before I do. He dives down the stairs in front of me.

"Christ," he says, walking into the scullery.

Henk wants to watch TV.

"We don't have TV here," I say.

"What? What do you do at night?"

"Read the newspaper, do the paperwork, check the animals."

"Paperwork?"

"Uh-huh. Nitrate records, health records for the vet, quality control records for the dairy–"

"I get it. What am I supposed to do in the meantime?"

I don't know how to answer that.

"You miss all kinds of stuff, you know, if you don't have a TV."

"Yeah?" We're sitting in the kitchen. Henk doesn't have anything else to say. I stand up and open the linen cupboard.

"Towels are in here. Come with me." I lead the way to the scullery. "The washing machine's here. You can throw your dirty clothes in the basket." I open the door to the bathroom. "The bathroom," I say. "The hot water is from a boiler. It's a big boiler, but it doesn't last forever." We walk back to the kitchen. "Can you cook?" I ask.

"I can throw a pasta dish together."

"Good."

He walks straight through to the linen cupboard, pulls a towel from the stack and disappears into the hall. As if he's following instructions. I hear him on the stairs. Then it's quiet for a moment. He comes back down the stairs. A little later I hear water running in the bathroom. Ten minutes later he turns off the taps. From the instant he left the kitchen I haven't done a thing. I've stayed sitting at the table with my arms crossed. The scullery door opens. "I'm going to bed," he calls.

"Goodnight," I call back.

"Goodnight." He climbs the stairs again. It gets quiet upstairs.

He has taken up half of the shelf under the mirror. Shaving gear, tooth-brush and toothpicks, shower gel, shampoo and expensive-looking deodorant. His damp towel is hanging over the shower curtain rail. I wipe the steam from the mirror. "A good thick head of hair," I mumble. Black hair, even now.

I'm exhausted, but can't possibly fall asleep. Not that far away a group of coots is swimming on the canal. The hooded crow is quiet and there is no rain drumming on the window ledges. Am I a kind of father now?

What am I? Can he sleep in that room up there? It's not just missing a wardrobe, there's not even a chair. Thrown-together pasta. I can't see Father being too happy about that. What is Father thinking about? Suddenly it's full of breath and life, upstairs. For the first time since taking over Father's bedroom, I feel some degree of regret about the move. Just before falling asleep, when all my thoughts are slipping away from me, I see the young lad who looked like Riet on the back of that bike. With his arms wrapped tightly around the girl.

30

I go into the yard through the shed door and a cold north wind hits me in the face. Surely it's not going to start snowing? On the far side of the farm it's already turning gray. I always do the yearlings after milking. If Henk was up, he could have done them for me. The light is on in the donkey shed, the donkeys are standing with their rumps to the entrance. They know I'll come later. Donkeys aren't stupid. I give the yearlings their feed first. While that's occupying them I scrape the shit out from under them and scatter some fresh straw. Then I give them hay. Yearlings are a lot less patient than cows, they snort and tug on their chains until they've been fed. Some mornings three or four will start mooing together and then there's no stopping them until they've all got hay. I cart out the dung from the gully then sweep the shed floor. Henk isn't up because I've left him to it. Two hours ago I was on my way upstairs and changed my mind four steps before the landing. Father must have heard me, he called out. I hurried back downstairs.

The broom is fairly new, its red nylon brush is still stiff and rings on the concrete floor. No matter how much I dawdle, the sweeping is finished too soon.

When I come in it's quiet in the house. Eight thirty. Before switching on the radio, I turn down the volume. I make a pot of tea and set the table. The sky over the fields is sallow. Snow sky. I drum my fingers on the tabletop. Now it's taking too long, I go upstairs. I tiptoe across the landing to the door of the new room. When I get there, I don't know what to do. Never in my whole life have I got someone out of bed. I knock on the door with limp fingers, then wait for a moment. "Henk," I say. I knock with my knuckles. "Henk!" Nothing happens. I stay there for too long without doing anything, motionless in front of the door. I don't dare to go into the room – in my own house, for God's sake. I walk back to the stairs seething with resentment.

"Helmer," I hear from Father's bedroom.

"Yeah, yeah," I mumble. "I'm not calling you."

In the kitchen I sit down at the table and start to eat. Only after a while do I realize that the radio is on.

I drive to Monnickendam and go in turn to the bike shop, a lamp shop and an electrical supplies shop. I pay cash for the mudguard, the reading lamp and the TV. The TV salesman wants to know whether I need a satellite dish and a decoder as well. "A what?" I ask. Do I have a cable connection? I think about it and see council workers digging channels in front of the lampposts, I see colored wires and I also see someone on his knees in a corner of the living room, a fatso with half his bum showing who's busy attaching a small box, more an electrical socket really, to the inside wall, after having drilled a hole in the outside wall first. I see a narrow strip of yellowed turf in the front garden. The TV salesman wants to know which road I live on. I tell him and he is sure that the cable was connected there a few years ago as a test run. I can't see Father, he must have made a point of avoiding the house that day. I'm lucky, the TV salesman adds. I ask whether I can connect the TV I just bought. Yes, I can, he just has to get a connector cable from the storeroom for me. Later, he says, the cable company will automatically send me a bill.

As I walk to the car, it starts snowing. Although it's not so very heavy, the cardboard box with the TV is awkward to carry. I pass a wine shop. I take the TV to the car, put it on the back seat and walk back. The snow isn't sticking to my shoes, but it's not melting straightaway either. When the shop assistant asks me what I'd like, I tell him a few bottles of red wine. And what kind of wine in particular? "One that tastes good," I snap. He sells me six bottles of South African wine for the price of five.

When I get home, the yard is white but not untrodden. A track leads from the milking parlor to the causeway gate next to the chicken coop. Henk is sitting on the causeway gate. He's smoking. I put the car in the barn and make my own track to the gate. The snow swirls around his red ears.

"How long do I actually have to stay here?" he asks.

"Huh?"

"How long do I have to stay here!"

"It's not a prison," I say.

He takes a drag on his cigarette and after a pause blows out a big cloud of smoke.

"You smoke?" I ask.

"I gave it up the day before yesterday."

"And now you've started again."

"Yep."

"I bought a TV," I say. "And a reading lamp and a rear mudguard and wine."

"Do I get money too?"

"What for?"

"The work I do."

"Have you done any yet?"

He looks at the cigarette he is holding between his thumb and his index finger, squinting a little. His eyes are gray. Then he flicks the cigarette away.

"Board and lodging," I say. "And pocket money of course."

"How much?"

"I don't know." I'm starting to get cold. If it keeps snowing like this, we'll have to move the sheep. From the field next to the windmill to here. And then throw some hay over the gate.

Henk jumps down and starts following my tracks.

"Where are you going?" I ask.

"Back to bed. I don't like snow."

"To bed?"

"Where's the reading lamp? That bright light is driving me crazy."

"I've got forty-watt bulbs."

"Twenty-five."

"Them too." We walk into the barn. Under the bonnet, the Opel Kadett is clicking. I open the boot and get out the lamp and the mudguard. Henk takes the lamp and walks off immediately. He disappears into the milking parlor. I am left looking incredulously at the mudguard in my left hand.

He's lying on his side with his face to the wall, the duvet with African animals pulled up high. The reading lamp is on the bedside cabinet, the plug is in the socket. Did he only realize then that it didn't have a bulb in it? Henk doesn't move when I come in. I don't know what to say, so I don't say anything. I put the chair I got out of Henk's room under the ceiling light. With some difficulty, I manage to unscrew the frosted glass ball. I remove the seventy-five-watt bulb from the fitting and replace it with a twenty-five watt. Next to the reading lamp is a book. I've never heard of the writer. It's been a long time since I read a book. A torn strip of newspaper sticks out from between the pages. I screw a forty-watt bulb into the reading lamp. Henk stays lying there, I can't tell from his breathing whether or not he's asleep. This morning he was sitting on the causeway gate smoking like a man, now he's lying in bed like a child. From the shape under the duvet, I can see that he is lying there with his legs pulled up. I put the chair against the wall next to the door and put his clothes on the seat. After a moment's hesitation, I also pick a pair of white underpants up off the floor and drop them on top of the rest of his clothes like a dollop of cream. The backpack is still on the floor under the window, which is half covered with a thin layer of snow. Before going out onto the landing, I turn on the light. A gentle light shines on the bed, illuminating the yellow giraffes.

I drag the sofa, which is in front of the fire, back a little and turn it ninety degrees. Now it's facing away from my bedroom. Moving the sofa scratches the paint. The living room was long, now it's wide. Before putting the TV in the corner, I get a potato crate out of the barn, brushing it clean with a rough brush. I put the TV on the crate, plug the cable into the hole in the back and the other end into the socket in the wall – in the connection with TV written above it. There's another one with an R. I turn on the TV. The picture comes on immediately and it makes a hellish racket. Since I don't know how to turn it down, I turn it off straightaway. I get the instructions, sit down on the wooden floor and read the booklet from cover to cover. An hour later I know how the remote control works, I've programmed about twenty channels and I've got a numb bum. Then I paint over the damaged spots on the floor.

In the evening I sit alone at the kitchen table. I haven't seen or heard Henk since I was in his room this afternoon. In a minute I'll take up Father's dinner. Not Henk's, he'll come when he's hungry. Over dinner I went through the paper for news from Denmark. Nothing. And nothing about Sweden, Norway or Finland either. As far as the newspaper is concerned all of Scandinavia is nonexistent, as if it's undiscovered territory. Now the paper is open at the TV page, although I know I won't watch it alone. The TV is for Henk. If he watches it, I'll watch it with him sometimes.

The donkey shed looks beautiful. It's stopped snowing, the sky has cleared and the moon is almost full. The snow on the roof is about three inches thick and nicely rounded at the edges. It's just below zero, but I don't think the frost will last until morning. I put some hay in the rack and sit down on the bales. In the light cast by the lamp I see my own footsteps walking here from the cowshed. The donkeys' breath billows through the bars of the rack. Except for their noisy chewing it's deathly silent. The silence of winter. An almost forgotten longing to smoke rises within me. How long does it take to smoke a cigarette? Five minutes? Ten minutes? Ten minutes of breathing in and blowing out, thinking to the rhythm of smoking, while the cigarette smoke mixes with the clouds of donkey breath. If Henk doesn't stay in bed tomorrow, I'll have him muck out the donkey shed.

31

"The day before yesterday he stayed in bed all day."

"See."

"What?"

"That he does that, just lying in bed. He didn't say a word either, I suppose."

"Sometimes he talks a lot, but when he stayed in bed he didn't say a thing."

"No, it's like he's in a kind of coma."

"You can say that again."

"As if he turns himself off."

"Yesterday he did the yearlings and put a new mudguard on Father's old bike."

"Good."

"But he refused to muck out the donkey shed."

"Did he?"

"Yes. He said he doesn't want anything to do with donkeys."

"I can understand that."

"I can't. Everyone loves my donkeys."

"He's scared."

"Why, for God's sake? The kids from next door lie down under them in the shed."

"Henk got kicked by donkey when he was little."

"No!"

"Yes. Wien had bought a miniature donkey as a treat for the girls. We used to keep it on the lawn between the pig sheds. For some reason Henk crawled around it on all fours and it lashed out at him. Got him on the side of the head. He was in hospital for a week."

"Is that how he got that scar?"

"Yes. He was four or five."

"And the donkey?"

"Sold it the next day. "'Just turn it into a big pot of glue,' Wien told the dealer." Riet is quiet for a moment. "What's he doing now?"

"I don't know, he's out the back." I'm quiet as well. "He wants money."

"What for?"

"The work he does."

"You know I never even thought of that?"

"Me neither."

"Don't give him any."

"Why not? He's working, isn't he?"

"Yes, but you're feeding him and putting a roof over his head. You're not rolling in it either, are you?"

"Riet, I've hardly spent anything my whole life. My father didn't either."

"Get him to do some of the cooking too."

"Yeah?"

"He's a decent cook. What do you actually make of him?"

"He seems like a nice kid. Touchy though."

"Yes, he's touchy all right. Is he . . . aggressive?"

"Aggressive? Not at all. Why do you ask?"

"No reason. When he's settled in a bit, shall I come too? Then I can do some of the women's work for a while. Cooking, washing . . ."

High time to end this telephone conversation. I try to say, "No, we'll manage" as conclusively as possible. For a while now I've been gazing restlessly at the wallpaper.

"I'll ring again next week."

"Fine."

"Bye, Helmer."

"Bye, Riet." I hang up.

I once went to Heiloo, to the Marian shrine. Mother wanted to see it, even though she didn't have a Catholic bone in her body. I drove her there on a weekday in May, about twenty years ago. "To Jesus through Mary" was written on the front wall in big letters (a mosaic, I think). Why am I suddenly remembering this? Riet is confusing me. I stop staring at the wallpaper and walk into the kitchen. Outside it's February. Hail, sleet and the odd bit of sun.

32

After Henk had urged me to be quiet and tiptoed out of my bedroom in his big, white underpants, I got up on my knees on my bed. I crossed my arms on the windowsill, rested my chin on them and stared out. There was a smell of warm ditch water and old, sun-baked roof tiles. The moon was shining so brightly I could see a hare in the field on the other side of the canal. The hare was alone, it seemed to be looking for something, walking back and forth and standing up now and then to listen, forelegs drooping. Behind the hare the field was empty as far as the dyke. No cows, no sheep. The colts are separate now, I thought.

The window of Henk's bedroom was open too. They were whispering, so quietly I couldn't understand a word. I imagined myself squatting barefoot in the gutter, tightly grasping the open window, head as close as possible to the windowsill. It was impossible just to lie down again and pull the sheet back up. I got out of bed, walked to the door, opened it cautiously and slipped out onto the landing. I waited a moment until my eyes had adjusted to the darkness. I took a few steps and knelt down in front of Henk's bedroom door. They're old panel doors, with oversized keyholes. At first I only saw movement, after a while shapes became visible too. Riet was hidden except for her lower legs, Henk filled almost the entire keyhole. I was down on one knee with the other leg up. I slipped a hand into my underpants. Back then we used to wear big, white underpants with strong elastic. Always clean, because – as Mother said – you never knew when you might end up in hospital. I was concentrating so much on watching that the warm throbbing of my penis against my belly took me by surprise. I began following Henk's movements, with my eyes and with my hand. Until I got a cramp in the leg that was raised. I had to stand up. In the process I looked at the small skylight at the end of the landing, which showed me moonlit poplars and myself, getting up in front of a closed door with one hand still in my underpants. I curled my toes to get rid of the cramp in my calf.

For some reason I couldn't go back to my own bedroom. Maybe because I could hear them there, and knew I would see them before me. I tiptoed to the ever-open door of the new room, went in and lay down on the blue carpet under the window. I fell asleep and woke up very early the next morning. Only then did I return to my own bed. Henk hadn't come back yet.

August 1966, almost forty years ago. Sometimes I don't understand how I could have grown so old. If I look into the mirror, I still see the eighteen- or nineteen-year-old behind my weather-beaten mug. And I still ask myself who I was watching that night.

33

"Where do you come from?" asks Ronald.

"Brabant," says Henk.

"Hey," says Ronald, looking at me, "that's where that lady came from."

"That's right," I say, "that lady was Henk's mother."

"Do you work here?" asks Teun.

"Yep."

"Where do you sleep then?"

"Upstairs."

"Is that lady here too?"

"No, Ronald," I say. "Just Henk."

"Can we have a look some time?" Teun asks Henk.

"Sure."

Teun and Ronald jump up immediately. I can't remember them ever going upstairs before. This is their chance. Ronald even leaves half his cake for it.

"Come on," says Henk. Suddenly he looks very big. Or is it Teun and Ronald who look small? They walk out of the kitchen. "These stairs are really steep!" I hear Ronald call a little later.

I go over to the side window and try to look into Ada's house. Her kitchen window is just a little too far away. Then I do something I've never done before. I walk to the bureau and take out the binoculars. From upstairs I hear the voices of Henk, Teun and Ronald, I can't make out what they're saying. I go back to the side window, this time with the binoculars. More than five hundred yards away, at the kitchen window of the next farm, Ada is peering at me through her binoculars.

Apart from the fact that we both have something before our eyes and can't look at each other directly, there is nothing advantageous about this situation. I don't know what to do, Ada doesn't know what to do. We are welded together by two pieces of plastic and a few lenses. The first one to lower their binoculars has lost and knows that the other will watch them slink off. Then Ada raises her hand and waves cautiously. I wave back, half-heartedly. "Let me go first," I hear Henk say on the landing. Without another thought about winning, losing or slinking off, I lower the binoculars, hurry over to the bureau and put them back where they belong.

"Henk let me try his Walkman!" shouts Ronald.

"And?" I ask, while pretending to look for something in the bureau.

"Henk needs posters on his walls," is Teun's assessment.

"They thought it was a bit bare," says Henk.

"And we're going fishing," says Ronald.

"When spring comes," says Henk.

"That's right," I say, "the fish are all in the mud now."

. . .

"The boys were upstairs a minute ago," says Father.

"Yeah, Henk showed them his room."

"They didn't come in to see me."

"Ronald is scared of you, didn't you notice that on New Year's Eve?"

"Scared? Why?"

"Because you're an old man."

"He never used to be scared of me."

"You used to be able to walk." I'm using Father's bedroom as a hiding place. Henk, Teun and Ronald are still in the kitchen. They drink tea and eat cake. I can't get a thing down, wet or dry, I'm too nervous. Ada and her binoculars, Henk and the boys together, the telephone conversation with Riet a few days ago. I had to get out of the kitchen and it's still too early to go and milk. Up here I'm surrounded by the old days, the dull ticking of the clock, the photos, the parental bed. Father himself. I sit on the chair at the window. On the branch in the ash, the hooded crow is washing its feathers. Even the bird is familiar now.

"How's it going with that Henk of yours?"

"Good."

"I never see him in here either."

"Does that seem strange to you?"

"Well . . ."

"Soon I'll get him to help me re-fence the donkey paddock."

Father is sitting up against the headboard with two pillows behind him. His eyes are clear today. He picks up the glass on the bedside cabinet and takes a mouthful of water. The glass shakes until he presses it against his lips. He has kept his eyes on me from the instant I sat down on the chair. "If only it were spring," he says.

"Don't drink too much. If you drink you'll have to piss."

"I do realize I'm finished."

"But?"

"I want one more spring."

Diagonally below us Teun and Ronald laugh.

"Why do you hate me so much?" he asks. "Why don't you call the doctor? Why do you tell Ada I've gone senile?"

My hiding place no longer provides any shelter. Until now the lethargic ticking of the grandfather clock has suggested an atmosphere of timelessness, now it changes into the ominous pulse of disappearing time. I stare at the six watercolor mushrooms and wonder who brought them into the house, and when.

"Helmer, what did I do?"

He asks me what he did and he calls me by name. The mushrooms blur, I have to get a hold on myself. Then a new voice sounds downstairs.

"There's Ada," says Father.

I look at him. He still has the glass in his hand, the hand is resting on the blanket. I clear my throat. "Just what we need," I say.

"I want to know, Helmer."

"A TV!" exclaims Ada, so loud we hear it upstairs.

"A TV?" asks Father.

"Yeah, Henk wants to watch TV, otherwise he gets bored at night."

"It seems like you'd do anything for him."

"Ah . . ."

"I want to know."

"You will," I say. "Now I'm going downstairs."

"You would have done anything for your brother as well. Anything at all."

"You too," I say. "For your son."

"Yes," he says. "Me too." Finally he puts the glass down on the bedside cabinet. It clatters on the marble top.

Henk is alone in the kitchen. He's standing at the front window. His long arms hang next to his body.

"How do you like it here, Henk?"

"It's okay."

"Will you do the yearlings soon?"

"Sure."

"Where's everyone got to?"

"That woman with the harelip has gone to get a rug."

"A rug?"

"Yes. She thought it was bare in the living room."

"Her name's Ada."

"I know."

"We'll get to work."

"Fine."

We both pull on our overalls in the scullery. I can tell how much Father has shrunk from the way his overalls sit on Henk. They ride up in the crotch, the sleeves are too short, a button is missing. There is something rectangular in one of the breast pockets; that'll be a packet of cigarettes. I see that the washing basket is full, I'll do a load this evening. We walk into the milking parlor together. I stay there, Henk carries on through the barn to the yearling shed.

Half an hour later Ada comes into the milking parlor with a rolled up rug under one arm. I'm sitting between the cows and only see her when she says my name. She blushes. "I've got a rug for you," she says.

I plug the tube into the milk line and step out from between the cows. "Put it in the scullery," I say.

"All right." She stays standing there.

"Caught out," I say.

"Yes, caught out."

Otherwise there's nothing else to say about it. She can say she's never done it before (which isn't true, I think), and I can say the same (and that is the truth). Or we can say that we'll never do it again. But what difference does it make?

"Nice lad."

"Henk."

"Teun and Ronald have already started playing farmhands."

"He showed them his room."

"Teun's given me a poster for him. It's in the rug."

"Put it in the scullery."

Ada walks past me. When she's almost at the door, she turns around. "Helmer?"

"Yes?"

"I . . ."

"Yes?"

"Forget it." She leaves the milking parlor and doesn't come back. A little later, when I'm back between the cows and look out at the road through the window, I see her outside. The road is wet, she's crossed her arms and that makes her gait a little jerky. Having waved to each other makes it less terrible, but it hasn't erased it. The two cows next to me raise their heads at the same time, the chains rattle on the rails. Get out of here, they say.

I walk to the open shed door. Henk is at the muck heap. The wheelbarrow is on its side next to the plank, the contents have spilled out. He's using a pitchfork to scrape the manure from the ground and throw it up onto the heap with a big swing of his arms. When he's finished, he scratches his head, rights the wheelbarrow and pushes it back to the yearling shed. He hasn't noticed me. What the hell is he doing here? I wonder. I put my hands in my warm pockets and look at the sky. It's cloudy, on the verge of rain, but the days are clearly lengthening.

Later I walk to the shed door again. He's leaning on the wall of the yearling shed, around towards the sheep shed. One leg is raised up with the foot flat against the wall. He's smoking a cigarette and staring past the muck heap at the donkey shed. He looks like a cowboy in an old cigarette ad.

Before dinner I roll the rug out in front of the sofa. It's ocher with a border of light-blue shapes: circles, squares and crosses. Henk unrolls his poster. It's a pouting girl with long blonde hair. She is very scantily clad.

"Who's that?" I ask.

Henk smiles. "Britney Spears," he says.

"Who?"

"A singer."

"So this is Teun's idea of what your room needs."

"Seems so."

"Pretty girl."

"Hmm. Childish."

"You going to put it up?"

"I'll take it upstairs. How old's Teun?"

"Nine? Ten?"

"He's not a Britney Spears fan anyway."

"Why not?"

"If he was he'd have put the poster up himself."

We cross the hall to the kitchen. While I'm thinking about whether or not to draw the curtain in front of the side window, Henk does it.

"What'd you do that for?" I ask.

"That window's like a mirror when it's dark."

"So?"

"I have no desire to look at myself constantly while I'm eating."

"In a month it'll be light when we eat."

"A month?"

"Yes."

"That's a very long time."

We're watching TV. I'm sitting on the sofa, Henk is lying on his side on the rug, resting on one elbow. He's got the remote control and races through the channels. I feel like shouting "hold on! stop!" the whole time; how can you know what it is if it's only on the screen for two seconds? I give up and watch Henk watch TV. After a while it starts to bore him. Before getting up, he lets out a few deep sighs. He hands me the remote control without a word and walks out of the room. I turn off the TV and go over to stand in front of the softly hissing fire. From her framed photo, Mother looks at me with that strange, mixed expression, at once seductive and haughty. For the first time I also see some degree of alertness. From up there on the mantelpiece she is keeping her eye on everything. I've seen Henk look at the photo a couple of times, but he hasn't asked who it is.

Just when I'm loading the washing machine, Henk emerges from the bathroom. He has a towel wrapped around his waist, his shoulders are still wet. "I'm almost out of cigarettes," he says.

"You'll have to go to Monnickendam."

"Is that far?"

"About three miles. We can go tomorrow by car."

"Maybe I'll take the bike," he says. He walks over to the staircase door, leaving wet footsteps on the cold floor.

"Doesn't that towel need to go in the wash?"

He turns. "Now?"

"Sure, why not?"

He pulls off the towel and bends to dry his feet. Then he straightens up and tosses me the towel. I catch it, the warm, damp material flaps around my forearm. For a moment he stands there, proud and embarrassed at once. The scar over his left ear is more visible than usual, maybe because of the hot water. Then he opens the door and disappears upstairs. His first steps up remind me of the supple way the young tanker driver leaps into his cab.

34

Henk and Helmer. At primary school here in the village there were twin girls in our class. Henk and I had a desk near the window, next to an enormous potted plant with dusty, leathery leaves. The twin girls sat behind us. Of course, we were boyfriends and girlfriends, that was expected. They were relationships in alternating combinations, and we were the ones who alternated. The twin girls looked a lot less like each other than we did.

Henk was faster than me; my reactions were always too slow. When I think back on those days, Henk is always doing something – turning onto the road on his scooter; jumping up from his school desk; answering a question while the headmaster stands waiting in his mustard dustcoat, fingertips brown from Camel Plains – I still have to say "eh?" before following him. I was never really with it. I daydreamed; he acted. After a while the twin girls knew when we switched. They didn't mind and neither did we, we had a role in the class to fall back on.

Henk and I wore the same clothes and got our hair cut one after the other by the village barber – "Nice and easy," he said every time to Mother or us – and we both had red scooters. But still, there were differences. When we wore shirts, Henk's was always hanging half out of his trousers or his collar was turned up. His hair was unrulier than mine (during the haircut he'd stop swallowing. Even before we were out of the door, he'd spit on his hand and run it through his hair. He didn't care if the barber was watching) and his scooter was always ten feet ahead of mine.

It was – looking back, always looking back – as if he knew exactly what he wanted, while I never had a clue. About anything at all. I can still see the bottle of birch lotion next to the barber's mirror, a bottle with a rubber vaporizer. Henk thought it was foul, I wasn't so sure. It had something, that smell.

It wasn't until we were eight that I moved to my own bedroom (where Father now spends his days). I lasted three nights alone. During the fourth night I sneaked back into my real bedroom and crept under the blankets with Henk. "What are you doing?" he whispered, just for something to say. I didn't answer. He turned onto his side and I nestled up against him, pushing my feet between his. Even though it had been more than seven years since we were breast-fed and the layer of fat had long since disappeared from our feet, it is possible that it was on that night that I formed the memory I can't possibly have: summertime, my feet feeling other feet and Mother's face seen from below, above a pale soft swelling. Her chin and, most importantly, her slightly bulging eyes, directed not at me, but at a point somewhere in the distance: thin air, the fields, maybe the dyke.

He never came to my room. My room was a lonely room, an abandoned room, I should have moved downstairs long ago. Father doesn't understand the loneliness of that room. Towards the end of primary school, when the twin girls had moved away and we were no longer obliged to be anyone's boyfriends, I stopped going into Henk's bedroom every night. It became once a week, sometimes twice.

When the frost flowers were on the windows, we lay in our pajamas under a pile of blankets. When it was warm, we lay naked under a sheet. We molded ourselves to each other's bodies. Together we rode our bikes to Monnickendam: Henk to the agricultural college, me to high school. We were separated all day, but in the afternoon we would come riding up from different directions and simultaneously lay our forearms on the handlebars to defy wind and rain together. We celebrated our birthday together, we had friends together and, up to fourteen, we showered together. Until the Saturday night that Father split us up. "First one, then the other," he said. "Now, now," Mother said later, when we went to her to complain. "You're not little boys any more." So what? we thought, but we didn't say it. Our grandparents couldn't even tell who was who from our voices. We still wore the same clothes, we had no need to differentiate. To the dentist together (even if I did always have more cavities than Henk), swimming together in Lake IJssel, getting clipped over the back of the head together when we gagged and tried to push away our plates of boiled endive. On that freezing day in February, when Father almost dared to drive out past the embankment, we did not have any difficulty at all in merging like a pair of Siamese twins. It was entirely automatic. If he had risked it and the ice, despite its thickness, had failed to hold the car, we would have drowned as one person.

In the summer we went to the Bosman windmill. Facing each other, we hung from the iron struts while the sheep looked on. Grease, sun-kissed skin, dry grass and salty sweat. High clouds and larks we couldn't see, no matter how hard we tried. We belonged together, we were two boys with one body.

But along came Riet. When I went into his bedroom in January 1966 and tried to climb into his bed, he sent me away. "Piss off," he said. I asked him why. "Idiot," he said. I left his bedroom and heard him sigh contemptuously. Shivering, I walked back to my own bed. It was freezing, the new year had just begun and the next morning the window was covered from top to bottom with frost flowers. We had become a pair of twins with two bodies.

35

The farmhand was as straightforward as his name: Jaap. Big hands, a square face, short blond hair, a sturdy build. His nose was crooked, one of his front teeth was chipped. To me he was always old – he came to work for Father when Henk and I were about five. In the autumn of 1966 he must have been about thirty. Old, in other words, then. Very young now.

Henk and Riet had done it (and I had watched), I had been banned from Henk's bedroom for more than six months, I wasn't Father's boy (especially now that I was left alone and would soon be going to Amsterdam to learn "big words"), Mother was at a complete loss (our alliance did not yet exist, she avoided looking at me) and August remained warm, golden yellow. It was weather for shorts, but my half-body was cold. I didn't know where to creep off to.

. . .

Jaap was always there, like a cow, a sheep, the harrow or the chicken coop – he was part of the farm. "Hi, boys," he said when he saw us. Apart from the skating, we were almost always together when we bumped into him. He kept a gentle distance, maybe because we were the farmer's sons, maybe because he didn't actually have anything to say to us. He hardly ever came into the house. He went to the laborer's cottage to drink coffee and eat. He was single when he came and single he stayed. At first his relatives sometimes came to visit, later that stopped.

During the night I lay on the floor of the new room and couldn't sleep because I kept seeing that movement, I remembered the incident with Father and the hand. Only then did I realize that Henk hadn't been there. It was Father, the farmhand and me. And I knew – lying under the window, with the keyhole as a disturbing, black, female patch still there behind my eyelids – that that was why the farmhand had looked at me, because I was standing behind Father alone.

It was the first time I had been in the cottage since Jaap had been living there. I didn't know what I was going to say, I hadn't come up with a reason for going there. I just felt that I had to. I went on a weekday evening.

He opened the front door. "Hi, Helmer," he said, as if I dropped by every day. He was wearing a short-sleeved shirt with the top buttons undone. His arms were tanned brown. It had been a good four months since he had been given his notice. I wasn't surprised by his knowing immediately who I was. I was pleased. Henk would never come knocking on his door. He walked through the small hall to the small living room. I closed the front door. One of the windows in the living room was open, propped with a long wooden slat. There was a pile of books on a coffee table in the middle of the room, a roll-up was smoldering in an ashtray. Next to the ashtray was an almost empty pouch of tobacco. Van Nelle, I read, medium-strong rolling tobacco. Next to the pouch was a packet of Mascotte cigarette papers. Quiet music was coming from a large radio. He sat down on a sofa and indicated a chair. I sat down and wiped my forehead.

"Hot," he said.

"Yeah," I said.

A summer evening cyclist rode past, and a little later another one.

"Would you like a drink?"

"Sure."

"A beer? I'm having one."

"Okay."

He got up and fetched two beers from a cupboard in the kitchen. He didn't have a fridge. He put the bottle, which was colder than I had expected, in my hand and sat down again, slouching slightly. One arm on the armrest, the hand holding the beer in his lap. The hand was clean after weeks without any manure, greasy cowhides, diesel or earth. The roll-up smoldered on.

"Where do you swim?" he asked.

"Near Uitdam," I said.

"I swim at the storm haven."

"The storm haven?"

"At the start of the dyke to Marken."

"Oh, there." I sipped my beer and wiped my forehead again. He hadn't taught me how to swim. I stared at the pile of books and pretended to read the titles on the spines, while trying to imagine how he would have gone about that, swimming lessons.

He moved on the sofa. Now he laid the arm that had been on the armrest in his lap as well, the fingers of both hands wrapped loosely around the beer bottle. "What's wrong?" he asked. He talked with his upper lip, exposing his uneven front teeth.

I didn't say anything, but kept staring at the books.

"Is it your brother?"

I nodded and swallowed.

"With that bird?"

"Yeah," I said.

It was still early, but the summer was drawing to a close. Most of the light was coming in through the open kitchen door. A ditch beyond the cottage had started steaming and a thin layer of mist was already forming over the fields. The roll-up had smoldered away, the smoke was still hanging in the small living room in a tidy horizontal layer. I looked at the farmhand, his short hair was touching the bottom of the layer of smoke. I saw what I expected to see: him looking back at me the way he had looked at me then – it must have been at least ten years earlier – simmering, feeling rebellious towards Father and looking for an ally. He stood up, the smoke swirled around his head.

"Come on," he said. He said it gently, the way he had always spoken to us all those years.

We put the bottles down on the coffee table simultaneously.

. . .

He didn't have a car at the time, maybe because he couldn't afford it. We went by bike to the storm haven, not to the dyke near Uitdam. I sat on the carrier and held on to him when he swerved. He had draped a towel over his neck and the ends blew back under his arms and flapped against my chest.

"I saw them," I said to his back.

"Your brother and that bird?"

"Yeah."

He turned onto the dyke and pedaled on stolidly. "I think it's for the best," he said.

"What do you mean?"

"You're not your brother."

"No. Of course not."

A few boats were moored in the storm haven. He lay his bike down on the grass and walked out onto the short breakwater. There was no one around. He took off his clothes and picked his way over the blocks of basalt and into the water. He looked like a racing cyclist: his arms and legs were brown, and his shoulders, back and bum were as white as white can be. Henk's was the only naked body I knew. This was a much larger body, a strange body, not a body you could simply mold yourself to. When the water reached to just over his knees, he fell forward into it. "Come on," he called. I took off my clothes as well. I didn't understand exactly what he had meant by "you're not your brother." He watched me clamber clumsily over the blocks of basalt. Then we swam: semicircles around the end of the short breakwater. A man on one of the boats raised a hand in greeting. For the first time I asked myself if Jaap usually swam alone. Or were there other farmhands in the area he did things with? I felt awkward, it was the first time I was doing something with him, the first time he was someone other than the farmhand. I was feeling a bit light-headed too, after that bottle of beer. He was a fantastic swimmer. A few long strokes would put him almost twenty yards ahead of me in no time. "You have to keep your fingers together," he said. I kept my fingers together. "Don't forget to use your legs." I kicked my legs in the water. "Try to keep your head in the water and then breathe on one side." I tried and choked. I thought I could already swim, but he disagreed. He didn't take hold of me with his hands during the swimming lesson, maybe because it wasn't convenient, maybe because I was no longer a kid he was teaching to skate.

He was already drying himself when I got out of the water and slipped on an algae-covered block of basalt. I fell forwards and had plenty of time to put out my hands to save myself, but still came down hard on my knees. Jaap had to laugh. Until I scrambled back up and walked over the grass towards him. "You're bleeding," he said. I looked at my right knee; it felt hot and now I understood why. He looked around, bent over and picked his underpants up off his pile of clothes. He knotted them around my knee. He handed me his towel. "Dry yourself off," he said. "I'll bandage it later, when we get home."

He sat me in a chair and went upstairs. I heard him rummaging around. When he finally came back, he was carrying an enormous first-aid kit, the kind with a round lid with a handle in it. Kneeling next to my chair, he very carefully removed the underpants before lifting a bottle of iodine out of the box. Home, I thought, and gritted my teeth. Then he bandaged my knee by wrapping a wide strip of gauze around it and sticking it down with Elastoplast. The radio was still playing quietly, some kind of jazz. Come on, I thought. From behind the cottage, through the open kitchen window, I heard a sheep's dry, barking cough. He stood up and ran his hand through my damp hair, like an elderly village doctor comforting an upset child. "Another beer?" he asked. "To get over the fright?"

"Okay," I said.

A little later we were sitting opposite each other again, like earlier in the evening, each holding a bottle of beer. Jaap had rolled himself a cigarette and was smoking serenely. A car drove by. It was so quiet that we heard it turning up onto the dyke in a lower gear a bit further along. When I'd finished my beer I stood up. "I'll be heading off," I said.

Jaap stood up too. "I don't know exactly how it works with twins," he said, "but I can imagine them having to split up eventually."

I still felt awkward, but not as much as I had an hour before. What with the swimming, his slow smoking, bandaging my knee and the way he raised the beer to his mouth just like me, he was hardly a farmhand at all any more. I nodded.

"Preferably on an equal footing," he said.

I nodded again and felt my lower lip start to tremble. He stepped over to me and put a hand around the back of my neck. "It'll come," he said. He checked the trembling of my lip by kissing me on the mouth the way you might kiss your grandfather on the mouth once in your life when your grandmother has died. "All that will come in time," he said again, pushing me softly towards the front door. His bloodied underpants were still lying on the floor next to the chair I had been sitting in.

. . .

Mother and Henk were in the kitchen. The light over the table was on.

"What happened to you?" asked Mother.

"Fell over," I said.

"Who bandaged it like that?" She was already going down on her knee to take the bandage off and do it better.

I stepped back. "Jaap."

"Were you at Jaap's?"

"Uh-huh."

"Have you been drinking?"

"Yes. Beer."

Henk frowned at me.

All the doors were open and I looked through the hall at Father, mainly to avoid having to look at Henk. He was sitting like a slab of stone in his chair in the living room, not saying a word. He gave an exaggerated rustle to the newspaper he wasn't reading.

Riet wasn't there. As I mentioned, it was a weekday and it was almost time to go to bed.

Afterwards, in late August and early September, I dropped in on Jaap a few more times.

"Why do you keep going to Jaap's?" Father asked suspiciously.

"No reason," I said.

"Has he found somewhere else to live yet?"

"Dunno."

"Or another job?"

"I don't think so."

"What do you talk about then?"

"All kinds of stuff."

"You never used to go to his place."

"Now I do."

"Strange," said Father slowly. "Very strange."

We drank beer and sat opposite each other. Him on the sofa, me in the armchair. I felt like taking up smoking, but didn't. It looked so peaceful. He never offered me his tobacco pouch. He never spoke about Father during any of my visits. He hardly spoke at all. If there was talking, it was me that did it. I was young. Mainly I thought about myself. I hardly asked him anything. I don't know how he got that crooked nose. I didn't even know where he came from. From early September onwards I had a lot to say about my first days at university, my lecturers and my fellow students. He wasn't surprised that I hadn't become a farmer. "You don't look at the animals the way your brother does," he said.

"How's that?" I asked.

He couldn't explain. "You're different. You see things differently. He probably looked at that bird differently too."

"I didn't look at her at all."

"See?"

Somehow he helped me through something: at home I could look Henk in the eye and more or less ignore Riet. "All that will come," I heard him saying for a long time, even after he had left.

The last time I went to the laborer's cottage was mid-September.

There were cardboard boxes in the living room. The bookcase was already half empty. The rug was rolled up behind the sofa. The radio was no longer plugged in.

"I'm leaving tomorrow," he said. "Tell your father."

"Where are you going?" I asked.

"Back to Friesland."

"Do you come from Friesland?"

He said something in Frisian.

"What?"

"I said, 'Haven't you ever noticed my accent?'"

"No, never."

"Drop by some time."

"I will."

He wrapped his big hand around the back of my neck one last time. "Will you be okay?"

"Sure," I said.

"Good."

Nothing I was waiting for came in time. I never saw Jaap again either. In the autumn I went into the empty cottage now and then. Here I had been someone. The tobacco smell lingered for a long time. Seven months later Henk was dead and a few days after that I was back milking cows.

I've been doing it ever since.

36

For a while now the weather has been very still. The weather report in the newspaper and the weather girl on TV – who's so cheery it always sounds like she's saying hello when she talks about a high – predicted sun, but we got mist. Cold mist. A couple of days ago the sun started shining after all, but it's still cold. Freezing February weather. There's a layer of ice on the ditches but I needn't bother going to Big Lake; the temperature creeps up above zero in the daytime. Ada's husband is muck spreading and he's not the only one. Ada herself has washing on the line. The weather is perfect for both things, but they're not a good combination: manure and clean laundry.

I love sun in February. This time last year Teun said, "Dead wood is beautiful too." I don't know what made him come out with it but he was right, even though the trees and bushes without leaves aren't dead. Low sun on bare branches *is* beautiful. On its branch in the ash, the hooded crow is more alert than usual and more cyclists come past than a few days ago. The sun has a different effect on Henk. He's in bed.

This morning I woke him up by knocking on the door.

"Go away," he shouted.

"It's five thirty."

"So?"

"Time to get up."

"Get up yourself."

"I already have."

"Ha-ha-ha."

I opened the door, felt for the light switch with my left hand and turned on the light. He had pulled the duvet up over his head. The African-animal cover was in the wash, he was now sleeping under dark-blue letters and numbers. Henk doesn't have an alarm clock. "What's the matter?" I asked.

"Nothing."

"Why aren't you getting up then?"

"Don't feel like it."

"Get out from under that duvet."

"Why?"

"So I can see you."

"Why?"

"Because."

"Don't be so childish."

"Look who's talking."

The duvet slipped down. His ginger hair had grown, it was time for him to get it cut again. He stared at me with drowsy eyes. There was a Walkman among the clothes on the floor next to his bed. A few butts lay in the ashtray on the bedside cabinet. Teun's poster – still rolled up – was against the skirting board.

"Could you move out of the doorway, please?" he asked.

"Why?"

"It looks horrible, you standing there like that. It's scary."

I walked into the new room and sat down on the chair. Henk slid up in bed so that his shoulders came to rest against the wall. The window was open, it was cold. Despite the twenty-five-watt bulb, I could see the hairs on his arms standing up. "What's the matter, Henk?"

"Nothing. I told you."

"Why don't you get up then?"

"I'm scared."

"What of?"

"I don't know."

"I don't understand."

"Me neither."

He keeps snapping back and forth between boy and man. Sometimes I feel like I should take him by the hand, at other times he towers over me. He is unpredictable. He took the packet of cigarettes from the bedside cabinet and lit one, blowing the smoke up at the open window.

"I'd rather you didn't do that," I said.

"No doubt," he said. And then, in a different tone. "I hear noises, at night."

"What kind of noises?"

"Animals. At least I hope so."

"That's no reason to be frightened, surely?"

"Short, high-pitched yapping noises."

"That's the coots."

"It drives me up the wall. And your father coughs in bed."

"Is that so terrible?"

"I feel sorry for him," he said quietly.

"Go in and sit with him sometimes."

Again he looked at me as if I'd asked him to lay out a dead body. "Coots," he said, "are they the black ones with those ridiculous big feet?"

"That's right."

He stubbed out the cigarette. The stench of smoldering filter drifted up towards me. He snuggled back down in bed and pulled the duvet up over his head again. "Will you turn off the light when you leave?" he asked.

Father called out when I walked past his bedroom. I opened the door but left the light off and didn't go in.

"Is Henk smoking in the new room?"

"Yes."

"Tell him it's not allowed."

"I did. He doesn't listen."

"I have to go to the toilet."

"Later."

. . .

I did everything myself this morning and I didn't find it easy, I wasn't back in the house until nine. The yearlings were restless, they're already used to Henk, I do things differently. In a few days, when it's a bit warmer in the daytime, I'll put the donkeys out again.

The young tanker driver is looking at the sight glass when I step into the milking parlor. In the time it takes me to reach him a number of names that start with G have run through my mind and I've latched onto his. Ever since Henk has been here, I've wanted to introduce him to Galtjo. I don't know why, I've just wanted to see them together and stand between them.

"How do you manage to get that thing so clean?" he says.

"I rinse it nice and hot," I say.

"They've found a replacement for Arie."

"You've got a new workmate then."

"Yes and no."

"Yes and no?"

"He's going to do this run, I'm moving to another district."

"You won't be coming here any more?"

"No."

His eternal smile becomes a crooked grin.

"Where?"

"Oh, near Bovenkarspel. I live up there."

"Well, all the best, then." I hold out a hand, which he shakes, somewhat surprised. I turn and walk to the scullery door. "See you round, Galtjo," I say, just before going into the scullery.

"Um, yeah," he says.

I close the door behind me and go over to the shed door on the other side of the room. One of the two light switches is next to it. I turn the light off and come back to stand in front of the window, four or five feet back. The young tanker driver stares at the door, shakes his head and looks in the storage tank. A little later he unscrews the hose and winds it round the reel. He unhooks the lid of the tank and carefully lowers it. He fills in a form, looks around the milk parlor one last time and pulls open the cab door. As supple as ever, he jumps up. The tanker disappears and bright light pours into the milking parlor. The storage tank shines.

Solidarity, a fine thing.

I go in, walk up the stairs and bring Father back down. I put him on the toilet.

"Ow," I hear him mutter.

"What is it?" I ask through the closed toilet door.

"It hurts."

"Wipe properly," I say.

"It hurts," he says again.

I pull open the door. He's sitting on the toilet like a half-dead bird, a piece of toilet paper in one hesitant hand. He looks at me with big, helpless eyes. "Just stay there," I say. I walk to the kitchen and get a flannel out of the linen cupboard. I turn on the hot water and moisten the flannel. I walk back to the toilet. "You have to bend forward a little." He does. Carefully I wipe his bum a few times with the warm flannel.

"Pants up," I say, while lifting him up under his armpits. He obeys. I carry him upstairs. A strange sound is coming from the new room, a shrill, rhythmic sound. I lay Father in bed and tuck him in. Then I walk to the new room. I pull open the door and in two steps I'm standing at Henk's bed. I tear the headphones off his head. "Now get up out of your bloody bed!" I shout.

"No," says Henk.

I tear the duvet off him and drag him out of bed by one arm. He doesn't have time to get his legs under him and falls onto the floor. "Get up!" I shout.

"Take it easy," he says.

"Get up!"

He scrambles to his feet.

"Get dressed." I hook my foot under his jeans and kick them towards him. They land on his bare feet. He looks down. I feel like hitting him, hitting him and kicking him. His semi-naked body here in this small room is too much for me. Instead of doing it, I walk over to the poster lying innocently against the skirting board, bend over and start to tear it up. Henk looks at me and pulls on his jeans. Then he pulls a T-shirt over his head.

"Teun will be pleased," he says sheepishly.

"Socks," I say.

He sits down on the bed and puts on his socks.

I grab him by one arm, jerk him to his feet and shove him over to the door. "Get to work," I say. But I think, What's he going to do?

He walks out onto the landing calmly, then runs to the door of

Father's bedroom, pulls it open and disappears inside. An artery in my neck pounds so hard I have to put my hand to it. I stand still for a moment, then turn around and go back into the new room. I pick the Walkman up off the floor and lay it on the bedside cabinet. The duvet is on the floor behind the bed, half of the girl singer's face whose name I've forgotten is lying at my feet. I flick the thick paper a couple of times with my big toe. I pick up the duvet, spread it out over the bed and lie down on top of the dark-blue letters and numbers. I close my eyes.

It must be a couple of hours later. I'm hungry. I haven't slept, but I haven't been thinking either. I've been lying on someone else's bed and seeing my own large bed before me. I used to go to bed to sleep and get up to milk. Now I notice more and more that my bed has become a place to rest. Not to sleep, but to rest. Sometimes I do my best to avoid falling asleep. Because too much happens in the daytime. The bed has become a safe place, like a shed full of cows in the winter or, until recently, Father's bedroom. Before getting into bed, I look at the map of Denmark and recite the names of a few towns or villages. I no longer concentrate on Jutland. I no longer wonder where Jarno Koper has settled. More and more often, I take a nap in the afternoon.

"Helmer?"

I open my eyes. Henk is standing in the doorway.

"What do you want?"

"Old Mr. van Wonderen . . . your father says you have to go and do the milking."

"Why?"

He turns. I hear him asking Father why. He comes back.

"Because it's already five o'clock."

"Tell him to do it himself."

He's about to turn around again but reconsiders. "He can't," he says.

"Why not?"

"He can't walk."

"No?"

"No." I can tell from the look of him that he's too scared to come in. It's his room, with his things in it. His eyes keep returning to the packet of cigarettes. It must be at least two hours since he's had a smoke.

"Maybe I should get moving then," I say.

"May I . . ."

"It's your room, isn't it?"

"You're lying on my bed."

"That's true."

He comes in, picks the cigarettes up off the bedside cabinet, takes one out and lights it. I sit up straight and swing my legs off the bed.

"Are you going to do the yearlings?"

"Of course."

"And are you going to help me tomorrow with the new fence along the side of the donkey paddock?"

"Sure."

"Good. Have you been in there with Father the whole time?"

"Yes. But he falls asleep a lot."

"He's very old."

"He sure is. Christ." He stubs his cigarette out in the ashtray.

"Come on," I say.

Going out onto the landing he looks over his shoulder quickly, as if to make sure nothing has changed in his bedroom. I see it because I have turned around to make sure he is following me.

"About time," Father mutters in his bedroom.

"Mind your own business," I say, closing the door.

"It is my business," he shouts.

"How old are you actually?" Henk asks me on the stairs.

"Fifty-five."

"Really? Your hair's still completely black."

In the scullery we pull on sweaters and overalls. Henk puts the packet of cigarettes in his breast pocket and runs his fingers through his hair. We set to work, the farmer and his hand.

37

"Henk?"

Henk turns and lets go of the concrete post he was trying to wrench loose. The sun is shining on the back of his head, it's a few degrees warmer than yesterday. Teun and Ronald are standing next to each other on the road like classic brothers: big and small; the oldest with a serious expression on his face, the youngest irrepressibly happy; the same hair, the same noses. All they need to do is hold hands. Teun is too old for that, but I can imagine Ronald still doing it. They could be orphans.

"Yeah?" Henk says.

"Have you put the poster up yet?"

Henk looks at me. I rest the head of the sledgehammer between my feet. Henk shakes his head.

"Don't you like it?"

"I like it a lot," Henk says, looking miserable.

"The poster got ruined by accident," I say.

Teun turns around to face me. "Ruined?" he says.

"Yes."

"By accident?"

"Yes."

"How?"

"Did you do it, Henk?" asks Ronald happily.

"No," I say. "I did it."

"But . . ."

"Did you want it back again?" asks Henk.

"Yes. I was lending it to you, didn't my mother say that?"

"No," I say, "she didn't say that."

"Can't you fix it?" Ronald asks Henk. "With sticky tape?"

"No, it's very ruined."

Teun looks from Henk to me and back again.

"Shall I buy a new one for you?" asks Henk.

"No," says Teun. "Forget it." Next to his right foot a lonely yellow crocus has come up in the verge. He doesn't see it and squashes it underfoot when he turns around. "Come on, Ronald," he says.

"I don't . . ." says Ronald.

"Come on . . ." Teun says. "We're going home." He takes Ronald's hand and pulls him away. A little further along, he lets the hand go again. Ronald looks back one last time, a bit less happy than usual.

"I want to do the pounding for a while," says Henk. He's managed to lever the post out of the ground and the new one is loose in the old hole.

I give him the sledgehammer, bend my knees and hold the post halfway down. He hits the top of it so hard I can let go after a single blow. A rip appears in the armpit of his old overalls, but he doesn't seem to notice. "Fucking hell," he says, swinging for the third time.

Of the thirty concrete posts in the fence along the road, eight need replacing. We did five this morning, now we're doing the last three. We started on the farm side and are working towards the north-east, to the remnants of the laborer's cottage. Once the posts are in place we will string green plastic-coated mesh along the whole length and put a rail on top.

"How was I to know?" he says.

"It's my fault," I say.

"It doesn't matter whose fault it was." He pulls on the concrete post as hard as he can.

"That's fine," I say. "One left."

We walk over to the last post that needs replacing.

"What's that?" Henk asks, pointing at the half-wall and the overgrown garden.

"That used to be the laborer's cottage."

"Did it blow over?"

"Burned down."

Henk slips the packet of cigarettes out of his breast pocket and lights up. Then he walks past the last post and up onto the road. A little later he's standing in the garden of the laborer's cottage. "Did the farmhand live here?" he shouts, tugging on a branch of the bare magnolia.

I nod.

From the garden he walks onto the concrete floor of the cottage. "It's tiny," he shouts.

I nod.

He looks around, walks to the half wall and tries to push it over with one foot. It's the wall the wooden staircase was once attached to. Henk is about the same age I was then. "Just a farmhand or a whole family?" he asks.

I shake my head.

"What?" he shouts.

"Just the hand."

He stubs his cigarette out on the wall, takes a run-up and jumps over the narrow ditch that separates the small patch of land from the donkey paddock. He walks up to the last post and starts jerking it back and forth. "If we just go at it for a while we'll be done," he says.

I see his neck muscles quivering.

Before starting the milking, I walk to the causeway. I see him riding towards me on Father's old bike. An Albert Heijn's bag is hanging on the handlebars. He's been to the barber's and done some shopping, that's why he's been so long. He gets off the bike. "Food," he says, gesturing at the bag. I raise a hand but he jerks his head away, as if he sensed that my hand was on its way to his cropped hair before I knew it myself.

"Why do you keep your hair so short?" I ask.

"No reason," he says. "Nice and easy."

. . .

I see the old village barber (dead more than twenty years now), swiping the comb over his white coat with a supple wrist to remove the hairs, and in the barber's mirror I see a Ford drive slowly past, blocking the view of the budding shrubs in the garden of the house across the road. An old Ford with wings at the back, the same color as the old ferries, light green. I smell the tingling smell of birch lotion and I see Henk's face, twisted into a grimace.

He's bought mince at Albert Heijn's, pale mince. Before he starts cooking I take him into the scullery to show him the freezer. "Open it," I say.

He raises the lid. "Christ," he says. "Is that all meat?"

"It's half a cow," I say. "Packed in bags." I pull out a rock-hard frozen bag with a red seal. "Red's mince: beef mince. Blue is steak, green is for roasting."

"What did you do with the other half?"

"The butcher sold it."

He lowers the lid again. "I've eaten pork all my life," he says.

Henk makes something with tomatoes, red peppers, onion, garlic and spices. It's ready in twenty minutes. I open the first bottle of South African wine with a corkscrew I had to search hard to find.

"Let me smell it," Henk says when he hears the cork pop.

I stick the bottle under his nose.

"No, the cork."

I hold the cork under his nose.

"Fine," he says, as if he knows what he's talking about.

I set the table and fill two glasses with wine. I had already noticed the days getting longer, but this is the first time dinner's ready before dark. I can't close the curtain in front of the side window yet.

"You'll have to take a plateful up to Father yourself later," I say.

"Why do I have to do it?"

"I don't know how he's going to react to this."

"He must have had red peppers before?"

"Never."

I like his food. I like the wine too. When I refill the plates, Henk tops up our glasses.

"If that house was still standing," he says after a while, gesturing over his shoulder with a thumb, "would I have to live in it?"

"No, of course not."

"Why not? I'm the farmhand, aren't I?"

"We're not living in the sixties any more."

"I might have liked it."

"Living alone?"

"Yeah. In a tidy little house."

"Isn't it to your liking here?"

He doesn't answer but sighs and scrapes his spoon over his plate. Then he takes a third helping.

I'm drunk from the wine and think of beer. Beer straight from the bottle, sitting in an easy chair in a house that only exists inside my head.

Jazz. There's something lonely about jazz, especially when it's quiet and coming from a radio somewhere in a corner.

Why did I let it all happen like this? I could have said "no" to Father and "do it yourself" or just "sell up."

Grandfather van Wonderen lived in Edam, he survived Grandmother van Wonderen six years. I visited him once a week for half an hour. He lived in an old people's home in a small room with a view of a pond that had a fountain in the middle. No matter where the sun was, it always seemed to shine in through his windows. Grandfather would pour me a coffee and I could never think of anything to say. I was glad when the half-hour was over. In the car on the way home I always thought, wouldn't it be kinder if I didn't come at all, because then he wouldn't know any better. That half-hour of mine made him a lot lonelier than no half-hour. If you don't know any better, you haven't got anything to miss. It's as if I already know that Henk is going to leave again. Of course he's going to leave, why should he stay? There's nothing for him here.

"More wine?"

I cover my glass with a hand.

"Do you ever go out?"

"Out?"

"Yeah, out. To a pub or . . . My father used to play cards, once a week."

"No," I say.

"I'd like to go out sometimes."

"You should go to Monnickendam on a Saturday night."

"Is that fun?"

"It used to be."

"A village like that must be really boring."

"You could always go to Amsterdam."

"I don't know . . ."

I stand up and clear the table. Henk disappears into the living room and turns on the TV.

After doing the dishes, I sit down at the bureau to do some paper-work, but my eyes keep wandering from the documents; I still feel light-headed. After a while he turns the TV off again. He walks into the hall and goes into the scullery, and a little later I hear the water running in the bathroom. I try to concentrate on the work in front of me, but actu-ally I'm waiting to hear him go upstairs.

He doesn't go upstairs. He comes into the kitchen, a towel wrapped around his waist. He holds the door with his left hand. "I'm glad my father is dead," he says.

"What?"

"I'm glad he's dead. My mother didn't even ask me if I wanted to carry on with the pigs, she just sold up."

"Would you have wanted to take it over?"

"No! Horrible. Selling up was fine by me."

"But you were annoyed she didn't ask you?"

"Not really. Maybe my sisters told her to sell. I don't know. They always shut me out."

"So you're glad?"

"Sure." He doesn't sound glad.

"What kind of man was your father?"

He thinks for a moment and raises one shoulder. "He was actually a very nice guy. We got on well together." He's still holding the door and has kept his eyes on the table the whole time, bare now except for the almost empty bottle of wine. Now he looks at me. "Goodnight," he says.

When I hear the door of the new room closing, I stand up and pour half a glass of wine. I see myself reflected in the side window and raise the glass – to myself or to Ada, I don't know which. Suddenly I realize that Father hasn't had any dinner yet and immediately I loathe that fellow in the window, who has raised his glass so preciously. Acting cool when he's anything but. I creep upstairs and cautiously open the door to Father's bedroom. He's snoring quietly and calmly. Peacefully. I let him sleep, it's already late. I go back to the kitchen and draw the curtain across the side window. Just when I'm about to sit down again at the bureau, Henk reappears at the door. Not with a towel around his waist, but wearing blue underpants and a yellow T-shirt.

"Your father hasn't eaten," he whispers.

"I know," I say. "He's asleep."

"But . . ."

"He'll survive."

He nods and disappears.

The electric clock buzzes, the tap drips. It's quiet in the house. I swallow something in the back of my throat and close the bureau.

.   .   .

"Ballerup," I say a little later. "Stenløse, Taastrup, Frederikssund, Holbæk." I run a finger over the top of the frame and blow the roll of dust off my fingertip. For the first time I see that Jutland could be a giant who is about to gobble up Funen, Zealand and all the smaller islands. I turn away, undress and slip into bed. Gradually my body starts to warm up the duvet. Upstairs something creaks, from outside there isn't any sound.

38

We roll the plastic-coated mesh out in the opposite direction, from what's left of the laborer's cottage towards the farmhouse, from post to post. Again it's a couple of degrees warmer than yesterday and now that I look I see more crocuses in the verge. The flower Teun trampled was less lonely than I thought. I keep looking up at the sky, expecting redshanks and black-tailed godwits, despite knowing full well that it's not even March yet. The concrete posts are designed for wooden rails, which you are supposed to attach with a nut. We twist wire around the bolts in the posts to hold the mesh. Henk is enjoying the work, I think. He whistles while rolling out the mesh, twists the wire together and smokes the occasional cigarette. He raises an index finger for cyclists and says "Hiya" – sniffing when the cyclists don't say anything in reply. Sometimes, while smoking, he stares at the high buildings and haze of Amsterdam. It's as if he was born here. All Waterland smells like manure.

. . .

"Do you ever get any other cheese?" he asks at lunch.

"No."

"Why not?"

"It's Edam from the dairy."

"So?"

"I get it cheap."

"It's pretty bland."

"You can always buy yourself some other cheese."

He lays down the cheese slice. "I don't have any money."

I stand up and walk over to the bureau. The wallet is in one of the square drawers. I flick it open and pull out two hundred-euro notes. "Here," I say.

He takes the money without a word, folds the notes in half and sticks them in his back pocket. He picks up the cheese slice and cuts some more slices.

The livestock dealer's truck goes past slowly.

"We've got a visitor," I say.

"You've got a visitor," Henk says. "Not me."

The livestock dealer knocks once on the jamb and appears in the doorway. "Afternoon," he says.

Now that I look at him properly, seeing him partly through Henk's eyes, even though *he* is sitting with his back to the door, I notice how old the livestock dealer is. He has a gray beard, the kind of beard you see in very old, severe photographs. The deep furrows in his forehead are dark along the edges. As usual he rubs the sole of one foot over the top of the other. He looks at Henk's back.

"This is Henk," I say.

"Nephew of yours?" he asks.

"A nephew? No, Henk works here."

"Oh."

Henk acts as if there's no one else in the kitchen. He hasn't turned around and keeps on eating. I've half turned my chair away from the table.

"Sit down," I say, pointing at the chair opposite me.

"Ye-es," says the livestock dealer slowly and unexpectedly. He takes his cap off and sits down. He glances sideways at Henk.

"I don't have anything for you."

"That's not why I'm here."

When he doesn't say anything else, I ask if he'd like a coffee.

"Yes, a coffee would hit the spot."

I stand up and get a mug out of the kitchen cupboard.

"So you work here," the livestock dealer says to Henk.

"Yes."

"Do you come from Brabant?"

"Yes."

Ada? Or is a single "yes" enough for him to hear where someone comes from? I put the mug down on the table in front of him.

He looks around the kitchen as if he's never been here before.

"How's old Mr. van Wonderen doing?"

"Fine," I say. I slide my plate, with a half-eaten sandwich on it, away from me. "Even if he's not all there any more."

"Too bad," says the livestock dealer. "I did a lot of business with him."

"Yes."

The electric clock buzzes, Henk fidgets on his chair.

"I'm here to tell you I'm quitting."

"Really?"

"Do you have any idea how old I am?"

"Just turned sixty?"

"Sixty-eight."

"Then it's getting time to stop."

"The wife said, 'If you don't stop now, I'm leaving you.'"

"Hmm."

"She wants to travel."

"Don't you have a daughter in New Zealand?"

"Uh-huh. The wife's already bought the tickets."

"Nice."

He sips his coffee. "Flying," he goes on. "Can you see *me* on a plane?"

"Why not?"

He has a slow way of talking and hardly looks at me. I suspect that his feet are now at rest and flat on the floor, and I feel like looking under the table to check. He's already become someone else. No longer a livestock dealer, he can speak freely.

Henk gets up. "I'm going outside," he says. "Goodbye."

"Bye, son," says the livestock dealer. Once Henk is gone, he looks me straight in the eye. "So that's your new farmhand."

"Yes," I say.

"Sturdy lad."

"Yes."

I hear the door to the milking parlor bang shut.

Finally the livestock dealer looks away, through the side window. "I was just at the neighbors'."

"You dropping in on everyone?"

"Yeah. That will take me a week as well." He puts the mug down on the table. "I'll be off."

"Okay," I say.

"I'll see you around," he says in the scullery.

"Have a nice time in New Zealand."

"It's summer there now," he says. He slips his feet into his clogs. "Say hello to your father."

"I will," I say.

He pulls open the shed door and walks around to the back.

I wait for a moment and then go out through the milking parlor. When the truck passes, I raise one hand. Henk is sitting on the donkey paddock gate, opposite the milking parlor. I only notice him after the truck has passed. A big plume of smoke is hanging over his head. He raises a hand to wave to me. A play without words for three men: one leaves without looking up, the second watches him go, the third looks at the second, and the second only sees the third after the first is gone.

It's hot in the kitchen. The sun is shining on the table. A brace of ducks fly over. I butter two slices of bread, cover them with cheese and walk upstairs. Father doesn't wake up when I come in. I put the plate down carefully on the bedside cabinet and sit down on the chair next to the window.

. . .

"The livestock dealer says hello," I say quietly, but without any spite. "He's going to New Zealand with his wife, to see his daughter." The hooded crow in the ash is my only witness. "I can't stand you because you ruined my life. I don't call a doctor because I think it's high time you stopped ruining my life, and I tell Ada you're senile because it makes things that much easier. If you're senile, then none of it makes any difference anyway. What I say, what you say. And you don't know the half of what I would have done for Henk. Henk was my twin brother. Do you know what it's like to have a twin brother? Do you? What do you actually know? In the months after you fired Jaap you didn't visit him once because you refused to see him as an equal. I saw him as an equal. He kissed me on the fucking mouth. Have you ever kissed me? Have you ever said a kind word to me? Do you know what I want? No, you don't know, because I don't even know myself. The livestock dealer is never coming back, that's why he says hello, and the tanker drivers are never coming back either, one's dead, you knew that already, the gruff one, but maybe you forgot because you're senile, and the other one, the young one who always smiles, is off to drive another route. That's your fault too. Not him going away, but making me be here for him to go away from. If I hadn't been here, I wouldn't have known him. And by the way, I don't think we'll be seeing much more of Ada, she prefers to spy on us from a distance and Ronald is the only one from next door who still comes here, we're in Teun's bad books because–"

"Helmer!" Henk shouts from the bottom of the stairs.

Father wakes up.

I stand up. "There's something to eat next to your bed," I say.

"Did I fall asleep?" asks Father.

"We going back to work?" Henk calls.

"Coming!" I shout. "Yes," I say to Father.

"Didn't even notice. I'm exhausted." He sits up and looks at the plate. "Cheese," he says. "Delicious."

Henk *is* actually a kind of nephew, I think when I close the door to the stairs and see him standing there. He is pulling on his overalls, the ones with the crotch that rides up, the sleeves that are too short and the tear in one armpit. A half-nephew, a could-have-been-nephew, a nephew-in-law.

39

"I'm not going behind those donkeys. Do it yourself."

"Go and stand in the yard over there then."

"I don't want anything to do with them."

"If you go and stand there, just past the gate, they'll walk straight into the paddock."

"And if I don't stand there?"

"Henk, they won't even touch you. These are *my* donkeys."

"What do you mean by that?"

"They're not your father's and they're not miniatures."

"What?"

"They're not like the one that kicked you."

"How do you know about that?"

"Your mother told me."

"Fucking hell."

"What's there to swear about?"

"What else did she tell you?"

"Nothing. Listen: the smaller, the meaner. Shetland ponies are vicious too, they kick and bite. These are real donkeys, they won't do anything. Teun and Ronald . . ."

"What else did she tell you? Why am I actually here?"

"I don't know."

"For no reason?"

"What?"

"Am I here for no reason?"

"No . . ."

"Why?!"

"Because you were at a loose end at home."

"At home? At home where?"

"You know, Brabant."

"Oh, fucking hell."

"What is it? Don't swear so much."

"What kind of bullshit's that! A loose end?"

"Yes, a loose end."

"How long do I have to stay here?"

"You don't *have* to stay anywhere."

"So if I want to, I can go?"

"Of course."

It's March and the sun has disappeared. We're standing in front of the donkey shed. It's drizzling. The donkey paddock fence is finished.

"Are you fighting?" Ronald is suddenly standing next to us. Like a faithful dog.

"Not at all," I say.

"We're having a difference of opinion," says Henk.

"What's that?"

"When Helmer says something I don't agree with."

"And Henk says something I don't agree with."

"Oh," says Ronald. "Are the donkeys going into the pasture?"

"Yep."

"Great! Can I help?"

"Sure. Where's Teun?"

"At home."

"Didn't he feel like coming?"

"No." He looks from me to Henk and back again before deciding to take us into his confidence. "He thinks you're stupid."

"Go and stand in the yard over there." I gesture in the direction of the causeway.

Ronald runs off straightaway – happy, always happy – and stops level with the door to the milking parlor. He holds up a hand to show he's in position.

"So if I want to, I can go?" asks Henk.

"I'm not stopping you."

He walks into the barn and comes out a little later on Father's bike. He takes the curve wide and rides off towards the causeway. Ronald looks at him in astonishment. "Are you going?" I hear him asking Henk. Slowly I walk to the house.

Maybe Henk says something. I can't hear because the hooded crow starts cawing. It comes swooping around the corner of the house and flies into the side of Henk's head. It beats its wings wildly to stay in the air and pushes off against Henk's skull with its claws, while the bike and Henk roll over beneath it. It stays hanging there for a moment, almost like a giant kestrel that's spotted a mouse, then flies away, between the trees along the donkey paddock, towards Marken.

"Henk fell off the bike," says Ronald.

40

"Henk fell off the bike," said Ronald. It looked to me more like he was "flapped off it." When I reached him he was trying to get up. He was still on all fours and blood was running down his forehead. I told him to stay put. Ronald pulled the bike upright but because it was Father's old bike, a heavy, reliable bike, the handlebars slipped out of his grip. The seat hit Henk on the back.

"Leave it, Ronald," I said.

"What happened?" asked Henk.

"I'll get the first-aid kit."

When I came back out through the milking parlor door, Ronald was standing over Henk with his hands on his hips and looking about. "He hasn't said anything," he said. "But he didn't have to cry."

I knelt down and dabbed the blood from Henk's head with a clean, damp tea towel.

Ronald watched over my shoulder. "What a crack!" he shouted and I immediately realized there was no question of my taking care of it myself. I decided to skip the GP and drive straight to the hospital in Purmerend. There were a few people waiting at Accident and Emergency, but they gave Henk priority, probably because of the blood-drenched tea towel he was pressing against his head. They cleaned and stitched the largest wound – the beak wound – but only cleaned the scratches from the crow's claws. The doctor wanted to know whether my son had had a tetanus injection in the last few years. I asked Henk and, because he couldn't remember any injections, they gave him one. The doctor was glad he had such short hair. He covered the stitched-up wound with a thick piece of gauze and pulled a kind of elasticated fine-mesh bathing cap on over Henk's head. He had never seen anything like it and didn't even know that hooded crows existed. "Pretty exceptional really," he told Henk with a smile, "getting your scalp ripped open like that." Henk couldn't see the funny side of it.

In the car on the way home, Henk sat next to me silently with a somewhat dazed look in his eyes. "My son," I said. Instead of laughing, he sighed deeply. His hair was hidden completely by the strange bathing cap and if the cap hadn't been there and he hadn't sighed so deeply, I would have touched it. When I turned into the yard, prepared to drive around Father's bike, I saw that it had been dragged over to the side of the house. Ronald had wanted to do something useful before going home. In the hall I took Henk by the elbows and turned him to face the mirror. He avoided his own eyes and for a moment it looked as if he was about to spit at his reflection.

. . .

Now he's been sitting on the sofa in the living room for at least half an hour. He's not saying anything, the TV isn't on. Once in a while he rubs his left arm with his right hand. He doesn't want any coffee, he doesn't want anything to eat. The hooded crow hasn't come back to its regular perch in the ash.

Of course, I don't need anyone else to get the donkeys into their paddock. I open the gate, walk to the shed, open the gate there and saunter back to the paddock. They buck and bray behind me, but don't pass. Just in front of the open gate, I make room for them. Only then do they leap past and start trotting in circles. When they've calmed down a little, they sniff the new fence. I close the gate, tie it fast and walk alongside the mesh to the road. The daffodils are about to come out around the trunks of the row of trees. I turn the corner and follow the new fence as far as the ruins of the laborer's cottage. The donkeys walk beside me on the other side for the last twenty or thirty yards. Glistening from the drizzle, they scratch their chins on the new wooden rail. They are contented.

I take a run-up and jump over the ditch. The Forestry Commission wants to build a visitors' center where the laborer's cottage used to stand. The day is coming when there won't be any farmers left in Waterland. Or one last farmer, to keep an eye on the Galloways or the Highland cattle, mow the grass, clear away empty soft-drink cans, cut the reeds and run tours from the planned visitors' center, in neatly painted flatboats, for instance. The Forestry Commission already owns the rest of our land, I just lease it. In spring I turn the Bosman windmill away from the wind, flooding part of the land for the peewits, godwits and redshanks. In return I get a provincial grant. I do it every year when I bring the sheep in. It's fine by me, but I still resist selling this bit of land.

Every six months a letter arrives from the Forestry Commission. Father's keen to write back but I'm not. I didn't even show him the last letter. It's in one of the pigeonholes in the bureau.

The floor plan of the cottage is still visible in the foundations. I brush aside leaves, dead branches and clods of soil with my foot. This was the living room, the kitchen was here, the toilet and hall were here. The cellar doesn't exist any more: it's a hole full of bricks and earth. Weeds grow out of wide cracks in the concrete. A few feet above my head was the large attic with its two dormer windows. I don't want children running around here screaming or a token farmer standing here giving his conservationist spiel. I want to come here now and then and rebuild the walls in my thoughts, see the ceiling close silently and fix the red tiles on the tile laths. I want to imagine the living room with open windows, bottles of beer and the smell of medium-strong rolling tobacco.

I run my fingers through my wet hair and rub my palm over my face. Water is good and clean, it washes away all kinds of things (dirt, dead skin, years), in water you're weightless, water makes you reckless and ageless. Henk will always remain nineteen. I see him sitting on the sofa before me, a bottle of warm beer in one hand, the top buttons of his shirt undone, his other arm over the back of the chair. Henk kissing me as if someone has just died. Lonely music, soft. I shake my head and kick a clump of weeds away with the toe of my boot. Jaap. It was Jaap. Was he a substitute? A replacement for Henk, telling me all kinds of things would come in time?

What happened to Henk?

What happened to Jaap?

I take the road back to the farm, to Henk with his aching head, to my worn-out father who wants to see one last spring. The donkeys let me go, staying where they are in the corner by the cottage. I pick up Father's bike, lift a leg up over the bar and cycle back in the reverse of the route Henk took earlier today. My muscles are still aching from the fencing. Inside the barn it is dark. Before going into the milking parlor, I turn on the strip lights over the workbench. I hang a pair of pliers up on the wooden board with the nails and the penciled outlines. What happened to me? I think, as I hang up the claw hammer in its outline.

"Where were you going?"

"Away."

"You didn't have anything with you."

"So?"

"You hadn't even taken off your overalls."

"So?"

"How's your head feel?"

"Itchy."

"That's good. Itchy's good."

He pours himself a second glass of wine. I cover my glass with my hand. We're eating steak, with potatoes and green beans. It's not completely dark outside yet, but I've already drawn the curtain over the side window.

"What makes a bird do something like that?"

I shrug.

"Why me?"

I shrug again.

"My arm's numb."

"Imagine if it had gone for Ronald, his head is still really vulnerable."

"So it's actually good that it attacked me?"

"In a way."

"Thanks."

I put the third steak on a clean plate and cut it into small pieces.

"You've actually got really big hands, you know," says Henk.

I spoon a couple of potatoes and some beans onto the plate and push it over to him. "Will you take it upstairs?"

"Okay."

He's gone a long time. I do the dishes and when I've finished I get the nailbrush out from the cupboard under the sink. The tub of mechanic's soap Mother bought when she was trying to get Father and me to take better care of our hands must be in here somewhere. After her death the tub moved deeper and deeper into the cupboard. I find it in a damp corner, under a threadbare rag. I scrub my hands with the sandy soap until my cuticles are almost bleeding.

In the scullery I take off my clothes and throw them into the laundry basket. I go into the bathroom, turn on the taps and step in under the hot water. It's only when the boiler is almost empty and the water is cooling off that I turn the taps off again with my shriveled fingers. I dry myself, wrap the towel around my waist and walk to my bedroom. On the way, I look at myself in the mirror over the mantelpiece, and at Mother, who looks back vigilantly. I was planning on putting on some clean clothes, but when I see my bed, I don't bother.

Tossing the towel into a corner, I go over to stand in front of the map of Denmark. "Værløse," I whisper. "Farum, Holte, Birkerød, Frederiksværk." My penis starts to swell and I slip into bed. I hear Henk coming downstairs. He walks through the house and seems to pause in front of my bedroom door. Then he turns off the lights – I can tell from the route he takes. A little later he goes back upstairs. The house is peaceful.

41

I've walked into the field to count the sheep. The sight of a sheep is always enough to make me feel a bit melancholy. They're such sorry animals. I often think of the three sheep I sold to buy the map of Denmark, mainly because I didn't even check which sheep I was getting rid of. It could have just as easily been three different sheep. Twenty sheep in the rain is not a pleasant sight, unshorn sheep look terrible in a heat wave and a lame sheep is almost unbearable. Worst of all is a sheep on its back. Incapable of getting up again under its own steam, intestines bloated and pressing against the abdominal wall, coughing and rattling, and, if it's windy, straining to hold its head up as long as it can while it slowly inflates. I try to remember when I took the ram out of the field. It must almost be time to take them in. I count nineteen sheep.

I'm not in the field just to count the sheep, I'm there to get out of the house. Riet rang. She asked again whether she shouldn't visit, not for any particular reason, just to have a look, and maybe to do some "women's work." Father was coughing upstairs. I called Henk, gave him the receiver and walked out into the field.

I sigh and count again. Nineteen. I walk to the closest ditch. The sun is shining on the smooth water. The lack of ripples doesn't mean very much: a sheep that falls into water gives up quickly, starts drowning and stands there calmly waiting for the end. Texel sheep are great drowners. Another point against them. I follow the ditch to the intersecting ditch. The nineteen sheep keep their distance, but follow. The sheep is in the third ditch. Almost everywhere the water is up to just below ground level: the banks of this ditch are no more than twelve inches high. I bury my hands deep in the wool and start pulling. Sheep legs are thin and fragile, but when those legs are stuck in mud, they're like leaden barbs. The sheep sways back and forth a little, turning its head towards me; water splashes against the ruler-high sides of the ditch. I plant my feet wider and try again. A couple of seconds later I'm sitting on my bum in the grass with a tuft of wool in my right hand. The sheep is no longer waiting for the end. It goes against its nature by struggling and bleating, its panicked eyes roll in its head. I stop thinking and step into the ditch, without taking my rubber boots off first. It's a shallow ditch, but when I squat down to get my arms under the belly of the sheep, I'm up to my neck in the muddy water. I struggle to lift the sheep, my boots sinking deeper and deeper in the sucking mud. Slowly but surely the animal rises, I've already got one of its flanks against the side of the ditch. Just when I think I'm going to manage it, the sheep feels solid ground and starts kicking wildly. I lose my balance, fall backwards, and the sheep rolls over on top of me.

My boots are standing upright in the mud as if in cement, I'm lying on my back with my legs bent, unable to exert any force. Just once I manage to get my head up above water – past the wet, enormously heavy fleece – and suck in a big lungful of air. Then the sheep's body pushes me down again. I think I can feel its heartbeat, a furious pounding, but it could be my own. I try to wriggle my feet out of the boots. No recklessness at all, now I'm running out of breath. Sideways, I have to try to get out from under the sheep sideways. No agelessness either, now I'm a half-drowned animal stuck under another half-drowned animal. The other way, to the left, pushing my left shoulder up and hoping the sheep will slide off. Strange, all of a sudden I see Jaap swimming away from me with his powerful strokes and myself, kicking awkwardly and thrashing my arms with my mouth wide open and great gulps of IJssel water disappearing into it. Clean? This filthy, stinking water? What is there to wash away? *His hair floated back and forth like seaweed.* I have to open my mouth, I can't help it. I don't see Henk, I see myself sitting in the Simca and my hair floats back and forth like seaweed while Riet looks in through the window. Not shocked, not frightened, not panicking. Smiling. She doesn't even do her best to open the door. I *have* to open my mouth. I can't get my arms between me and the sheep. Even if I tried to roll it up over my head to get it off me, I couldn't.

III

42

Helmer,

You lied to me. Henk told me about your father. I thought he'd lost his mind. But he's dead and scattered, I said. No, he's not, Henk said, he's upstairs in bed, I can hear him coughing now. He even told me he quite often takes his dinner up to him. Why did you lie to me? I didn't expect that sort of thing from you. Henk (your brother, my fiancé) would never have lied to me like that. I always thought of you as a nice, honest, gentle guy, but it turns out I was wrong. I sat in your house and walked around with your father there as well, behind closed doors! It puts my visit in a brand new light. I hate your father, he sent me packing, he ruined my life. (Or do you think I spent dozens of years happy and contented with Wien? That I like living in Brabant?)

Why did you do it? Because you thought I wouldn't come otherwise? You only think of yourself. There isn't a day goes by I don't think of Henk. Henk was a boy, but he was a real man as well, and he gave me what I wanted. Wien was completely different. In a way he was more interested in his pigs than in me. I came second. If only you knew the pictures that haunt me every night. Always that car and Lake IJssel. You're more like Wien than Henk. And to think that I found some degree of peace on the farm in the days after Henk's death. Your mother was a comfort to me and I thought there was also some kind of connection between us (you and me). There was something we could build on, I thought.

And something else: I want Henk back (not your brother, my son). Having him round the house wasn't easy but I see now that not having him is even worse. I want to learn to talk to him, I want to understand him. He's my son. What's more, I realize now that he doesn't belong there with you, because you're a liar and a cheat, and a bad example for him. And what's this story about the crow? Didn't you realize it was such a dangerous animal? Why did you expose my son to that kind of danger? Did he at least get proper treatment at the hospital? You're an irresponsible man.

I'll write to Henk as well, telling him he has to come back to his mother, that she needs him.

It can't go on like this.

Yours,

Riet.

43

Fog. All I can see are the bare branches of the ash. Empty branches. Beyond that, nothing. It's always a bit damp in Father's bedroom. I can't remember it being clammy when I slept here. It's still March, but to me it feels like it could just as well be May or even June. Father agrees entirely.

"I've had enough."

"You just said that."

"It's taking too long."

"It's not spring yet."

"I know. That's why."

I look at the crowded walls: the photos, the samplers, the watercolor mushrooms. Do people take photos for later, for when they're gone? "And?" I ask. "What do you want to do about it?"

"Stop eating."

"What?"

"I'm not going to eat any more. I'll just drink."

"But . . ."

"Is that so bad?"

"If I don't bring you any food . . ."

"You'll be guilty of killing me? Bah. If it bothers you so much, bring up the meals anyway. I just won't eat 'em." He's lying there cheerfully, as if it's a joke. Maybe he's thinking, If my son can joke, so can I.

The last few days I've kept looking at Henk's wrists. He has strong, broad wrists. Covered with fine ginger hair. After ending the telephone conversation with his mother, he followed me out. He hung around for a while at the causeway gate, where he couldn't see me, but noticed the sheep clumped together and staring in the same direction. There was something funny about it, he said later. In retrospect I think that must have been the moment I managed to get my head above water for the last time. He climbed over the gate just in time, and walked just fast enough to reach me before I drowned. He saw the sheep lying there and a limp arm draped over its flank. He too stepped into the ditch, slid the sheep off me with ease and pulled me upright with those strong wrists. My boots stayed behind in the mud; they're still there now. He heaved me up out of the ditch. When I opened my eyes I saw an ear, a hand and a scar. He kissed me on the mouth, I thought, and the next thing I knew a powerful stream of air was forcing its way into my lungs – I felt like I was suffocating. There was nowhere else for the air to go, he had my nose pinched shut. I made a noise and Henk's head moved away.

My diaphragm contracted and the next thing I knew I was lying on my side – helped by his strong wrists – and vomiting a wave of muddy body-warmed water. "Just stay there, don't move," said Henk. I obeyed. I was gasping and glad to be breathing air instead of water. A little later a few drops splashed onto my face from a bale of wool that came wobbling by. He'd even managed to get the sheep up out of the ditch.

Now he's in bed. He says he's come down with something. I see his wrists on a background of African animals. I vomited a few more times in the course of the day and that was that.

"How's Henk?" Father asks.

"Okay," I say. "Better." It's as if I can still taste the mud in my mouth. Or feel the gritty soil between my teeth. I can well imagine death tasting like mud. I stare at the ash.

"You were going to tell me why you hate me and what I did to you."

"Yes," I say.

"Why you tell Ada that I'm senile and why you refuse to call the doctor."

"Yes," I say.

"I understand."

"What do you mean?"

"You put me upstairs as the first step. You keep people away from me."

I stop answering and stare out of the window.

"At first you hardly brought me anything to eat. And now I've said I don't want any any more, you start grumbling. Just let me go."

Slowly I turn my head towards him. He is no longer cheerful. He's about to say things he's never said before.

"You tell people I'm senile so that whatever I say, no matter who I say it to, it won't be true."

I stay silent.

"That time you brought me bread and cheese, on that beautiful sunny day."

"Yes?"

"And you thought I was asleep."

I don't say yes again. He said, "thought," that's enough.

"I know, son. I know." He smoothes out the blanket next to his legs with one hand. It's a strange, feminine gesture. "No," he goes on, "I suspected it. And I don't want to hear another word about it. Ever."

The fog is thinning out, thinning and paling. There is a silver glimmer to the road and almost imperceptible ripples on the surface of the canal. I get up and walk to the door. What exactly does he know or did he suspect? He doesn't want to hear another word about it, ever, but that's not as easy as stopping eating.

I see myself kneeling next to the bed and laying my head on the blanket and I see Father's old hand stop rubbing the blanket. He raises his hand, lifts it up over his legs and lays it on my head. The hand feels dry and the skin scrapes over my hair, and it feels warm as well. I open the door and look at the plate on his bedside cabinet. A cheese sandwich, an apple and a knife. I leave the plate where it is and go out onto the landing.

. . .

Everyone else is in bed so I lie down on my bed too. It's just gone mid-day. I feel even more that I don't belong here. Henk should have lived here. With Riet and with kids. Despite the age difference, Riet would have been as thick as thieves with Ada, and her children would have gone to school with Teun and Ronald. No, her grandchildren. I should have been an uncle. Henk would have told the young tanker driver from his heart that he was sorry to see him go and wished him all the best, maybe even patting him on the shoulder. When I look in a mirror, I see myself. Sometimes I look through myself and see Henk, who generally looks back with a strange expression on his face. What would it have been like if the two of us had been standing there with Father just now, united? Would he still think we were conspiring against him? Would we have still been capable of provoking him by looking him straight in the eye? Would Henk have stood up for me or would he quietly but clearly have called me an idiot?

I've been doing things by halves for so long now. For so long I've had just half a body. No more shoulder to shoulder, no more chest to chest, no more taking each other's presence for granted. Soon I'll go and do the milking. Tomorrow morning I'll milk again. And the rest of the week, of course, and next week. But it's no longer enough. I don't think I can go on hiding behind the cows and letting things happen. Like an idiot.

44

His arms are next to his body, I can't see his wrists. The fog has lifted and I have set the window ajar. The new room smells of illness, even though he's been better for a day or two now. It also smells of cigarette smoke. He refuses to get up. The letter his mother sent him is lying next to the bed. The letter she sent me is downstairs, on the kitchen table.

I changed the bandage on his head once, pulling the gauze cap back on over the top. When I went to do it a second time (he had already taken to his bed), I saw that the wound was dry and left it. The ends of the blue stitches are longer than his hair. "They always go for my head," he mutters. "Animals."

I wonder when the stitches need to be removed. Is that something you can do yourself? I like the idea of doing it myself. I'd clamp his skull against my chest and use one steady hand to remove the threads with a pair of tweezers.

I hear the milk tanker turning into the yard. The new driver is a determined woman in her mid-forties. I've only exchanged a word or two with her, she is standoffish and, like the old tanker driver, a bit surly.

"Do you miss your brother?" Henk asks.

"What?"

"Do you miss your brother. Henk?"

I don't answer.

"I don't miss my sisters at all."

"They're still alive."

"True. Were they really going to get married?"

"Yes."

"And you looked like each other?"

"You've seen the photos in Father's bedroom, haven't you?"

"Yeah, but . . ."

"We were twins."

"Why did she fall in love with your brother and not with you?"

"I don't know."

"Or did she see him first and you afterwards?"

"No, both at the same time. We were at the pub together."

"Why?"

"I don't know, Henk. Things just happen like that."

"It could just as easily have been different."

"I'm not so–"

"What if she'd–"

"Stop it."

"I think she wants to marry you."

"I thought so too."

"Not any more?"

"No."

"I think she's even using me for that."

"How?"

"By sending me here."

"You watch too much TV."

"She's going to be disappointed." He sniggers.

I look at him. "It's time you got up."

"No. I'm staying here."

"What's she say?"

"That she needs me and you're a liar and I have to come home."

The tanker drives out of the yard. It grows quiet outside. I can feel from my back that I'm still standing under the window, under the sloping wall. I slide his clothes off the chair and sit down.

"She's angry. With my father, my sisters, me. Always has been. She's angry with everything and everyone. Even the pigs. She's probably angry with you too."

"Yes."

"Why did you tell her your father was dead?"

"It's a long story."

"I've got time."

"No, you don't. We have to get the sheep in."

"Why?"

"They're about to yean."

"You mean lamb."

"Yes."

"Can't you do that by yourself?"

"No. I need your help."

"Will I have to run?"

"Maybe."

"I'm ill."

"You were."

"I'm scared."

"You're young, you should take things in stride."

"I want to stay here permanently. I don't want to go back to my angry mother, to Brabant. I hate it there, there's nothing for me in Brabant. What good are sisters?"

"Is there anything for you here?"

"Yes." Two wrists appear. He fumbles for the packet of cigarettes on the bedside cabinet. "It must be weird," he says. "Having a twin brother. Someone who's exactly like you." He lights his cigarette.

I get up off the chair and open the window a little wider.

"Exactly the same body."

"What are you actually scared of?"

"Summer."

"What?"

"Summer is long and lonely and light." The duvet has slipped down a little, baring his chest. A smooth young chest with a timorous heart. He blows out a cloud of smoke. Not at the window, but straight in my face. "With a twin brother that's not a problem. You're always together."

. . .

Of course he runs twice as fast as I do. He runs too fast, scattering the sheep in all directions. I tell him to take it easy, reminding him that he's dealing with pregnant animals. When I check after milking, two lambs are already walking around the sheep shed. A fence in the middle of the shed divides it into the drop pen on one side and the lambing pen on the other. I pick up the two lambs and an ewe starts to stamp. That is the mother. I put the ewe and the lambs in the lamb pen. Henk watches from the doorway. His face is flushed. Wisps of steam are rising from his shoulders.

"Come on," I say.

We walk through fields that are sheepless but not empty to the Bosman windmill. Two graylag geese are standing next to the ditch. I also see two peewits, a flock of wood pigeons, a pair of white wagtails and a solitary black-tailed godwit. When I'm almost certain that the redshanks haven't arrived yet, two fly past. The sun is about to set. The vanes of the mill are turning very slowly. I fold the tail forward to disengage it and wipe my hands on the legs of my overalls. Let the water come.

"We spent a lot of time here," I say, "in the summer."

"You and Henk?"

"Yes."

"Like now," he says. "But it's not summer yet."

"No," I say. "It's not summer." The geese take wing, one flying higher than the other, the way geese do. "Your mother used to come here too, just after Henk died. With my mother."

That doesn't interest him. "What did you do here?"

"Hang around."

. . .

Hang around. Stand, walk, sit. Stare at the yellow water lilies in the canal, watch clouds drift slowly – always slowly – by. Watch the water bulging in the ditch. When we closed our eyes to listen to the larks, the squeaking of the windmill's greased axle and the wind blowing through the struts, time stood still. All kinds of things flicked back and forth under our eyelids and it was never dark. It was orange. When it was summer and we were in another country here – almost like America – nothing else existed. We existed and even stronger than the smell of warm water, sheep droppings and dried-out thistles was our own smell. A sweet, sometimes chalky smell of bare knees and bare stomachs. Sitting on the itchy grass. When we touched each other, we touched ourselves. Feeling someone else's heartbeat and thinking it's your own, you can't get any closer than that. Almost like the sheep and me, merging together just before it drowned me.

"Helmer?"

"Yes?"

"What's it like, having a twin brother?"

"It's the most beautiful thing in the world, Henk."

"Do you feel like half a person now?"

I want to say something, but I can't. I even need to grab one of the struts to stop myself from falling. I've always been forgotten: I was the brother, Father and Mother were more important. Riet demanded – no matter how briefly – her widowhood, and now Riet's son stands opposite me and asks me if I feel like half a person. Henk grabs me by the shoulders; I shake him off.

"What are you crying about?" he asks.

"Everything," I say.

He looks at me.

I let him look.

We don't really eat. Henk has opened a bottle of wine, there's bread and cheese on the table, butter and yogurt, a ripped-open bag of chips. "She acts like you set that crow on me," says Henk. He's got the letter his mother sent me spread out in front of him. "And here, 'some kind of connection between us' and 'something we could build on.' I told you she wanted to marry you. Then you would have been my father."

"Of course not," I say. "If I was your father, you wouldn't be who you are."

"What?"

"You know what I mean."

"Not at all. Shall I fry a couple of eggs?"

"No, thanks. What are you reading that for anyway? It's rude to read other people's letters." I am tipsy and keep looking out of the side window. I hope Ada is watching through her binoculars and can see just what's going on in here. Booze, bad food, general agitation.

"I could have been your uncle," I say. "But not really, because if Henk was your father, you wouldn't be who you are either."

He gives me a fuzzy look. "Uncle Helmer," he says slowly.

I wonder where the tweezers are. In the first-aid kit, in the linen cupboard, somewhere under a pile of clean towels. "Henk," I say. "Get the first-aid kit out of the cupboard, will you? And turn the light on." He gets up and does what I ask. Keep watching, Ada, I think, digging the tweezers out of the first-aid kit. I push my chair back from the table and signal for Henk to come closer.

"What are you going to do?" he asks.

"I'm going to remove those stitches."

"You sure? Don't I need to go to the hospital for that?"

"No. Kneel down."

He kneels down in front of me and I use one hand to press his head against my chest.

"Careful," he says.

"Of course," I say. There are four stitches. Two come out without any real tugging. The third is more difficult.

"Ow," says Henk.

"It's already done." The fourth stitch is another easy one.

Before standing up, he runs one finger over the wound that has almost become a scar.

Slightly befuddled, I stand in the sheep shed. Not much is happening. The two lambs are drinking from their mother, the rest of the sheep are lying down and quietly chewing the cud. There's nothing for me to do in here and I put off whatever else might be about to happen by sitting on the floor of the lambing pen, my back to the fence. Sitting is easier than standing. A shed full of sheep in spring is just like a shed full of cows in winter. I tell myself that I mustn't think like that any more. I don't want to think like that any more. Henk pulled me out of that ditch and something has changed. The re-la-tion-ship, I think with my boozed-up brain. I wonder if you have to do something in return if someone saves your life. One of the lambs comes up to me, the ewe stamps a forefoot. Sheep in a shed aren't as sorry as they are in a field. When I walk out of the shed I leave the light on.

In the scullery I take off my clothes and throw them in the basket. The sound of TV is coming from the living room. I go into the bathroom, turn on the taps and start by washing my hair with Henk's shampoo. Just when I'm putting the bottle back on the shelf under the mirror, the door opens. He comes into the bathroom and closes the door behind him.

"What are you doing?" I ask, wiping the lather out of my eyes.

"I want to get in the shower," he says.

"Can't you see I'm in here?"

"Yes," he says. He pulls off his T-shirt. "You using my shampoo?"

"Yes."

"It doesn't matter."

"Go away, Henk," I say.

"Why?"

"Because I say so."

"Ha!" he says.

"Who's the boss here?"

He's standing opposite me, the T-shirt dangling from his right hand. He looks surprised. "What's got into you?"

"Who's the boss here?" I repeat. The foam on my skull is starting to itch, my head is buzzing. I have become my father. I'm not embarrassed, I don't have the slightest urge to conceal my nakedness. Henk keeps looking at me, I see him turning things over in his head, searching for something to say. But he doesn't have any allies, there isn't anyone standing behind me and off to one side.

"You're the boss," he says. Very calmly, he puts his T-shirt back on before disappearing from the bathroom.

When I emerge, all the lights are on. In the kitchen voices drift from the radio; in the living room the TV is on a music channel. Henk is nowhere to be seen. I do a circuit of the house and turn off all the lights, the radio and the TV. Finally I turn the fire down to the lowest setting and go into my bedroom. I turn on the light and go over to stand in front of the map of Denmark. "Skanderborg," I say quietly. Generally three or four other names follow, but not this time. I get into the enormous bed and close my eyes. A little later I hear the whirr of a passing bicycle. After that it gets very quiet.

I wake up when someone climbs into bed with me. He sighs and shuffles back and forth. The pillowcase on the pillow next to mine rustles. He hasn't turned on the light. I wait.

"I don't want to sleep in that room any more," he says. "It's cold and horrible."

I know that. It *is* cold and horrible. It's also empty.

He lies very still, I can't even hear his breathing.

"Your father hasn't eaten," he says after a while.

I clear my throat. "He doesn't want to eat any more."

"Does he want to die?"

"Yes."

"I don't," he says, with a satisfied sigh. Then he turns over onto his side. It's too dark to see which side.

I have already said something else. I answered him. Now it's too late to send him away. Maybe this is what you have to do in return for someone saving your life.

45

I sit on the side of the bed and look at him. He is lying on his back and wearing the T-shirt he had on yesterday. His chest rises and falls calmly. Exhaling, he puffs a little. He's lying in my bed as if he's never lain anywhere else. That annoys me. I get up and pull on my work trousers. "You going to come and do something?" I ask loudly. *Wake up, Henk* is something I can't bring myself to say.

He gives a slight groan, rolls over and snuggles down on his stomach. "Yeah, sure," he mumbles into the pillow. "Not yet."

"It's five thirty," I say.

It takes a while before he says anything else. "Those animals."

"What about them?"

"The ones that go for my head."

"Yes?"

"I have to do something about it."

"What do you want to do about it?" I'm almost in the living room.

"I don't know. Something."

"Protect your head."

"I don't know."

"That miniature donkey's been dead for years and the hooded crow's flown off."

"Still."

"I'm going," I say. "Will you do the yearlings?"

"Yes," he drawls. "Later."

Late March and the sun is already up when I start milking. When I've milked ten cows, I walk to the shed door. There's a blackbird somewhere, the muck heap is steaming, the pollarded willows could sprout tomorrow. The yearlings are restless in the shed, but otherwise it's so quiet I can hear the donkeys trotting in the paddock.

It's been almost thirty years since I read a poem – not counting death notices – and now I'm thinking of a poem. I didn't learn much in my seven months in Amsterdam, but one thing I still remember is that poems are almost always retrospective. A poem (incredibly, instead of the muck heap, I now see our energetic modern lit. lecturer before me: his tangled curls, his owlish glasses, as if he's a poet himself) is "condensed reality," an "incident that has been reduced to its essence," a "sublimation." A poem is never about what it seems to be about (gushed our energetic modern lit. lecturer). If only I smoked, I could go now and lean against the shed wall to gaze pensively – smoking, as I imagine it, is a pensive activity – at the motionless Bosman windmill. I go back into the shed, plug the claw into the milk and pulse tubes, and put the teat cups on the eleventh cow.

After milking I fill a couple of buckets with water, tip them into the barrel on the other side of the gate in the donkey paddock and chuck a couple of winter carrots down next to it. Rather than rushing straight to the gate, the donkeys stroll casually towards me, side by side. These animals are mine, really mine, I bought them. Nothing else here is really mine: not the cows and not the sheep, I even inherited the Lakenvelder chickens. The old Opel Kadett, the muck heap, the willows – I drive it, I throw my dung on it, I pollard them, but none is mine. I'm a tenant, doing things someone else should have been doing.

The sun is shining, there is hardly any wind. Spring. Something glistens on what's left of the side wall of the laborer's cottage, maybe a snail trail. It's not good, I think, feeling like a poem. It's because of what Henk said yesterday. The carrots disappear with a crunch in the donkeys' mouths. I scratch the animals behind the ears. It's only when they've both had enough and start shaking their heads, the two of them at the same time, that I stop, almost without thinking. Then I do the yearlings, much too late. Henk hasn't got up.

46

Father is turning grayer. He hasn't eaten for a week now and he's only drinking water and orange juice, and less and less of the latter because it's "so tart." Every now and then I find a trickle of dark yellow urine in the bedpan. In the last seven days I haven't carried him downstairs once. His wish has come true all the same, he's getting a final spring. For a few days now it's been sunny and mild and the buds have started to swell on the ash, turning it into a skeleton tree. Father's voice is weakening, although I don't know if that's because he's stopped eating. How long does this sort of thing go on? If a body is tough, I imagine it being able to go weeks without food. I go up to look in on him more often than usual and sometimes I get a shock because he looks dead when he's just sound asleep. He often asks for Henk. He talks to him. Yesterday I couldn't resist and crept up onto the landing behind him.

"How's the dying going, Mr. van Wonderen?" Henk asked cheerfully.

"Fine," Father answered, just as cheerfully, but quietly.

After that Henk must have picked up the gun, because they spent a long time discussing its action. Henk asked Father what he shot. Hare and pheasants, long ago. If the thud against your shoulder wasn't heavy. No, the recoil was nothing special. If the gun was loaded. No, of course not. Whether he had any bullets ("Cartridges," Father said, and then a little louder, "cartridges!") and where did he keep them. In the cupboard in the hall, next to the toilet. And how do you load a gun? You have to undo that little catch, then it breaks open, then you put in two cartridges and close it again. Do both cartridges shoot out at the same time? No, you get two shots and the cartridges stay put. How does it work then? You have to take them out, after you've fired it. Or shake them out. The gun went back to its spot, next to the grandfather clock. I heard metal tap wood. It was quiet for a moment.

Then Father asked, "Are you nice to Helmer?"

"Yes," said Henk.

"And is he nice to you?"

"Nice enough," said Henk.

Father didn't say anything. He sighed, very deeply. I crept down the stairs.

He hardly says a word to me. He asks how many lambs have been born and why no one ever visits. Where Ada has got to and why he never hears the voice of the livestock dealer any more. Teun and Ronald? Maybe malnutrition really is starting to get to his memory.

. . .

I haven't written back to Riet. Or phoned her. Henk hasn't responded either. "Who does she think she is?" he says. "She can go and move in with my sisters."

I force my way through the old rubbish in Henk's bedroom. I have to push a lot of stuff aside to open the door of the built-in wardrobe. The cardboard box is on the bottom shelf. "Dutch language and literature, University of Amsterdam, September 1966–April 1967" is written neatly on the top flaps. I don't remember doing that. I remember grimly stuffing my textbooks into the box when Henk had hardly had time to settle in his grave. I lift the box up onto Mother's dressing table and look for *H. J. M. F. Lodewick's History of Dutch Literature*. I lay Part One ("From the Beginning to Around 1880") to one side and sit down on Henk's bed with Part Two ("Around 1880 to the Present"). I hear Father snoring softly, he can't even do that at full strength any more. Because I don't know where to find what I'm looking for, I leaf through the book. Gorter, Leopold, Bloem, Nijhoff, Achterberg, Warren, Vroman. I am impatient, reading the odd line that strikes home or will strike home soon (*a flood has covered the land, a flood of tepid water and blood, / I am a fatherless man and rooted in the mud*), then leafing on quickly. I notice that I am trying to recall faces from my months in Amsterdam – I hear the coots yapping at the same time and finally, on page 531, I find a poem that I read from the first to the last word.

to yearn & pursue

Why do I always see
– when I have closed my eyes
in bed or in my thoughts –
your nose, your hair, your chest?

I sometimes see myself
in mirror or in windowpane
just after I've seen you:
my own half body.

For all your youth and beauty,
I think I look like you –
my nose and chest and hair
are all identical.

I see the poet's name but don't read what Lodewick has to say about him, or his verdict on the poem. None of that matters. I close the book and put Part One back in the box.

Thinking of Denmark, I go downstairs with Part Two in my hand.

Henk is on the sofa watching TV. He's not sitting, he's draped, with the remote control dangling from one hand. His shirt is unbuttoned. It's as if he's taken the place over.

"Have you looked in on the sheep yet?" I ask.

"No."

"Why not?"

"I'm watching TV."

"It's two o'clock."

"So? It's war. Look."

I look at the screen. Buildings with scattered palm trees. An explosion somewhere. Empty streets. Subtitles at the bottom of the picture. Is this what war is like these days? Live on TV? With kids like him slumped on the sofa to watch it? "Do you think the sheep care?"

"Come and sit down for a while."

I stare at him until he looks up. "Go and do the sheep," I say. I turn around and go into the kitchen to sit down at the bureau. I turn to page 531, take a pad and a pen and start copying out the poem. When I have finished and torn the page from the pad, I wonder what I'm doing. I stand up with the page in one hand and don't know where to go. I look out of the front window, out of the side window, I look at the dishes on the draining board and the newspaper on the table, I hear the electric clock buzzing. Because I hear the clock buzzing, I realize the TV is off. I'm standing here holding a neat copy of a poem and I haven't got a clue what to do with it. I hurry through the hall to the scullery, take the stairs with big strides and catch my breath on the landing. Cautiously, I open the door to Father's bedroom. He is asleep. His small head is motionless on the pillow, his ears and nose look enormous, his mouth hangs open. Somehow or other, he is very dry. Once again I don't have a clue what I am going to do next. I look around the bedroom and walk up to the bed. I lay the neatly copied poem on his chest. It rises and falls calmly.

There is a swish outside. It swishes, lands and jerks its wings in, like a farmer in Sunday black making a vain attempt to wipe his big hands. It's back. Quietly I click my tongue. I suspect it would have done better to stay away.

47

"Am I a kind of Henk now?" Henk had spent a couple of nights in his own room, but tonight it apparently got colder again and he slipped into bed with me for the second time. He was asleep for a while, but woke up and asked me if he is "a kind of Henk." I was already awake. I was lying on my side looking at the light that comes into the room through the venetian blinds. I was listening. Someone just rode past on a bike, a few ducks landed on the canal, the coots yapped quietly. Father said something, maybe in his sleep, maybe staring into the dark like me, at his curtains, behind which the hooded crow was dozing on its usual branch. I wasn't entirely relaxed in the first place, but now I feel even more tension entering my body. I know what he's getting at but I don't answer.

"Well?" he says. "Am I a kind of Henk?"

"What do you mean?" I ask cagily.

"Your brother. Am I like your brother now?"

Something is going badly wrong here. When did this start? "No," I say.

He is quiet for a moment. Then he says, "I think your father's brave."

My shoulder blades are itching with annoyance. The selfishness of the boy: talking when he feels like talking, even if it's the middle of the night. I have to get up to milk, he stays in bed and gets up around eight to do the yearlings. If he gets up at all.

"You could just as well call him a coward," I say.

"How's that?"

"You wouldn't understand."

"Oh."

"Go to sleep," I say. I'm still lying on my side, but feel like turning over. I stare at the slats of the blinds, but see Ada's head appearing around the corner of the kitchen door. There is a mischievous look on her face and she says "in a big bed you've got room to stretch." Then she gives me a meaningful look, which still looks funny now, with that hare-lip. "Two pillows, Helmer, two pillows." When I think he's fallen asleep again, I roll onto my back and rub away the itch. I look at the dark frame next to the door. I wish I was *in* the frame and thinking of here.

"If you ask me I am," he says, half asleep. "A kind of Henk."

God almighty, I think.

A little later he's asleep and I think about the ditch and the sheep. One of the sheep took too long and yesterday I removed two dead lambs. Was that the sheep that fell in the water? I try to remember what I thought or saw, what happened to me in the black minutes between drowning and regaining consciousness. Or was it seconds? Was it like that for Henk too? Or was he already unconscious when the car hit the water? I notice that my hands are clasped together over my stomach. As if I'm laid out. I'd like to lie on my right side, but that's where Henk is, so I turn back onto my left. Outside it is totally silent.

How does he do it? Asking Father how the dying is going, as if he's asking him if he'd like some more gravy on his potatoes? And how does Father do it? Answering "fine," as if looking on contentedly while he pours the gravy?

48

The magnolia is in flower. Like a glacé cherry on a cowpat. Its large flowers are neither white nor red, but pink with a white edge. If the laborer's cottage was still standing, the top branches would be up to the dormer window. April has come and spring has gone away again. It's sunny but cold, and at night the temperature falls below zero. But still the magnolia is in flower. None of it makes any difference to a tree and the frost doesn't seem to have damaged the flowers. A very long time ago, maybe in the days when the farmhand was still living there, a night frost froze all the flowers. Two days later they turned brown, as if they had been scorched by a fire, and the petals, which normally fall from the branches one at a time, didn't fall. It's incredibly clear: from Father's bedroom you can see the lighthouse on Marken. The wind is blowing from the north or northeast. From Denmark.

· · ·

"When your mother died," says Father, "you were the only one left."
He is lying on his side because I've told him not to lie on his back all the
time. The piece of paper with the poem is next to the bed, halfway under
the bedside cabinet, blank side up. "And now everyone's gone. I would
have liked another chat with the livestock dealer, even if he hardly ever
said anything."

"He must be in New Zealand by now," I say, more to myself than to
Father.

"Life is such a mess. Ada hasn't been here for weeks because she
watched you through a pair of binoculars, and you watched her. And
why doesn't Teun come any more? Teun is a nice boy. What are you playing at, Helmer?"

"Me?"

"Yes, you."

I look out of the window. "The ash is in bud," I say.

"How many lambs?" No matter what happens, he doesn't want to
lose count.

"Fourteen."

"From?"

"Ten."

He sighs. "No one could tell you and Henk apart, not the barber,
not your teacher, not your grandparents. Even I had to look closely
sometimes. Only your mother and Jaap always knew who was who.
Jaap always knew that you were Helmer and Henk was Henk. How
did he know that? What did he see that I or other people didn't see? I
never trusted him." He's lying on the edge of the bed. His nails haven't

been cut for a long time, a clawlike hand hangs down next to the bed. He moves his fingers, as if reaching for the poem. I'm surprised that so many words can come out of such a worn-out person. With the bed up on blocks, his searching fingertips will never reach the ground. Then he rolls onto his back. His arm follows the movement of his body and falls next to him on the blankets like a dry branch. He's panting slightly. "I don't know what went on in the laborer's cottage, but I was glad he left," he says, almost inaudibly.

"What?"

"Kissing," he sighs. "Men don't kiss."

Until this instant I hadn't noticed the ticking of the grandfather clock. It's ticking irregularly, slowly. It's been a long time since I raised the weights. "He . . ." Then I let it be, I let him be. I stand up and open the glass door of the clock. After I've raised the weights, the ticking is as good as ever.

"You never said anything," Father says. "You never said you didn't want to."

"You didn't have much choice." I walk back to the window and follow the line of the dyke until I can see the lighthouse again.

"No."

I clear my throat. "I didn't have much choice either."

He doesn't answer that. He's still panting.

"And now Henk is here." A car drives along the dyke, very slowly. The windows catch the sunlight so that it looks as if the sun is shining from inside the car. The chariot of the sun god. "I'm not sure that's such a good idea," I reply.

"No, maybe not," says Father.

The chariot corners and changes back to a car. I turn around.

Father's eyelids droop, but his eyeballs are still moving. "I . . ." he says. Then it's quiet for a long time. "I have almost no body any more." I knew it. I knew he had read the poem.

49

"What's your name actually?"

"Greta."

"I'm Helmer van Wonderen."

She gives me an insolent look. "Yes, I know that."

"What's your surname?"

"What's it matter? I'm only the driver."

"Fine," I say. "Whatever."

Greta bends over and unscrews the milk hose. She's wearing train-ers, but doesn't raise her feet to avoid the last bit of milk that runs out of the tank and hose.

"How's your boy going?" she asks.

"My boy?"

"Your helper."

"Henk?"

"How would I know what he's called?"

"Why do you ask?"

"No reason."

"It seems like a strange question to me."

"Yeah?" She's finished and walks over to the cab. She climbs up. The young tanker driver always leapt up like a cat, pulling the door open as he leapt. Greta clambers, pants, grabs hold and hauls herself up. She has to pull the door twice before it shuts properly. I can't see her any more, but imagine her sliding her fat ass back and forth to make herself comfortable before setting to work on the gear stick, clutch and accelerator. After it's been quiet for a while in the milking parlor, I start to hose out the tank and wash off the tiles.

There's someone in the field. Near the Bosman windmill. I stand at the causeway gate and watch him approach the farm. He gets bigger and bigger and smaller and smaller at the same time. It's Ronald.

"It's all wet there," he says after reaching me.

"That's the idea," I say.

I can hardly remember the last time it rained and yesterday evening I saw on TV that there have been dune and heath fires because of the drought, but still the field near the windmill has got boggy. This isn't dune or heath here, it's peat meadow.

"What for?"

"For the birds, Ronald. They like that, wet land."

"Oh, right." He stays standing on the other side of the gate.

"Aren't you going to climb over the gate?"

"Yeah." He looks around. "Nice weather, isn't it?"

"It's like summer."

"Yes. But it's only April."

"How's your mother's garden?"

"What about it?"

"Is it looking good?"

"Uh-huh. Where's Henk?"

"Henk's gone to Monnickendam to get some cigarettes."

"By bike?"

"Yep."

"Smoking's bad, isn't it?"

"Smoking is very bad. But enjoyable."

"Why didn't he take the car?"

"Because he doesn't have a license."

"Is he scared?"

"No. He's only just eighteen."

"How old are you?"

"Old."

"What did you do with Henk's head?" He's still standing on the other side of the gate.

"What do you mean, Ronald?"

"The stitches."

"I took them out."

"Doesn't a doctor have to do that?"

"No, it's easy."

"Oh." He looks a bit unhappy and puts one foot on the bottom bar of the gate.

I take him under the arms and help him over the gate.

"I'm going home now," he says.

"Fine."

"Just going to see the donkeys first." He crosses the yard to the donkey paddock. The donkeys are over near the cottage and come trotting when they see him at the gate. Ronald sticks his arms through the bars and rubs them both under the chin at the same time. When he tires of it they stay there for a while using the top bar of the gate to scratch their own chins. Slowly Ronald walks to the road, kicking stones along in front of him. Not once does he turn back to look at me.

Not much has changed when I see Henk come riding up. I'm still standing at the causeway gate and the donkeys are still standing at their gate. They start braying and shaking their heads when they see Henk. He ignores them. He rides straight at me, brakes and stretches a hand out towards my head. I step aside, just like he pulled back when he'd been to the hairdresser's – how long ago now? – and felt my hand moving towards his shaven head.

He puffs a little, leans Father's bike against the gate and takes off his coat. He drapes the coat over the gate, then pulls a new packet of cigarettes out of an inside pocket. "It's boiling," he says, pulling the cellophane off the pack, flicking the lid up and taking a cigarette. The lighter appears from his back pocket. He lights the cigarette and inhales deeply, selfishly. The way everything about him is selfish. "Boiling," he says again. "And it's not even summer."

"No," I say, "It's not summer by a long shot."

. . .

After we've eaten, Henk goes upstairs with a plate. I clear the table and start washing up. He comes back down – plateless – just when I'm wiping the last knife. He has the gall to say, "He's not dead yet."

I turn to face him, still holding the shining clean knife in my right hand and with the damp tea towel over one shoulder. "Henk," I say. "Shut your trap."

"Goodness," he says.

I yank open the cutlery drawer and throw in the knife. I drape the tea towel over the back of a chair and walk into the scullery.

"Where you going?" he calls out after me.

I don't answer. In the shed the cows are calmly chewing the cud. It's quiet in the sheep shed as well. One sheep has started in the afternoon and isn't making any progress. I roll up a sleeve, make my hand as narrow as possible and feel my way round a warm tangle of legs, bodies and heads. There are three: this is the first sheep with triplets. Number eighteen. In a few minutes I've got them out. One is dead. A dead lamb is always a shame, but triplets almost invariably mean that at least one of them will need bottle-feeding. With just two sheep left to go, it's looking unlikely this year. Ronald has already complained, he loves mucking around with bottles and teats. His father doesn't have sheep. I lift the two remaining lambs into the lambing pen, then pull the gate open a little to herd the sheep through to the other side. I lay the dead lamb outside the sheep shed next to a dead lamb from yesterday. I'll have to call the incinerator tomorrow morning. Twenty-nine from eighteen. It could be better.

. . .

Coming back into the house, I go straight to the bathroom. I leave the taps running until the boiler is empty. I dry myself and wrap the towel around my waist. It's quiet in the house. Henk isn't watching TV. He's sitting at the kitchen table with his back to the side window. The curtain is drawn. He's smoking. The table is completely bare except for the butt-filled ashtray. I walk into the living room.

"Where are you going?" he asks.

"I'm going to bed."

"Oh," he exclaims indignantly, "I'll go to bed too then."

"Your own bed," I say.

"Upstairs?"

"That's right, upstairs, that's where your bed is."

"But . . ."

"But what?" I've reached the bedroom door.

"Nothing. Nothing at all."

I close my bedroom door and go over to stand in front of the map of Denmark. "Helsingør," I say. "Stenstrup, Esrum, Blistrup, Tisvildeleje." Five names spoken slowly are not enough tonight. I do a few extra islands. "Samsø, Ærø, Anholt, Møn." The big bed is ready for me. When I pull back the duvet, I smell Henk. I lie down and tug the light cord above my head. It's dark. I hear him enter the living room. I hear him walking up to the bedroom door. He breathes in front of the closed door, I breathe here in bed. Then he walks away from the door. A few seconds later the TV goes on. Cigarette smoke drifts into the bedroom through the cracks. He rips open a bag of crisps. An hour later the TV goes off. He stamps upstairs and slams the door of the new room behind him. He doesn't think of Father, he doesn't think of me. He is young and thinks only of himself.

50

Riet,

You're right: I am a liar and a cheat. I said that Father was dead because I thought you wouldn't come otherwise. And I wanted you to come. I wanted to see you and I wanted to talk about Henk. I was curious about you. Just like you – presumably – were curious about me. That's why. But you didn't ask me anything, you just talked about yourself in relation to Henk. That hurt. I felt forgotten then and I felt forgotten again now.

I could also question your motives for putting Henk in my care. Everyone wants something, but what you want is not entirely clear to me. Did you think he needed a father figure? Well, I can be all kinds of things if necessary, but I'm not a father. I'm not an uncle either. I'm a son. I'm a brother. But I don't want to go into that. I think Henk's "apprenticeship" is over, I believe – no, I am certain – that it is time for him to go back to Brabant. To you, or maybe to something of his own. He has been here for two and a half months now and I think he's learned quite a lot, and I'm not just talking about looking after livestock or different

kinds of farm work. He gets along well with Father. Lately they've spent a lot of
time talking together, but that might be something you'd rather not hear. Either
way: he has to leave.

If you ask me there's not too much wrong with him or about him. I think
that, if there is anything, he's more than capable of working it out for himself. In
time. I can't do anything else for him. You're his mother. It's your responsibility.
I suggest you come and get him. It's hard for me to get away because of the cows
and the sheep. Surely one of your daughters has a car? I'll ring you up about the
details. It is very likely – and this time I'm not lying – that Father really will be
gone by then. He's had enough and stopped eating a while ago.

Best wishes,
Helmer van Wonderen

Some things have ceased to amaze me. Henk hasn't got up yet, so it
wasn't until after nine this morning that I sat down at the kitchen table.
In the sheep shed the count is now thirty from nineteen. One sheep to
go. After breakfast I put on some coffee and sat down at the bureau to
write the letter to Riet, signing it with my full name. Maybe I did that to
show her I'm serious. The letter is already in an envelope with a stamp
on it; I'll post it later today.

I'm sitting on the sofa in the living room. Mother watches from the
mantelpiece while I smoke a cigarette. She was already seductive,
haughty and alert, but now she is disparaging as well. The sunlight
through the narrow slats of the blinds is beautiful. Last night Henk
left his packet next to the sofa. I look ridiculous with the smoldering

cigarette in my hand, I can see that in the mirror. A filter cigarette is slender and elegant, my hand is coarse and bony. No matter how I hold the cigarette the smoke drifts up to my left eye, which is watering. I look back at Mother's photo. It's impossible, I know – a photo is a photo and Mother is dead – but still I seem to see a mocking smile flit over her lips. Maybe I'm more a roll-your-own kind of bloke.

Father is sleeping. Without snoring. His chest, or what is left of it, is moving up and down very slightly. I have to look closely, otherwise I would miss it. It's actually high time he had a shower, but I no longer dare to do it. I'd rather not have him die, like Mother, in the bathroom. Two parents dying in the bathroom, no. The plate of food Henk brought up last night is sitting on the bedside cabinet untouched. A couple of dry potatoes, shriveled green beans, a meatball. Next to the plate, a glass of water he's hardly drunk from. He moves.

"Henk?" he says, with his eyes closed.

Which Henk does he actually mean? I wonder. Was he dreaming about his son? "No, it's me," I say.

"Have you been smoking?"

"Yes."

He opens his eyes and looks at me. "You're a weird one," he says quietly.

"Yep."

"Do you know what I keep thinking about?"

"No."

"That drive on the Gouw Sea. Do you remember?"

"Yes. The ice was two and a half feet thick."

"I wanted to go out onto Lake IJssel, but I was too scared. We sat there near the embankment for hours."

"It wasn't hours," I say.

"It felt like it." He closes his eyes again. His arms are lying next to his body like the legs of a dead calf. "I was too scared," he whispers. "I was too scared."

I don't say anything. I listen.

"And you sat in the middle of the back seat like one boy."

I stand up. It's as if he's fallen asleep again and is dreaming of that arctic winter forty years ago.

"Helmer?" he says, when I'm at the door.

"Yes?"

"I want to be buried with your mother and Henk. And don't put a notice in the paper until afterwards."

"You sure? No one there?"

"No one there," he says.

"Okay," I say.

"And I want an egg."

"What?"

"A hardboiled egg."

"You haven't eaten for weeks. It will kill you."

"If I could laugh, I'd laugh. I feel like an egg."

"I'll bring you an egg later."

I close the door and cross the landing.

Am I doing the right thing? I wonder.

When Father's dead, I'll be the only one left, I think, as my hand moves up to the handle of the door to the new room.

So be it, I think, as I open the door.

51

The Velux window faces north and casts a strange light in the new room. The only direct sun it gets is late in the evening in June and July. Henk doesn't know yet that it's summer outside, more so even than yesterday. He doesn't know what he's going to do this afternoon either. The duvet with dark-blue letters and numbers is pulled up to his ears.

"Henk?"

"Bastard."

"What you say?"

"I called you a bastard."

"Now, now."

"Are you saying you're not?"

"I don't know."

The duvet slips down, exposing his chest. A hand moves towards the bedside cabinet. The strip of newspaper that was serving as a bookmark is lying on the cover of the book.

"Your cigarettes are downstairs," I say.

"Shit." He crosses his arms and stares at the wall opposite the bed. "What have you come up here for anyway?"

"You didn't do the yearlings this morning."

"So?"

"I did them myself."

"Serves you right."

"That's all I've come up for."

"You can go away then."

"Fine." I turn and walk out onto the landing. I'd forgotten the cigarettes; I can go downstairs and bide my time.

A little before twelve he comes down, dressed and all. He walks straight through to the living room and lights a cigarette. Then he comes into the kitchen, fills the coffee pot with water, spoons coffee into the filter and goes over to the side window. "What kind of weather's this?" he says after a while. The water gurgles through the coffee machine.

"Beautiful weather," I say.

"It's like summer."

"And you haven't even been outside."

He stays there by the side window until all the water has dripped through. Then he pours himself a mug and sits down at the kitchen table. He doesn't ask whether I'd like a cup of coffee as well.

"Don't you want anything to eat?"

"Later."

"Have you got plans for this afternoon?"

He stares at me in disbelief. "Plans?"

"Uh-huh."

"No."

"In Broek there's a small canoe rental place that doesn't bother about the official seasons. If you mention my name, he'll give you a canoe without any problems. He's got maps too. East Waterland."

"A canoe." He lights a fresh cigarette and looks at the canal through the front window.

"You have to take advantage of weather like this."

"How do I get there?"

"Right at the end of the road, then straight ahead and in Broek it's the seventh house on the left. You can take a route that comes past here."

"Do you want me out of the way?" he asks.

"What for? You never go anywhere. You've only been to Monnick-endam."

"You're still a bastard."

"Sure. Maybe I am."

Just before he gets on the bike, I give him fifty euros in ten-euro notes. His coat is in a plastic bag hanging from the handlebars. He rides out of the barn with a wide curve. I stroll over to the chicken coop and pick up four eggs. I take the eggs inside, put them in an empty egg box and leave it next to the stove. I take off my overalls, lie down on the sofa and close my eyes. It will take him a while to get back here.

It's April 16th and a young lad passes in a canoe. That doesn't happen often, especially not this early in the season because the official canoe-ing routes don't pass my farm. He has taken off his shirt, it's unusually warm for the time of the year. I'm standing at the side of the house, on the north side, as yet unseen. Because the canoeist is alone, there's no talking. He doesn't make any comments about my farm, the trees or my two donkeys. A hooded crow sits on a branch in the crooked ash. The crow is preening itself and now and then pulls its large beak out from under its wings to check the progress of the canoe. The paddle doesn't slap at the yellow water lilies; there aren't any yellow water lilies in April. There aren't any noisy redshanks either; there are two oystercatchers in the field on the other side of the canal, calmly foraging.

The young man has ginger hair and sunburnt shoulders, he has underestimated the strength of the spring sun. The paddle is resting on the canoe in front of him, water drips into water. The canoe slides forward slowly. There's nowhere for me to go, there's nothing on the bare north side of the house that I could be working on. I don't want to go anywhere. I want to stand here and be seen.

He sees me. His canoe gets caught with its nose against the side of the canal. He looks at me and he looks at the dormer window. He looks at the hooded crow, at the trees lining the yard, he even looks – if briefly – at the two inquisitive donkeys that have come to stand at the new fence along the road. I can't tell whether he is surprised to see me here. He doesn't raise a hand, I don't raise one either. If it's worked out, he sees what he is seeing as an old, yellowed postcard, with buildings, people, animals and trees frozen in time. Something to pick up for a moment and then lay aside again. A place with nothing to offer him.

Then he picks up the paddle and pushes off from the bank. A little later he turns right, into Opperwoud Canal. He must have studied the map carefully. I walk up to the road to watch him. Opperwoud Canal empties into Big Lake. Past Big Lake is a narrow ditch, whose name I don't know, that leads to the Die near Uitdam. Beyond Uitdam is Lake IJssel.

He comes into the shed when I'm almost finished milking. He stays standing there just past the open sliding door. The sun is around him, I see only a silhouette. I feel the weight of my twenty cows, the weight of the straw in the hayloft, the heavy rafters, the tiles on the roof (not one of which is crooked), the neatly pollarded willows. I can hardly stand.

"You want me gone," he says.

"Yes," I say, lowering the milking claw to the floor.

"Shit."

When will the swallows arrive? Or have they already come? I wonder. I've lost my sense of time. It's summer outside.

52

"It's almost over," says Father.

"Yeah," I say, thinking of earlier in the day.

The window is wide open.

I correct myself. "Yeah?"

"And I haven't had a spring, but a summer instead."

"Are you going to eat your egg?"

"Soon. I'm going to look at it for a while first."

I have already shelled the egg for him. It is lying on a saucer and the salt dish is next to the saucer. Mosquitoes dance in front of the open window. I've sat down on the foot of the bed. He says he's going to look at the egg, but he looks at me. The sheet of paper is no longer sticking out from under the bedside cabinet. I wonder where the poem has got to.

"Will you manage on your own?"

"I think so."

"You're a grown man."

"Half a grown man."

Now he looks at the egg as if he's got a little marzipan cake in front of him, the kind the baker in Monnickendam calls "castles." In the old days he would sometimes drive all the way into town on a Saturday to buy four. On some occasions he might have got five. Later it became three and, after Mother died, very rarely, he went in for two. I never told him that castles were not my favorite cake.

"I was second choice," I say. "That was the worst. Always feeling I wasn't good enough."

"I did my best," he says.

"And I didn't?"

"Of course you did. We all did." There's a lot more life in him now than there was this morning.

"Where's Henk?"

"I don't know. Outside, I think."

There is something I want to ask him. Despite everything, there is something I want his permission for. "Shall I . . ." I say. I stand up, go down on my knees and stick my head under the bed. There's the poem, covered with fluff. I stand up and sit back down on the bed, close to his feet. He's still staring at the egg, a bit frightened now.

"Father, shall I sell up?"

"Feel free, son. Feel free." He takes the saucer off the bedside cabinet with his claw hand and puts it on his lap. The egg rolls onto the blanket. "Dead is dead," he says. "Gone is gone and then I won't even know about it." He gropes for the egg and lays it back neatly on the saucer. "You have to decide for yourself."

I stand up. Watching him eat the egg is too much for me.

For weeks now he hasn't said a word about the hooded crow. It's as if he's forgotten it.

Henk isn't outside. Henk is in the kitchen, half sitting on the worktop. In his right hand he is holding a torn-open envelope, in his left he has my letter to his mother, which I should have posted in time for today's collection. He has already changed: exactly the same but different, the way a house seems strange when you've spent a day somewhere unfamiliar. The farmhouse seemed different to me after the old tanker driver's funeral, after skating on Big Lake and after picking Riet up from the ferry. I realize now that I felt just the same when I came home after picking up Henk. I haven't worked out why that is. Maybe because you yourself have grown older, even if just a few hours (I had already got that far) and everything at home has stayed still, except the hands of the clock. Then it takes a while to smooth over the time you've missed at home.

I'm not going to tell him that it's rude to open other people's letters. I notice now that his forehead and nose are burned as well. He turns away, screwing up the letter as he turns. I recognize the gesture, but unlike Father almost forty years ago, Henk is carrying a lighter. He pulls it out of his back pocket and holds the flame under the piece of paper, letting go just before he burns his fingers. The letter burns away in the sink.

"What kind of letter was that?" asks Henk. "Do you think my mother would have understood any of it?"

"The last bit, at least."

"There's no need," he says. "You should be glad I've burned it."

"What do you mean, there's no need?"

He looks at me and raises his eyebrows. Then he strolls out of the kitchen. I hear him go upstairs and walk into Father's room. Is he going to sit and watch Father eat the egg?

I look around. The buzzing clock says eight twenty. I've boiled an egg for Father, but I haven't eaten myself. I don't know whether Henk has eaten. It feels much too early for the sun to have set but I need to turn on the kitchen light. Summer in April.

Before going to bed I look in on Father. I don't turn the light on, the light shining in from the landing is just enough to see the empty saucer. Father is lying on his back and I can hear him breathing in and out through his nose. The curtains are open. I tiptoe over to the window and close them.

53

The cows virtually ignore the shot. Cows are strange creatures: the least little thing can spook them, but they don't look up or around when they hear a sudden noise. No, that's not entirely true; the cow I am milking rolls her eyes back. Cows can roll their eyes a long way back, showing so much white that it looks as if they're completely panicked. It just doesn't occur to them to turn their heads. Father doesn't like me saying so, but it's true: cows are stupid. Even more stupid than sheep. The only clever animals around here are the Lakenvelder chickens and the two donkeys. The second shot comes as even less of a surprise than the first: if you've never fired a gun, there's a good chance you'll miss the first time. I pull the tube out of the milk line, pat the cow on her side and put the claw down on the dirty floor. No more shots follow.

When I open the door between the scullery and the hall, I see that the front door is open. Sunlight from the east is falling into the hall at an angle, the gleam of the copper-tipped cartridges is bursting out of the box. There's a sour smell in the hall – sour and metallic. The kitchen door is open too, all the doors are open. Henk's backpack is on one of the kitchen chairs. I walk up to the front door. A feather floats down, a black feather that spins like an ash key as it falls. It must have been balancing on a twig for quite a while because at least four minutes have passed since I heard the shots. The hooded crow itself is still sitting on its branch. With its back turned towards us, as if insulted. Father's bike is leaning against the iron railing of the bridge. Henk is standing under the ash, more or less level with my bedroom window. From that distance he could have hit a mouse. He's got his coat on. It's colder than it was at the same time yesterday morning, summer is a few degrees further away today.

He waves the gun around, as if he's about to throw it away, but when he hears me he rests it on the ground next to him, clasping the barrel with his right hand. "I'm going," he says.

"Where?"

"To the train station."

"How?"

"On the bike." He gestures at the bridge.

"And how's the bike going to get back here?"

"Your father doesn't need it any more."

"Do you know the way?"

"I'll follow the signs." He's talking to the crow. He doesn't look at me.

"You got any money?"

"Uh-huh," he says. "Plenty. What have I had to spend it on here? Even that shitty canoe cost almost nothing." It's not easy, but he does it, he tears his eyes away from the crow. He turns and walks into the hall. A little later he re-emerges with the backpack. He's still holding the gun in his right hand.

"Didn't you even wing it?" I ask.

"No. It just stayed sitting there. As if nothing had happened. When I fired again, it turned around, with a little jump. That bird is weird."

"Why did you do it?"

"It's as if things don't exist unless you see them. You think it was me?"

"Who else?"

"You really think I'd shoot an animal dead like that off my own bat?"

"You had a score to settle," I say.

He hands me the gun. He looks at me and smiles contemptuously. Then he walks over to the bike.

I don't expect him to say anything else.

"Your father asked me to do it last night. 'Blast that bird out of the ash,' he said."

I walk over to the bridge too. "And you thought, fine, I'll do it."

"That's right. He couldn't do it himself."

"You could have just left it."

"I think your father's a nice guy. Nicer than you."

"Maybe he is," I say.

" 'Then throw the gun in the ditch.' He said that too."

"But you haven't done that."

"No. Because you suddenly appeared in the garden. And it actually seems like a waste."

"Have you said goodbye to him?"

"Of course." He takes the handlebars and pushes the bike onto the road. "Maybe I'll see you sometime."

"What are you going to do, Henk?"

"I don't know. I'll see." He swings a leg over the back of the bike. "Thanks," he says, riding off.

He came with one scar, he's leaving with two.

He says, "thanks." Not mockingly, not spitefully. He says it without any kind of emotion. But why does he say it? I don't know how to answer, so I say nothing. He pedals hard and soon disappears behind Ada and Wim's farm. An early Thursday cyclist passes, an old man, a bit older than me, in shirtsleeves. He rides onto the verge, and from the verge he almost crashes into the canal because he can't keep his eyes off me and the gun. I wait until he's back on the saddle and riding in a straight line again. I don't throw the gun into the ditch, I walk up onto the road and throw it in the canal. On the way back I stop for a moment on the bridge. The crow turns around again. It preens itself and steps from side to side. "What do you want?" I ask quietly. It doesn't answer.

Your father doesn't need it any more. What did I say myself, months ago, when Father's bike caught my eye and I knew what Henk's first job would be? "That's my Father's, but he can't ride a bike any more." That's not the same as "not needing it any more." First I'll finish milking, then

I'll go upstairs. The bloody cows always come first. Whatever you do, even if you know your Father is lying dead in his bed, you milk the cows first, idiot that you are.

People always want to know what someone has died of, even if their curiosity diminishes as the age of the deceased increases. But who can I tell that Father died of an egg? The GP I am about to call? The undertaker? Complete strangers or people I hardly know? I have to laugh, but suddenly the ticking of the clock annoys me so much that I open the glass door and seize the pendulum with both hands to stop it. Then I sit down on the chair by the window. The buds of the ash have burst open: tender, purplish-green plumes waving back and forth on the breeze. It's early: the hands of the grandfather clock point to half past nine. I can't look at him yet. First I'll stay here in the chair and stare out at the dyke through the plumes of the ash.

54

I've taken a photo of Henk from the wall in Father's bedroom and put
it on the mantelpiece – on the other side of the mirror. The photo is
in an old frame, the kind you can either hang or stand up. Dressed in
brand-new overalls, my brother is sitting on a milking stool next to
some bony hindquarters and beaming as if nothing in the whole world
is more beautiful than milking a cow. Now we're all together in the living room.

This morning I left Father alone to go to the tobacconist's in Monnickendam. It didn't really feel right, leaving him in the living room
like that. That's why I locked the hall door and the front door before
I left. There were two people in front of me at the tobacconist's and I
was nervous. When it was my turn the shop assistant asked me what I
wanted and I hadn't had time to study the shelves behind her. "I'd like a
packet of rolling tobacco," I said. Fortunately no one had come into the

shop after me. All right, which brand? I didn't know. Which brand did I usually smoke? Van Nelle, I read, to the right of her hip. "Van Nelle," I said. Strong or medium strong? "Medium strong," I said, no longer guessing, because suddenly I saw the almost empty pouch of rolling tobacco on the coffee table in the laborer's cottage. Papers? Mascotte, of course, they'd lain next to the pouch that first time and I had seen them later in his hands, when his practiced thumb brushed the shag off the packet after he opened the pouch. "So, have you worked it out yet?" the shop assistant asked. "Mascotte," I said. It came to four euros and eight cents. That was a shock, I had no idea tobacco was so expensive.

Afterwards I searched the bureau for Father's papers and found the letter from the Forestry Commission. I've put it on top of a pile and soon, but not now, I will go through it again thoroughly. Then answer it. The second part of Lodewick's history of literature was still lying on the desk. I didn't need it any more. I went up to Henk's bedroom and put it back in the box – which was still sitting on Mother's dressing table. I re-taped the box carefully and put it back in the wardrobe.

I locked all the doors yesterday as well – before driving to the ferry. By the time I arrived it was getting dark. It had occurred to me that Henk wouldn't have taken the bike with him on the ferry, because what use would it have been to him on the other side? You only have to cross the road and you're in the train station. I wanted Father's bike back. Henk wouldn't have bothered to lock it (I wasn't even sure it still had a lock), because you only do that if you're coming back to use it. I drove a circuit, but from the car all the bikes looked the same. Although there were less of them than I had expected. Then I walked past all the bike racks twice. Father's bike wasn't there. Could Henk have taken it onto the ferry with him after all? No, it must have been stolen. After a ferry had left, I stood for a while on the bank of the IJ. The other side was white with ships, the kind of ships that take elderly people on river cruises. I wondered why Riet hadn't called. Or had she called, but I wasn't at home? I wasn't home now either. I pictured the hall and heard the telephone ringing. A telephone ringing in a house where there's no one to answer it. When a ferry came sailing towards me, I felt it was time to leave.

The last lamb was born last night. Thirty-one lambs from twenty ewes.

I've finally managed to roll a cigarette that looks reasonable. I should have bought two packets of papers. I turn the roll-up around in my fingers. The cooling unit clicks on, Father shudders. They didn't mention that: that the deceased shudders when the cooling unit clicks on or off. I'm sitting on a kitchen chair next to the coffin, I don't know where else to sit. The box of matches is lying on the edge of the coffin. I light the roll-up. "You're a weird one," he said. When was that? The day before yesterday? Three days ago? Everything is different when you have a coffin in your living room. I wonder, for instance, whether it's proper to have the blinds open? I definitely remember the curtains being half drawn when Henk was laid out in here. I've forgotten how the curtains were with Mother. On the other hand, I'm hardly going to sit here with the blinds closed, am I? It's Sunday tomorrow and Monday will be like another Sunday. Two Sundays in a row. Easter. I inhale the smoke. It's not too bad. I breathe out through my nose and, for the first time in my life, smoke comes out of my nostrils.

Someone's in the scullery. "Quiet, now," she says as the door between the scullery and the hall opens. She comes into the room, the boys stop at the door.

"What are you doing?" she asks in astonishment.

"What do you mean?"

"You're smoking!"

I look at the roll-up in my hand, then stub it out in the ashtray on the arm of the sofa. I get up.

Ada doesn't say anything else. She comes up to me and wraps her arms around me. Her hair smells nice and fresh, she presses her fingers into my shoulder blades. Teun and Ronald look at me with big eyes. I wink at them over Ada's shoulder. Ronald thinks it's funny and starts grinning. Teun's expression stays serious. Ada lets go and plants a wet kiss on my lips at the same time. Then she looks at Father.

"I'll put some coffee on," she says. Although Ada is still Ada, nothing has been quite the same since the day she brought me the rug and Teun gave Henk the poster of the singer whose name I've forgotten. She walks to the kitchen saying, "If you'd like to, it's all right. You can have a look."

Teun and Ronald approach very slowly. Teun stops at the foot of the coffin and pretends to look. Ronald comes closer. He's not as tall and has to stand on tiptoes to see over the side.

"Is it scary?" he asks.

"No," I say. "Do you think it's scary?"

"A bit."

"When's the funeral?" Ada calls from the kitchen.

"Tuesday," I call back. "You don't look scared," I say to Ronald.

"Did you have to cry?"

"No."

"Is there anything I can do?" Ada calls from the kitchen.

"Why not?" asks Ronald.

"Well . . ." I say. "You either have to cry or you don't, there's not much you can do about it."

"Why is he dead?"

"He ate an egg, Ronald."

It makes him laugh. "*I* eat eggs, they don't kill *me*."

"I'm glad to hear it," I say. "Come on, let's go into the kitchen. Would you like an almond cake?"

"Yes!" shouts Ronald.

"Please," Teun says politely.

We go into the kitchen. The coffee machine is on, its gurgling drowns out the buzzing of the electric clock. Ada has put out two mugs. I get a packet of almond cakes out of a kitchen cupboard and tear it open.

"I'm just happy you've come over," I tell Ada, in answer to her question.

"Of course I've come," she says, almost indignantly. "And I'll come tomorrow as well. It's horrible, especially now it's Easter, without a soul around. You have to come and eat with us, and shall I phone farm relief, to send someone for the milking? Wim wanted to come as well, but the bulk tank's not working properly and he has to be there when the supplier . . ."

"You have to cry now," says Ronald. "Your eyes are wet."

I don't answer. The boys are sitting together on one chair, because the fourth kitchen chair is in the living room.

"Has Henk gone?" Ronald asks.

"Yes, he's not here any more."

"Why's he gone?"

"He'd been here long enough," I say.

"Has he gone back to Brabbend, where his mother lives?"

"Ronald," Teun says through a mouthful of cake, "just shut up for once."

I *really* am happy they've come.

Ada, Teun and Ronald have gone, it's quiet again in the house, but a different kind of quiet. Better. I don't want to sit down on the kitchen chair next to the coffin any more. I walk through the scullery and the shed to the yard. It's almost time to put the cows out again. I check the sheep and then walk over to the chicken coop. The wheelbarrow is in front of the donkey shed. I should actually muck it out. Not now. I go back inside and get the binoculars from the bureau. I stand with my legs apart in front of the side window and raise the binoculars to my eyes. Ada is standing there five hundred yards away. When she sees me she immediately raises one hand and waves. She gestures with her other hand. Teun and Ronald come into view. They raise their hands as well. I wave back and lower the binoculars. For a moment I stay there, in front of the side window, binoculars at chest height. Letting them have a good look at me. How long has she been standing there? How long has she been waiting for me? She knew I would appear at the window. Just as I knew she would be standing there. Relieved, I put the binoculars down on the table. Now she can come back with a light heart and take charge of things around here again.

After smoking another roll-up next to the coffin, I go out through the front door. I walk over to the bridge and sit on the rail. The hooded crow has taken a few steps to one side and has turned to face me. It looks at me. I look back. Until I see a car pulling up at the remains of the laborer's cottage out of the corner of my eye. A man gets out of the car. It is bleak and gray and there are no sunny-day cyclists. A large group of coots is bobbing in the canal. The man has walked from the car to the magnolia. He grabs a branch and shakes it. Then he walks to the half-wall. When the man has been standing there motionless for a while staring up the imaginary staircase, I slide off the rail and walk up onto the road. The donkeys come over to the new fence and follow me to the former laborer's cottage. He turns around when he hears me approaching. It is an old man with a weather-beaten face. An outdoor face.

"Helmer," he says.

"I thought you were from the Forestry Commission," I say.

"And I didn't know whether I could expect to find you here."

"Henk's dead," I say.

"Really?" he says. "Since when?"

"April 1967."

"That's a long time. And now you're the farmer."

"Yep. Mother's dead too and Father is laid out in the living room."

He screws up his eyes. It is a lot of deaths in one go. Then he turns around. "And the cottage burned down."

"Yes," I say to his back. "Amsterdammers. Holiday home." I shiver, I've come out without a coat.

He stands there staring for a while, then turns back. He lays a hand on my shoulder. "Come on," he says. "I'll go and pay my respects to your father." He walks over to his car. His back is straight, the stubbornness hasn't disappeared. I follow and get in next to him. He puts the car in reverse and backs onto the road. We drive slowly to the southwest.

"It smells of dog in here," I say. I can smell that, even though we never had a dog.

He looks at me and smiles. "He always sat where you're sitting." Because he's looking at me, he sees the donkeys. "Are they your donkeys?"

I nod.

Again he smiles. "Yes," he says. "You're a donkey man all right."

IV

55

There's a sand dune here with an English name. A long time ago a rich Englishman came to this shore. He had a large house built on the highest dune and laid out a garden with ponds, paths and low stone walls. Because the whole dune had been covered with heather he named his estate Heather Hill. He drowned while swimming in the sea and the house disappeared long ago. All that's left of the garden is a silted-up pond and a few shrubs. It's grazed by sheep of a breed I don't recognize, with dark heads and long floppy ears. They are much tamer than my sheep; they're used to people coming here to walk or swim. Along the coast, the dune is actually a cliff, with a straight drop to the narrow, rocky beach. It's not the North Sea here. There are no bare dunes held together with difficulty by planted marram grass and wind-blasted pines. Here the grass grows almost all the way down to the sea and even beeches and oaks thrive ten yards from the high-water line. I've tasted the water: it's brackish, a little saltier than the water of Lake IJssel. I know almost the whole map of Denmark off by heart, especially Zealand, but Rågeleje is new to me, and that's where we are now. Not that you'd know it when you hear the locals say the name of their village. Danish is a strange, sloppy language. I don't understand a word of it; he says he can follow it. I wanted to know how that was possible. "I'm Frisian," he said. The owner of the Heather Hill Grill, located next to a car park on the coast road, told him the story of the Englishman, though it's possible it was all very different in reality. We often go there for a sausage. The Danes love their sausages.

We swim every day. The water is cold, but clear. Every three days we have to toss aside the rocks we tossed aside three days before to make it easier to get into the water. We always swim in the same place, at the end of the path that skirts Heather Hill on its way from the coast road to the rocky beach. There's a gate at the road and another one just before the beach. The sheep have to stay on Heather Hill to keep the grass short and eat the birch seedlings. It's quiet on the rocky beach, the Danes aren't on holiday yet. If we look to the right on clear days we can see the coast of Sweden in the distance. "We should go there sometime too," he says. I nod. It's not far to Helsingør, from there we can take the ferry to Helsingborg. Hooded crows glide above the cliff. They hold their wings still and float on the updrafts without moving forward. At the weekends the hooded crows aren't there. Then men and women leap off the cliff with parachutes. Sometimes they float for miles before turning around and coming back to land on top of Heather Hill again. The height they fly at is determined by the height of the dunes. We swim naked: we're almost always alone and if someone does show up we ignore them. "We're too old to worry about that," he says. I nod and then, like two kids at a swimming pool, we joke about each other's scrotums, which the cold water has shriveled up. He can't help giving me instructions: "Keep your fingers together" or "Move those feet of yours for once." Afterwards we warm up again by playing a game of badminton – a little stiffly, and with him a bit stiffer than me – in the holiday house garden. He found the racquets and shuttlecocks in a rack at the Spar. I paid.

Father was laid out in the house for four nights. I didn't touch him once.

When he went into the living room he immediately sat down on the kitchen chair next to the coffin. I stayed standing by the door. He rolled a cigarette, maybe because he saw an ashtray on the arm of the sofa. While smoking, he looked at Father. His glance moved from Father to the photos on the mantelpiece. "She was a beautiful woman, in her own way," he said, nodding at the formal photo of my mother. "I don't think many people saw that." A horizontal layer of smoke formed in the living room. All the times I sat there smoking next to the open coffin, I didn't manage that once.

"Are you alone?" he asked.

"Yes," I said.

"Things have changed a lot in here."

"I did that, a few months ago."

"That recently?"

"Yes."

He took a couple of deep drags from his roll-up then nodded in the direction of the mantelpiece again. "Dead brother," he said. He stubbed out his cigarette and laid the backs of his fingers lightly on Father's forehead. Then he stood up and shook my hand, with the fingers that had just touched the dead body. "Your father's dead, Helmer," he said.

He didn't kiss me on the mouth, although someone really was dead now.

As if I didn't know it yet myself: beautiful mother, dead brother, dead father. Twenty cows, some yearlings, two nameless donkeys, twenty sheep, thirty-one lambs and a few Lakenvelder chickens.

"Do I smell coffee?" he asked, crossing the hall to the kitchen, where he didn't just sit down on the first chair he came to. He walked around the table and sat down with his back to the side window. Henk's chair. He drummed on the tabletop, as if waiting impatiently for me to pour him a cup of coffee. He looked with mild surprise at the binoculars, the open packet of almond cakes and the mugs Ada and I had drunk out of. He said this was the first time he had sat at the kitchen table. Still standing there in the doorway of the living room, I looked from his drumming fingers to Father's forehead and from Father's forehead to my hand.

I didn't pour him a coffee right away. I went over to stand by the front window. The hooded crow was staring at me from its usual branch. It lowered its head a little as if shrugging its shoulders. I wondered whether birds have shoulders, whether you can call the elbows of folded wings shoulders. It looked like an animal that can stalk, somehow feline. It had been sitting there since autumn. Sometimes I forgot about it and some days I noticed it again and felt like I had the first time I saw it, the day I sat down on all four chairs, as if trying to avoid eating alone. It pulled its shoulders up a little bit more and fell forwards, not spreading its wings until just before it would have hit the ground. I stepped back; it looked like it was going to sail straight through the windowpane. During the sharp turn it had to make, its wingtip touched the glass. It flew off towards the dyke, the Lake IJssel dyke. I watched it go until there were tears in my eyes.

He cleared his throat. I turned around. Yes, he would like some coffee – black with sugar – and yes, he wouldn't say no to one of those almond cakes either.

Dead is dead. Gone is gone, and then I won't even know about it. That's why I wasn't the only one to attend Father's funeral. A funeral is not for the dead, it's for those left behind. It was egotistical of Father to want to be buried on the sly. Jaap was there, Ada and the boys (not Wim, he hates death, and what's more he had something else to do, something important) and the young tanker driver. "How did you . . ." I started and Ada, who was standing behind him, formed a telephone receiver with her little finger and thumb and held it up to her ear and mouth. She shrugged apologetically, holding her head a little to one side.

"Solidarity, that's important," he said to Jaap.

"You're right about that, lad," Jaap replied, "absolutely."

I didn't mind, even if I was beginning to suspect the young tanker driver of making a habit of going to as many funerals as possible, which was something of an aberration. Once again there was a white sheet, hardboard by the look of it, at the bottom of a grave that actually went deeper. It didn't last long, there weren't any speakers. The sun was shining and the temperature was around average for late April. I threw earth in the grave. Not a handful, a shovelful. Because I like that at funerals. I don't regard a handful of earth that blows away before it hits the coffin as any kind of conclusion. Only Ronald followed my example.

"How do you like the new driver?" Galtjo asked when we were sitting in the kitchen later. Ada had put on some coffee and I had bought marzipan castles at the baker's in Monnickendam. All in honor of Father. There was jenever for the men. Teun and Ronald drank something with bubbles.

"She's a bit mouthy for me," I said.

"Yes," he said, smiling as ever. "I've heard that." His smile no longer moved me.

"Are you farmers too?" Jaap asked Teun and Ronald.

"We're kids," Teun corrected him.

What surprised me was the number of cards that appeared in the green letterbox on the roadside in the days after the death notice appeared in the paper. Dozens of cards. There was one from the livestock dealer, who returned from New Zealand two days after the funeral. There was even a card from Klaas van Baalen, the farmer who was the same age as me and had had his sheep removed because he neglected them. Jarno Koper's parents sent one and so did the old tanker driver's widow. And, of course, there were cards from all kinds of distant relatives, second and third cousins, none of whom I knew and none of whom were called Van Wonderen.

I sent a card to Riet and Henk, who obviously wouldn't read our paper all the way down in Brabant. Riet didn't respond at all, although it was from her that I had expected to receive a perhaps not-so-friendly card in return. If I never hear from her again, I won't be surprised. Henk sent a postcard in reply. *I already knew,* he wrote on the back. *And I think it's a shame, because he was a nice man. I'm using his bike here now. I brought it with me because I couldn't lock it up and it would have just been stolen otherwise. So I think of him now and then. Cheers, Henk.* I had to smile at the card he had chosen, showing a tower of animals: a donkey, a dog, a cat and a rooster. "That's cute," said Ada. "They're the Bremen town musicians. One of Grimms' fairy tales." The donkey in particular appeals to me. He didn't just grab a card from the rack. I think.

Two weeks ago I turned fifty-six. In Germany. He wanted to drive over the Lake IJssel dam, I wanted to go through the new polders. Since the Opel Kadett would almost certainly have broken down halfway through Denmark, we took his car and drove over the dam. At the monument – we'd only been on the road for an hour – he pulled over. We smoked a medium-strong Van Nelle each, looking out over the Wadden Sea. Then we drove to his house – in a small village past Leeuwarden. He showed me the shed where he makes the owl boards he sells to customers from all over Friesland, without having to advertise them. "How do you think I can afford to buy my jenever?" he said, pouring two glasses. "From the pension?" He also took me out to where he'd buried the dog, in a far corner of the garden, under a gnarled pear tree that had long since lost all its blossom. He had welded two pieces of metal together to make a cross and stuck it in the ground. The turned soil was still raised. In his living room there was a large bookcase with at least twice as many books as he had had in the laborer's cottage. He poured me another generous glass of jenever but no more for himself, because he was driving. I knocked it back: I didn't want to be in Friesland, I wanted to go much further north.

Past Nieuweschans, just over the German border, we stopped again because he was hungry. "We're going to eat now, Donkey Man," he said. It was fine by me.

If you keep driving it's easy to reach Denmark in a day, it's not even five hundred miles. But we didn't keep driving and stopped for the night at a *Raststätte* just past Hamburg. "Double room?" asked the disinterested woman behind the counter. "Of course," he said. "It's cheaper, isn't it?" In the enormous bed we both lay on our backs, me with my hands clasped over my stomach. I don't know how he was lying. When I woke up it was my birthday. I was planning on keeping it secret from him, but there was no secret to keep. He had remembered. I wanted to know how that was possible.

"For about thirteen years in a row I wasn't invited to you and your brother's birthday," he said. "Do you think that's the kind of thing you forget? I worked as usual while you two ran around with your chests puffed out and party hats on your heads. Sometimes you'd even come and stand in front of me to proudly shout, 'It's our birthday!'"

I don't remember this at all. He says that's what it was like, so that must have been what it was like.

. . .

Sometimes I forget that he knew me as a brat. Sometimes I also forget that he came to work for Father when he was a boy himself. About Henk's age.

The boat sailed from Puttgarden and landed at Rødby. The crossing only took forty-five minutes. I drove the car off the ferry and wanted to pull over to the side of the road straightaway.

"What are you doing, Donkey Man?" he asked.

I told him that we were in Denmark and I wanted finally to feel it with my own two feet.

"There's a lot more Denmark to come," he said. "Down the road."

Driving along I had a sense of having been here before, I knew almost all of the place names on the signs. We stopped to buy something to eat in a roadside restaurant outside Copenhagen and only then did we discover that we couldn't pay with euros in Denmark. The guy at the cash register accepted them, but grudgingly, it seemed to me. Past Copenhagen ("Much too big," he said. "Much too busy, we'll drive on.") I put a bank card in a cash machine for the first time in my life, typed in my PIN number, and pulled Danish kroner out of the slot. He doesn't have a bank card; either that or he hasn't brought it with him. I pay for everything. Since we didn't know where we were going, we decided to keep driving until we couldn't go any further. That was how we ended up in this village with the unpronounceable name.

Here there are rolling hills and no ditches. There are hardly any cows either, apparently they're mostly in Jutland. With Jarno Koper. When we do see cows, they're usually brown. "Beef," he growls and we look the other way. There are wheat, barley and rye fields. And rapeseed: entire hilltops covered with yellow flowering rape, bordered by cow parsley. A few days ago I saw a rhododendron and a purple lilac in flower in a garden, next to a few red tulips. Everything here seems to flower at the same time.

When it starts to get dark we hear the melancholy call of a wood owl.

Dead is dead. Gone is gone, and then I won't even know about it. The new livestock dealer couldn't have come at a better time. He was driving the old livestock dealer's truck, he said he'd been able to take it over at a good price. He was a young tearaway, there were dents in the truck that hadn't been there two months before. He was a windbag too. He called me Helmer from the word go, as if we were old friends. I asked him whether he could offload twenty cows, some yearlings, twenty sheep and a whole lot of lambs at short notice.

"Easy!" he shouted.

"How are you going to do it then?"

"I'll see."

"It has to be fast, and preferably all at once."

"Just leave it to me." On his way back to the truck, something occurred to him. He turned around. "And your milk quota?"

"That's none of your business."

"Okay, fine."

Two days later he roared back into the farmyard. Stony-faced, he quoted a price. "But then you're done with it in one go," he shouted immediately after. "And I'm sticking my neck out, I have to make sure I can shift the whole lot before too long, my sheds aren't that big–"

"I've changed my mind," I said.

"What?!"

"I'm keeping the sheep, and the lambs too."

His eyes seemed to pale a little while he was doing the calculations. After a while, he came up with a lower total. "But it's still true," he said, "that I'm the one sticking my neck out and if–"

"Fine," I said.

"Really?" he asked, stunned.

"Yes."

"Oh, well, then–"

"When?"

"Soon," he said, running out of steam. "Soon."

I spent the day the animals were picked up in Father's bedroom. I put the photos, samplers and watercolor mushrooms neatly in a potato crate. I stripped his bed, washed the sheets and pillowcases, took down the curtains, cleaned the windows and vacuumed the blue carpet. When I stuck the nozzle under the bed, the vacuum cleaner almost choked on the poem that was lying there.

A weird one. He told me I was a weird one. Coming from him, at that moment, it almost sounded like a term of endearment.

I sat down on Father's bed and read the words once again. I felt ashamed. Giving an old wreck of a man a poem to read. I folded it in half and shoved it in my back pocket. A week later I took it out of my newly washed jeans as papier-mâché. I didn't look in the shed until evening, when it was already getting dark. It was emptier than empty: everything was still there – straw, shit, dust, warmth – except the cows. The yearling shed was the same. No – it was even emptier, because going in I was just in time to catch sight of the tail of a mangy cat, shooting off.

The next day I wrote a letter to the Forestry Commission. I informed them that I was not in the least inclined to sell them the land on which they wanted to build a visitors' center. And that I would be grateful not to receive any further correspondence on the subject until I contacted them again. Up to the day of our departure for Denmark I hadn't received a reply. Just as I had requested.

I looked around for something to put my traveling things in and found a suitcase in a cupboard in the barn: a massive, old, leather thing. I soaped the leather to make it a little suppler. I haven't had a single holiday in thirty-seven years of milking day and night. I wonder when in God's name Father and Mother used it. They never went on holiday either.

I also went to the Rabobank to apply for a bank card. If you go to other countries you need a bank card. I had to wait two weeks before I could go and pick it up. I still don't understand why, but I used the time to do up the kitchen. I repainted, threw out the old curtains and put up venetian blinds. I cleared out the bureau. I almost drove to Monnickendam to look at kitchens in a furniture shop. "Did you have a bonfire?" asked Ronald when he came by the next day and found a smoldering heap behind the donkey shed. "Without calling us?" added Teun, who was there as well.

. . .

We're sitting outside, on the roofed patio. Earlier in the day it rained, but it's not cold now. The garden is steaming and the bamboo along the side of the holiday home rustles gently against the wooden planks. For dinner we had beetroot with meatballs you buy ready-made at the Spar. During the meal we drank a bottle of red wine. Wine is expensive in Denmark.

"What are we going to do tomorrow?" I ask.

"Whatever we feel like. We'll start by getting up and drinking some coffee."

I've asked him about his nose, his parents, Friesland and his dog. About how he came to work for Father and Mother. "You've got a lot of questions, Donkey Man," he says. "What are your intentions?" The only thing he was willing to discuss was his dog. It died just before the New Year. On a Saturday night, after he'd come home from playing cards with three friends. He sat down on a chair and the dog laid its old head on his lap. All at once the dog's head turned heavy and it was as if he felt its blood stop flowing under his hand. "He just folded up," he said, "like one of those toys, one of those little puppets you collapse by pressing the button under its feet."

"So you do have friends in Friesland?" I asked.

He sighed and didn't say another word.

He points at the damp cherry tree in the middle of the garden. "We'll have to stay here at least another month."

"Fine by me," I say. "I like cherries." I go inside and pour two cups of coffee. When I come back I see that the dark clouds have disappeared. The sun is shining again. Here in the north it doesn't get dark until very late. I put the coffees down on the garden table and lay a bar of dark chocolate next to them.

"Why didn't you get a new dog?"

"You can't go on forever."

"No?"

"It hurts. Every time one dies."

"I believe that."

"It was because the wife of one of my card buddies died. He came over to my place and drank my jenever and talked about "not wanting to lose her" and "having to let her go." It got on my nerves: someone either dies or they don't, wanting doesn't come into it. My dog felt his sorrow and laid his head on his lap, something he never did otherwise. The guy just ignored him. I couldn't bear it. That dog was close to death himself, but he took the trouble and was kind enough to lift his head to someone who was grieving and that person didn't react." He breaks off a square of chocolate, lays it on his tongue and takes a mouthful of coffee. His mouth is shut, but I can see the chocolate melting. "Friends," he goes on, with a wry smile. "Is that enough? Friends to play cards with, a well-kept house and garden, messing around in the shed, a dog, jenever and a bit of money in the bank?"

He no longer has that one chipped tooth. A crown?

"How did you actually know that Father was dead?" I ask.

"I didn't."

"So it was just coincidence, you coming back on that day of all days?"

"Yep."

"There's no such thing as coincidence."

"Of course there is. I thought: I'll go, and I went. I wanted to see the West Friesland orchards in blossom. But it was misty so I didn't see very much. I might just as well ask you why you came out of your house just when I arrived at the laborer's cottage."

Coincidence, I think.

"I might not have gone to the house at all if you hadn't come to me." He repeats the chocolate ritual. In the distance the wood owl starts to call. For the first time it is answered, from very close by. "And where would you have been now, in that case?"

"Yes," I say. "Where would I have been now?"

We both stare into the garden. I think about Riet and Henk. Little Henk. The young tanker driver, the livestock dealer (who he had known as well), Ada. I wonder what kind of things I am going to tell him, or will want to tell him. Suddenly the time between his departure and return no longer interests me. Or even the time of his arrival. What difference does it make? Tomorrow we'll "start by getting up and drinking some coffee," and afterwards we'll do "whatever we feel like."

"I've never actually learned how to do things by myself," I say.

Slowly he turns his head towards me. "Drink your coffee, Donkey Man. It's time for a game of cards." He gets up and walks inside.

He's right, it's time to play cards. I roll a medium-strong Van Nelle, light it, stand up and walk around the garden with my head back. I stick the pouch of tobacco and the lighter in a back pocket. I like smoking, it suits me. He hasn't mentioned it, maybe he thinks I've been smoking for years. He has turned the light on over the table. Not because it's necessary, but because he's used to having a light on over a card table. I feel like I could reach out and touch the wood owl, its mournful call sounds that close. It might just as well be a long-eared or short-eared owl. I don't know a thing about owls; there are lots of woods here, that's why I think it's a wood owl. Hearing it call is even worse than seeing wet lame sheep or unshorn sheep during a heat wave. It gives me an empty feeling in my chest. As if I haven't just eaten.

"You coming?" He's standing at the open door, but doesn't sound impatient.

I don't say anything, raising one hand.

He calls me Donkey Man. Now that I'm away from the donkeys for the first time ever. Teun and Ronald have promised to look after them. No, not too much mangold, carrots or stale bread. Yes, inside if it rains for a long time. Yes, always check the big water trough. ("But a bucket of water's heavy," says Ronald.) They're also looking after the Lakenvelder chickens. Their mother can use the eggs in cakes and pancakes. Teun will walk through the sheep field once a day. He is strong enough to help an overturned ewe up on her feet, and maybe even strong enough to get a lamb that's fallen into a ditch back onto dry land. If not he can fetch his father. Ada has promised "to keep an eye on things" and "run the hoover around the house now and then." She wanted to know how long I would be gone. "I don't know," I said. Just before I left, she came on Wim's behalf to ask what I was planning to do with my milk quota.

"This is his chance," she said. "Our chance," she added.

I told her I wanted to think about it and asked why Wim hadn't come himself to ask me what I was planning with my quota.

She looked at me as if she was about to make up another excuse for him, then said, "He doesn't have the nerve."

A little later she asked me why I'd kept the sheep.

"I haven't got the foggiest," I said.

Donkey Man. That's fine by me.

When someone addressed me by name, as Helmer, I always added "Henk and" in front of it in my thoughts. No matter how long he had been dead, our names belonged together.

Maybe Riet was right, on that cold day in January at the cemetery, when she said you could become a new person. It annoyed me at the time, that statement of hers, but if I'd opened my eyes I could have seen it in that run-over duck. It had become a new person in next to no time. A dead person.

No, no rows of swallows on sagging electricity wires. The poles are still here but the wires are gone. For miles around, men in orange suits are lugging thick cables and digging narrow trenches along the roads. If I'd come a year later, I would never have known that they'd had poles here with wires strung between them.

56

I'm still searching for the owl. Smoking is a pensive activity. While searching I think, without any clear idea of what I'm thinking about. I didn't say, "I'm coming." I raised a hand. That can mean all kinds of things. Jaap has sat down on a stool at the window. He too is smoking, waiting serenely for me to come in. I throw the butt on the grass and squash it with the toe of my shoe. Then I walk past his car to the gate, which is open.

I go by the sun, which I lose sight of now and then because of trees and other holiday homes. This place is a maze of paths and unpaved roads. This is the first time I've tried to cut through on foot. We do everything by car, usually with Jaap driving, very slowly. Two old codgers on holiday in a foreign country. Who knows, maybe sometimes an elderly Danish woman sees us passing slowly by and thinks, Oh, they're alone, are they widowers? The lawns in front of the cottages are impeccable. Everywhere, Danes are at work with clippers, hand mowers or hoes. I wouldn't mow the lawn if it had rained earlier in the day, but there you have it, I'm no Dane. They say *hej* to me. There's a smell of resin and wood fires. I'm away from home, in a foreign country I knew only from a two-dimensional map without smells or shapes. In a way I find Donkey Man a more beautiful name than Helmer. With so many paths and side paths, there are a lot of junctions as well. A few Icelandic horses are out in a field. They come up to the electric fence when I pass on the path. I don't stop to rub their noses. It's annoying that I can't head straight for the sun, I have to keep choosing left or right before I can take another road that leads west. "*Hej*," I say to a friendly woman with a dog, before asking her the way in English. At least I'm headed in the right direction. She reminds me of my mother.

I was hoping to come out at the Heather Hill Grill, but went wrong somewhere and hit the newly tarmacked coast road midway between the village and Heather Hill. There's no footpath or bike lane beside it. A little further along is a campground. As yet there are only a few tents and no one is out jumping on the trampolines, which are at ground level. Three cars pass by, five come from the other direction. The sky has started turning orange, I speed up a little. "Idiot" is the word I think of when I remember Henk, even though so many other words were spoken in our eighteen years. The Grill is shut, the small car park is empty, no one is eating any sausages (*pølser* they call them here). I turn right and push open the sheep gate. A few minutes later I am standing on the rocky beach.

I raise a hand to look at the sun through my fingers. It's hanging half a thumb's width above the smooth water. Off to the right is the village, with the first houses built on the dune. In front of them a few brightly painted fishing boats are lying on the beach. The stuff of postcards. Off to the left a tall cliff – higher than Heather Hill – plunges into the sea at the end of the rocky beach. Wooden stairs climb up to a black-painted holiday home with a veranda. The beach is deserted. There are no hooded crows in the sky and even the busy gray sandpipers are missing. No planes, no ships, no oil rigs. I take off my jeans and walk a few steps into the sea, using the path we had to clear again this morning. I am the only one for miles around making any noise. Behind me, I think, very far behind me is Lake IJssel, which the sun can never set into. When I'm up to my knees in the water, I cross my arms and turn slightly to the left, towards the sun, which is now a fingernail above the horizon. When the bottom starts to melt into the water like warm wax, I turn back and climb the cliff. I sit down on top of Heather Hill and only then do I see my jeans lying there, alone between the rocks, as if left there by a suicide.

It's faster than I expected. It's not so much the sun that sinks below the horizon, it's more the water of the sea swallowing the orange ball. Warm air blows across my neck. It's a while before I realize that it can't be the wind: wind doesn't blow in regular, short blasts. Very slowly I turn around. Less than eight inches away, at face height, is the dark head of a lop-eared sheep. She looks at me impassively with her yellow eyes, in which the pupils are not round but almost square. Now her breath is blowing in my face, smelling like herbs. This sheep is no sorry creature. This is a noble beast. When I can't bear the gaze of her yellow eyes any longer, I look forward again. The sheep stays where she is. I imagine that she, like me, is looking at the sky over the sea, which is blue, orange and yellow – almost purple in places. My breathing adjusts to the warm air blowing over my neck in gentle blasts.

I know I have to get up. I know that the maze of paths and unpaved roads in the shade of the pines, birches and maples will already be dark. But I stay sitting calmly. I am alone.